MISTAKES BY THE LAKE

PRAISE FOR *MISTAKES BY THE LAKE*

"In *Mistakes by the Lake*, Brian Petkash writes, 'I learned then, and I know now, that there is no insulation from tragedy.' Part adventure narrative, part love letter to Cleveland, this collection uses history to illuminate and elevate trailblazers, troublemakers, and tinkerers. This book is a tribute to the American experience."

—Tasha Cotter, author of *Astonishments*

"With a tender and transportive love note to a city—with shades of Richard Powers's feel for people and land, spiked by flashes of the odd experimentalism of underground poet d.a. levy—Brian Petkash has written a muscular, inventive, and engrossing novel in stories, each one set in a different Cleveland decade. From 1796 to 2013, we travel from wilderness to street car, from the day a steer escapes the stockyards to the awful day a star little leaguer disappears. Each chapter about this city in Ohio throbs with love, intensity, devotion, and creativity. Epic, ambitious, gorgeous, and deeply felt, all of the stories in *Mistakes by the Lake* add up to a book at least as old, important, and beautiful as the grand old city of Cleveland itself."

—Nathan Deuel, author of
Friday Was the Bomb and frequent *Los Angeles Times* book critic

"Evidently, Brian Petkash was somebody's big secret until now. I don't know how they kept him from us. No one writes this good the first time out, do they? Well, secret no more, folks: this genie's out of the bottle. Brian Petkash's *Mistakes by the Lake* is a stunning literary achievement. The prose is luminous and compassionate, the themes are complex and resonant, the characters are riveting and heroic. You won't soon forget them, and you won't want to. They'll haunt your dreams. This is not a book that you can put down until it's through with you. Yes, it's that good, and you're going to thank me for telling you about *Mistakes by the Lake*."

—John Dufresne, author of *I Don't Like Where This Is Going*

continued on page 194 . . .

MISTAKES BY THE LAKE

Brian Petkash

Lake Dallas, Texas

FIRST EDITION

Requests for permission to reprint material from this work should be sent to:

> Permissions
> Madville Publishing
> P.O. Box 358
> Lake Dallas, TX 75065

ACKNOWLEDGMENTS

These stories, in slightly different form, appeared in the following journals: "And the Moon Shimmered" in *Bridge Eight Literary Magazine*; "Flood" in *Southword*; "Our Lady of Cleveland" in *Midwestern Gothic*; "Up in the Sky" in *El Portal*.

Grateful acknowledgment is given to Reason magazine and Reason.com for permission to use the quote by Drew Carey.

Grateful acknowledgment is made for permission to reprint an excerpt from "What the ants are saying" from *THE LIVES AND TIMES OF ARCHY AND MEHITABEL* by Don Marquis, copyright © 1927, 1930, 1933, 1935, 1950 by Doubleday, a division of Penguin Random House LLC. Used by permission of Doubleday, an imprint of the Knopf Doubleday Publishing Group, a division of Penguin Random House LLC. All rights reserved.

Grateful acknowledgment is given to Western Reserve Historical Society for permission to use "Seth Pease's Map, 1796/Pillsbury, I.H., 1855." Comments: "A plan of the city of Cleveland" reprint "Jan. 5th, 1855".

Author Photograph: Adrianne Mathiowetz Photography
Cover Design: Jacqueline Davis; Cleveland skyline in black watercolor on white background, Cristina Romero Palma / Shutterstock; Cleveland USA city skyline silhouette, YurkaImmortal / Shutterstock.

ISBN: 978-1-948692-32-8 paperback, 978-1-948692-33-5 ebook
Library of Congress Control Number: 2020931925

for my parents

TABLE OF CONTENTS

Skywoman and the Cayagaga, 1796–1797. 1

The Last Ride, 1928. 12

Up in the Sky, 1938. 26

Dispossessed, 1946–1947. 31

Our Lady of Cleveland, 1954. 57

Butterflies on Fire, 1969. 66

Flood, 1975. 76

And the Moon Shimmered, 1984. 83

In the Shade, 1999. 91

Mistakes by the Lake, 2013. 96

Afterword and Acknowledgements. 191

About the Author. 193

Yet herein will I imitate the sun,
Who doth permit the base contagious clouds
To smother up his beauty from the world,
That when he please again to be himself,
Being wanted, he may be more wondered at
By breaking through the foul and ugly mists
Of vapours that did seem to strangle him.
—Henry IV, Part 1

Experience is simply the name we give our mistakes.
—Oscar Wilde

I love the normalcy of Cleveland. There's regular people there.
—Drew Carey

Skywoman and the Cayagaga, 1796–1797

The story is thus, or so I've been told: Skywoman, the mother goddess—pregnant with her daughter, Tekawerahkwa, Breath of the Wind—fell through a hole in the sky, a celestial being cast out, an Eve without her Adam. In her attempt to hold fast to Skyworld, her grip stripped the branches of the Celestial Tree. And as waterbirds carried her down, down, down to the back of Turtle Island, her hand released the Tree's seeds, sprinkled the land with plenty.

Here, in this New Connecticut, this Western Reserve, there grew oak and walnut and beech and chestnut and maple and sycamore so thick and breakless that day seemed night and night seemed pitch. Skywoman, she planted in spadefuls.

This land, this endless land, ripe for exploration and settlement, summoned me. My failures in Old Connecticut, my failures to my wife and child, could here be washed away.

I'd had to play catch-up; my surveying party left without me while I stayed behind to finish interring my son's empty casket. I made my way from Connecticut to Schenectady where I purchased supplies: lantern, surveying compass, porringers, yarn for wicks, cooking utensils, bread, pork, and liquor. I also encountered an impossibly weird beast, an elephant on display beside an old tavern. I marveled at it for hours. As it lumbered in its too-small pen, the impressive footprints it left in the mud—larger than any animal's prints I'd ever seen—were washed away in a storm that left me wondering why we do anything in this world.

It was September, what was once called by the people of this land The Full Corn Moon. My route took me up the Mohawk and into Oneida Lake, up the Oswego into Lake Ontario, and I arrived at the landing above the falls. It was breathtaking. I dropped a stone at the top; it took three seconds to fall. Esau, my son, dwelled deeper than three seconds.

I fell in and out with various traveling groups. Some were moving from one fort or garrison to another. Others were like me: looking for fresh starts in virgin lands. After getting some help over the portage to skirt the falls, I continued along the southern shore of Lake Erie, passed Catawaugus Creek, Presque Isle, and, finally, I crossed into the eastern confines of New Connecticut and into a new world.

The first night after I'd overtaken my party at Conneaught, we encamped by a pond. It was now November, The Frost Moon. After our fire, our meal, our storytelling, our bed-making, I lay in the open land and enjoyed the sensation of an unusually warm rainfall dripping through the thick canopy. Drops struck my face, rolled and glided down my nose, cheek, and neck and melted into the soft earth. And I could swear the wind, in my Sukey's voice, whispered my name. "Jacob," it said. A plaintive plea.

Much of the land had already been surveyed in the summer of 1796 by Moses Cleaveland and his team. But the Connecticut Land Company wanted additional and re-confirmed information prior to opening it up for settlement. And we needed to finish quickly: there was already talk of a few men, Lorenzo Carter and, separately, Judge James Kingsbury, on their way behind us, champing at the bit to start anew.

The first few months of our surveying went as it should even with considerably fewer men than Cleaveland had at his disposal: twelve miles a day, axeman clearing the straight-line path through the forest, the flagman sighting the surveyor, and my fellow chainman and I running the lines with a Gunter's chain, measuring distance and setting marks. By the time of The Long Lights Moon, the winter snow proved difficult, chest-high at times, but surveying in the winter could keep Indians at bay.

While our work continued in earnest, I couldn't help but feel my vague hopes were cursed. In rapid succession: one of our packhorses, carrying a fair amount of our supplies, wandered off, never to be found; our other packhorse succumbed to the blind staggers; we lost Samuel, our jocular and watchful trailing spy, to an unlikely accident involving a felled tree; Gideon, our lead hunter, took ill—the ague, the Cayagaga Fever, often blasted him into feverish fits; and my eyes, which had started to degrade in Connecticut, seemed anxious to fully hobble my vision. My wife had said, even before Esau's death, that pinpricks of fog had erupted from within the centers of my eyes and had sought to usurp them slowly, wholly. Abraham, the surveyor, often wondered aloud how any of my survey lines could be straight.

As we settled in for a cold night, I got the fire going. I dragged Gideon near to it. He was a young humorless man but physically powerful. More than once we'd overtake his three-hundred-yard lead to find a bear felled by his knife, a claw mark across Gideon's cheek, a patch of his heavy beard abraded. He'd smile in a way that reminded me of Esau just after we'd had a row, and Gideon would say we'd be eating well tonight. He'd leave the carcass for me and continue ahead to scout more game or savages. His ague now weakened him and he felt lighter, so much lighter, than I expected.

I prepared our food. Gideon ate little; instead, he took some rhubarb and a dose of tartar emetic which puked him several times while the rest of us ate. Seth, our axeman and my fellow chainman whose eye-to-chin scar seemed to brighten when he got agitated or excited, left briefly for his nightly constitutional.

"Anyone a song, a story?" Abraham said. He'd removed his hat, a black squirrel-and-beaver mixture that, when donned, swallowed his head. He cleaned his glasses with dirty fingers.

Gideon said, "No fucking songs." His ears had turned sensitive since the fever's onset. "For the love of God."

"A story then," I said.

Gideon waved his hand at me, pulled his blanket over his head.

I stabbed at the fire. Tendrils of flame reached for the branches that held the full moon at bay. "Skywoman," I said, "lived on Turtle—"

"Go fuck yourself, you and your nackle-ass Indian shit." Gideon's words emerged stilted and muffled from underneath his blanket.

3

Abraham squinnied his eyes and tweaked his brows, aping movements I made when my eyes bothered. He affected my voice: "The Moon of the Shit, The Moon of the Beard-splitter, The Moon of the Fucking Pickerel."

Seth was back. "Come on, Jacob, enough of these Red Jacket stories. Give us stories full of women and sex and drink and gambling and, I don't know, adverbs." The firelight's glow—or was it my eyes?—limned them all and seemed to illuminate Seth's scar from within.

I pulled a glove off with my teeth and pulled out my compass. The brass iced my hand. The needle shifted back and forth. Its inaccuracy had befuddled us for months; the wavering and imprecise magnetic needle kept our running lines from running parallel. Something about this land. "Look," I said, "these stories, these bits of Indian shit, as you say, made this land. It's what and why—"

"Here we go," muffled Gideon.

"My wife and I, we're rebuilding. Here. When I draw my ticket, when this is all done, we're packing. Everything."

Gideon flipped the blanket and uncovered his hirsute face. "Not your son." His teeth chattered and the "n" repeated.

Gideon could be a bastard, but he looked like my son, like my Esau, and even though he often held Esau's very same contempt for me, I paused my hate, stayed my fist.

I put the compass away. "You prove the stories of this land." I replaced my glove. "Sky-Holder and Flint. Good Mind and Bad Mind. Admiration and loathing." I stood and pointed my gloved hand at Gideon. "Don't speak of my son, you regular fucking incorrigible shit." I collected my blanket and most of my gear, moved a few hundred yards away, brushed and cleared some snow, wrapped myself tightly in my blanket, and lay on the frozen ground. Sleeping near the fire wasn't safe. The others would join me soon, place their blanket beds side by side to generate warmth.

I dreamed of a blacksmith business on the edge of the Cayagaga, on the edge of the world, my wife by my side. Only my wife by my side.

I awoke alone. I heard laughter and coughing and laughter. I unwrapped myself from my blanket, stood, approached the fire. Gideon looked a bit healthier, at least he wasn't shaking now, and

4

he and Abraham were sharing a bottle. My bottle. Gideon must have taken it from my things. I kicked a flaming log at Gideon. The log struck Gideon's arm and he cough-yelled-laughed as he skittered backward, the log tumbling back into the fire.

Gideon swiped at a small flame that had erupted on his sleeve. I didn't wait to see how it turned out and returned to bed.

In the morning, Abraham nudged me awake, gave the signal for me and Seth to check the area surrounding the smoldering fire for signs of ambush.

When we returned, Abraham had covered Gideon with a worn blanket.

"This," Abraham said, pointing at Gideon's body, "changes nothing."

"The ground's frozen," Seth said. "We won't be able to—"

"We don't," Abraham said.

Seth futilely banged his axe into the frozen ground. It would take him at least a day to dig a grave. While Gideon had reminded me of my son in appearance and perturbable nature, Seth gave life to my son's wild and exuberant spirit, but Seth was kinder, tamer. He was Sky-Holder to Gideon's and Esau's Flint.

On the sixth or seventh strike, all of which rang like my hammer on its anvil, Seth yelped, dropped his axe, and held his hand to his chest. "I think I've put my wrist out of joint."

Abraham sighed. "We have miles and miles to survey before we finish. Hundreds of sections and aliquots. We don't stop."

We hastily covered Gideon's body with leaves, rocks, and branches. Seth marked some trees nearby with Gideon's name and the date of his death.

We pushed on, we three, for weeks. Seth nursed his wrist, but we both served as axemen, chainmen, forward hunter, rearward spy. The Full Snow Moon, a time of a coldness unlike the other months, felt pink. I know pink isn't palpable. But that's how—I cannot explain.

The forest thickened and the snow melted. The chest-high drifts shrank first to our waists and then to our knees. The hoarfrost departed from my beard and tiny fissures cracked my lips; thin bloodlines smeared the back of my hand. There were many forenoons and afternoons when I'd peel off a layer of clothes and let the cold air chill my sweating body.

When we would run our lines, one catching up with the other before we turned and ran the line again, Seth would tell me of his dreams. He'd first build his cabin, and he'd be the sort of kind- and free-hearted man to always leave the latchstring out. Then he'd grow a farm, a small one to start, but one that could ultimately feed a town. His import would make him worthy of the prettiest woman of good upbringing. A family would follow. His name and his issue would echo throughout time, mainstays of the Western Reserve. I heard his dreams fifty times or more. Seth held all the good parts of Esau, even his dreams, and I could only hope Seth's turned out differently.

During The Full Worm Moon, we lost sight of Seth as the skeletal trees prematurely added muscle and flesh. He wanted this over. We all did. I wanted to get back to Old Connecticut, hold Sukey, kiss her face with lips no longer bloodied. She would tell me how proud of me she was, how everything that had happened was forgotten, that it was time for the two of us to let go of the past, let go of the shame, and embrace the new land. And I with cloudy eyes would whisper, "Enough."

My reverie broke at a yawp and a crack. Or was it a crack and a yawp? I ran from my trailing position and caught up to Abraham.

"What is it?" I said. "What did you see?"

"Wasn't me."

We hurried forward. Slushed snow crunched underfoot. Felled branches from Seth's blade kicked before us. I yelled for Seth, but Abraham quieted me, said we might be heading for an ambush. What did it matter? We sounded like an elk at a charging run. Indians would know we were coming, yelling or no. I yelled again. Abraham did not stop me.

We emerged from the trees, the trees that held night all day long, and into a brightness to which my clouded eyes could not adjust. Abraham grabbed my coat, held me from tumbling into a fairly frozen river—the Cayagaga, presumably—a hole twelve feet from shore splintered and spidered outward. I stared at that ice, at that hole, at that water, and tried to will Seth's scar to glow and show us the way.

I searched north. Abraham searched south. The river bowed and curved and bent back upon itself. I had no Indian story as to why the river ran so crookedly. And I had uncovered no trace of Seth. Neither had Abraham.

Abraham and I checked our inventory. I'd given my compass to Seth. I had an axe, my chain, a blanket, a canteen, and bits of fetid deer. Abraham had his plotting instruments, a thermometer, his field notes, his blanket.

"Now?"

"We run lines," Abraham said, "and we push back to Lake Erie."

The Gunter's chain began to warm in my hands. Each line seemed to run true although Abraham's survey told otherwise. Lines narrowed and widened, narrowed and widened. None of it mattered to me. When we finished I would head home so we, Sukey and I, could create a new home. Maybe I wouldn't see it clearly, no, but Sukey would. And we would be blessed in this Cleaveland, this Forest City, this land gloriously seeded by God or Skywoman or both, and acquired through trinkets, whiskey, wampum, and trickery.

Maybe we'd make it, I thought, as more weeks passed. And I was encouraged by smaller game—raccoon and muskrat and squirrel and chipmunk—running alongside my hatcheted trail and by fish—bass and pickerel and trout and perch—swimming close to the breaking surface of the Cayagaga. All seemed to offer themselves to us, sacrificing for our strength.

I led Abraham by several hundred yards. With night coming, I paused at the edge of the river, dipped my canteen into the chill, and drank warmly. We had maybe a week of surveying till we reached the mouth. I gathered twigs and branches and built a small fire, the smoke billowing into my eyes. I coughed and spat and once I had recovered I coughed and spat some more. I waited for Abraham.

Wood popped in the fire and branches broke nearby.

"Lost?" I said. I couldn't see well and I wiped my eyes with a glove so full of holes it barely held together.

An elk, through the flames, stared at me. "Jesus!" I jumped and slid along the slush. For a moment I thought Gideon or Seth or Esau had turned elk. Myths slid through me.

The elk's breath tendrilled toward the flames, mixed briefly with the fire's smoke, and dissolved. The elk turned its head left, right, gave me a final look—a nod? a benediction?—and plodded away.

I stood and fumbled for words. The trunks of the trees surrounding me in the firelight appeared to hold carved and gnarled visages. They stared at me, these false faces; who they were, I knew not. My eyes, were they true?

The elk reappeared, its head joining the audience. Its antlers brushed the boughs and then it, and the trunks' faces, disappeared. "Esau," I called. My son's name sounded hollow.

I followed the elk. No, I chased the elk. But night and trees muddied my muddy vision, so I chased blindly, loudly, reaching, snapping, cracking, groping, tripping, gasping. I fell. My face slapped into the mud and I inhaled earth. I lay like that for seconds, minutes, inhaling and exhaling air and slush and mud. I rolled over. Maybe I spied a break in the trees, maybe I spied a starless sky. I heard my breath, heavy and ragged.

I reached a hand out beside me, searched. Dirt. Slush. Twig. Rock. Root. Leaf. Rocks. Leaves. Slush. Roots. Fur. My wet and aching hand felt into the softness, sought warmth. The elk, it had to be the elk. It had waited, my spirit guide, it had waited for me. I felt for more, sought elk snout or elk hair or its unshed antlers. But there was no warmth, just Abraham's hat. I cast it aside. I crawled only a few feet before I bumped into him. I gently pushed—a shoulder, perhaps—and pushed. "Abraham," I said. "Please." I felt for his face and held my hand below his breathless nose.

I didn't bother sleeping away from the fire. I doubted I could go on, I doubted I should go on. This virgin land was tainted. A miasma. Maybe the river's crookedness was a curse. What river bent its way around its land so raggedly?

In the morning, I covered Abraham with branches and leaves and dirt. I scratched his name on a tree two or three rods from the river. His body would rot here, seeding the earth in a way Skywoman never did.

I abandoned my axe, my chain, and I left Abraham's field notes. I simply followed the river, that muddy river, north.

I didn't care anymore about finishing the survey. Maybe I never did. It just increased my—our—chance to stake here. It was a chance for this failed man to make good for failing his son.

Esau had been nineteen. A contentious nineteen. But he'd always been contentious. We'd play-wrestled when he was little; sometimes I'd let him win, sometimes not. As he got older the wrestling became fiercer, combative. I was a good father, I thought. I was a good husband, I thought. But he had it in for me and I knew not why.

I often dumbly wondered why I'd agreed to name this child Esau. The biblical Esau was a right and regular shit. But Esau was my issue, my heir, my son. Sukey would often say she saw him in me and me in him. And when Esau, in few words, for Esau spoke directly, begged us, his parents, for land of his own—my uncle had left his land, tracts of it near Bennington, Vermont, and the Taconic Mountains, to me—I denied him. He cracked our wooden door when he crashed out of the house in protest.

When Sukey had pleaded on his behalf, I knew I had lost. Sukey loved me, but a mother's love is something special. Something more. And Sukey wished more for her son. She had that right.

After packing his things, he patted my right check, kissed the left, hugged his mother, and departed, leaving me and my wife childless again.

I wished I could say I checked on him often, that Sukey baked him pies and redecorated my uncle's Spartan house, that I even worried a little, but it wasn't like he was next door. Western Vermont and Suffield, Connecticut, were plenty far apart and making that trip took time, took preparation. We heard, though. Letters from cousins—never from him, never from Esau—proved Esau'd made good, forested and farmed better than anyone my cousins had ever seen. I even had admitted to Sukey, much to my surprise, that I might be proud of Esau. She kissed me and said of course I was, that deep down I had always been proud. Perhaps she was right.

On his birthday, during The Green Corn Moon, Sukey and I approached his land. We'd made the long trek, our first, to surprise him with new tools and wares we'd purchased from Sterling Feed and Goods. Low stone walls, walls I know my uncle hadn't built, stretched in several directions and seemingly endless fields had been plowed and sown. The land had been generous to Esau.

Within the walls, in the middle of the land—it was hard to

see at first for it was overcast and the shadows played tricks with my trickster eyes—a hole bigger than two wagons revealed itself. We could've gone to his small house, the one in the distance with numerous wood-framed expansions in progress, and looked and yelled for him there, we could've searched his land and yawped his name. But two dogs waited impatiently beside the hole, barked into its abyss. We knew, Sukey and I, we knew.

We yelled into that hole, cried out for Esau. But it was so deep. Terribly deep. We dropped rocks whose silences lasted five or six seconds before a faint knock would reach back out to us, cause the dogs to begin their barking afresh. I tied one end of a rope to our wagon, the other to my waist, and descended. Down nearly two hundred feet and I still could not see the bottom. My yells taunted me with echoes: "Esau, Esau, Esau." We spent hours, days, searching and waiting and hoping. In the end, we were simply spent. We planted a cross deep into the ground at the edge of the hole, anchored it, and let a rope dangle as far down as it could go. Hope was a funny thing.

Sukey had blamed me. Used appellations I didn't know she knew. I made a promise. I would take all of Esau, the best parts, the parts Sukey loved, and the worst parts, the parts I loathed, and I would see us through, will us together. But I could not do that here. Here, in Vermont, in Connecticut, there were demons. So I would see. I would see this Western Reserve that others in Suffield had invested in. I would make it ours.

The Cayagaga widened, its slow eddies quickening as the forested land rose. I considered climbing into the muddy river, considered letting it wash over and into me, considered letting it fully accept me as its own.

Instead I climbed a high bluff as rain fell. I was close, I was close. I tossed my gloves. Branches clawed at my forest-stained coat and shirt. I let them strip me. The rain dripped through the dark-but-thinning canopy, ran down my shoulders and chest and back. The rain quickened into a storm. The mud tripped me and my feet slipped and slid as I ascended higher and higher until the edge of the bluff forced me to stop.

I overlooked a vast river that flowed slowly around a small spit of land and then joined a choppy yet beatific and endless-to-the-horizon body of water. At least that's what I thought I saw.

Rain dripped over my clouded eyes. "Yawp!" Another. "Yawp!" Another. "Yawp!" One for Esau. One for Sukey. One for me. The storm, it now raged.

I yelled and yawped and cried for the skies to crack and blow and destroy the mould of my life, for Skywoman to try her hand again. I knelt on the promontory and tried to pray but I had nothing. My voice, my eyes, were empty.

I knew I'd never see this land fully settled, that I'd never see a bustling New Haven or a booming Boston born on these shores. I knew I'd never see who would live on what parcel, on what yet-to-be-named streets and corners, who would run what business, open what school, start what church. And I knew houses and towns and cities and colonies were no more permanent than that elephant's grand footprints.

Maybe Sukey and I would make it back to live here at the edge of the world. Maybe Sukey would see me as I would soon be unable to see her, her and this land.

Felt it now. My knees sank into the muddied earth, rooted me.

If we did come, I thought, I hoped it changed us. I hoped we'd thrive.

And I hoped it wouldn't all be another mistake.

THE LAST RIDE, 1928

When Oswald "One Track" O'Malley was six years old, Abraham Lincoln's visit changed his life, kindled in the young lad a want—no, a need—to do something by which he'd be remembered.

That morning, all those years ago, young Oswald was awakened by the sound of cannon fire, cannon fire, cannon fire.

His father, pus snowflaking an eyepatch received in a mill accident, urged Oswald out of bed. "He's coming." While his father dressed Oswald in a too-small black suit that was his in miniature, he said, "You'll see, son. This man: goodness made him great." Oswald didn't understand why viewing the body of a dead president, one making his final journey back to Illinois, was so special.

People thronged Public Square. Young Oswald shifted from foot to foot, peered between the tightly packed and solemn crowd. He glimpsed snatches of the gray sky, the tops of buildings, a bit of Perry's monument, and beyond it a flag-topped pavilion. Rain began in a light drizzle, then within minutes turned into a steady curtain parted only by the emergence of six brilliantly white horses gleaming in the mist. Oswald released his father's hand. The rain created a mix of puddles and muddy patches through which Oswald moved. The horses were festooned with crepe detailed with small rosettes and silver stars. Time slowed for Oswald as the horses' somber gait piaffed to the raindrops splashing in the street, rippling the puddles. Behind the horses trailed a finely crafted hearse bearing the body of the country's president.

Tapestries of black velvet and of red, white and blue dripped from the hearse.

The horses stopped. Several men carried the coffin to its temporary resting place in the middle of Public Square. A band played a dirge and its powerful solemnity startled young Oswald. Time quickened. He had lost his father in the crowd. After moments of panic and incorrect adults, he found his right hand safely gripping the threadbare sleeve of his father's coat.

Through the noise of the rain, young Oswald heard phrases that sounded like prayer: "the Lord hath taken away" and "man hath a short time to live" and "life is full of misery." The pious words filled his bowed head.

The crowd surged, movement pushing him and his father first toward then away from the president's catafalque. Oswald couldn't see. Bodies pressed against him; his one-eyed father tugged him closer, draped his arm over Oswald's shoulder and chest. The newspaper plugging the holes in Oswald's shoes had long since given way to rain and mud. He shivered. Oswald thought no one could be this important, no man this praiseworthy, to warrant such a display.

The fifth hour: young Oswald—hungry, sullen, angry—thought the rain had stopped as he entered the pavilion. But he heard the drop drop drop on the covering above, knew he was wrong. And he heard the dripping gasps and sobs and mutterings of "shameful" and "too sorrowful" and "what of our country?"

When he saw the foot of the casket, young Oswald marveled at the length of it. A white-bearded gentleman held aloft a young girl at the open end and when he whispered something to her she nodded seriously. Oswald hoped his father would hold him high.

Standing on tiptoe, young Oswald moved up the casket—the finest mahogany, his father had later told him—and his hand flew quickly to cover his mouth, shocked at the serene and hirsute face. Oswald pumped up and down on his toes. Lincoln's face was leaden, the eyes deeply sunk. The thin lips seemed glued together. Given the spectacle, young Oswald almost expected these lips to part, utter a joke or a phrase of condolence to the distraught city.

He reached out a shaking hand to touch one of the petals that comprised the large floral "A.L." resting on Lincoln's chest.

His father swatted Oswald's hand away. "Show some respect."

Oswald took in the scene and he knew what he wanted: a life of awe that might someday cause some future father to swat a child's hand away, a life that would generate this kind of sadness.

So, it was Abraham Lincoln's fault. That simple truth insinuated itself daily into Oswald O'Malley's thoughts near the end of his twelve-hour shift.

Oswald, now sixty-nine years old, stood outside his electric streetcar, his dinkey, and pulled the trolley rope down, releasing the spring-loaded troller from the overhead wires. He shuffle-footed his way to the opposite end of #111, feet dusting through the sand he'd forced over the tracks moments before, and swung the center- and swivel-mounted pole behind him. Once he had it lined up, he eased the tension on the rope so the troller snugged against the wire. He tied off the loose end of rope to a metal loop on the side of the car, clapped his hands several times to warm them against the late-October Cleveland cold, and readied for his return trip to the West Side Market.

It was a short run, his route: six-tenths of a mile. He'd heard that now, in 1928, there were over four hundred miles of track in Cleveland. Four hundred! And here he was, Oswald O'Malley, delegated to a back-and-forth trolley covering less than a single mile.

Six stops, three minutes to run one length, a two-minute lay-over at each end. Every hour he'd raise and lower the trolley pole twelve times. That meant, in his three decades as Abbey Avenue motorman, he had—

When his mind drifted toward working the math, to the tens of thousands of miles traveled on this single stretch of track, he became lightheaded with fear, queasy with loss.

Out of habit, he mentally recited a mantra that had served him well early on, a mantra that for a time heralded a brighter day: "This is only temporary."

He had, once, believed that. It was only a few weeks after that sad and glorious day in the rain, after disassembling his mother's Singer sewing machine to see how it worked, after discovering he had an aptitude for such things, that young Oswald became a tinkerer, an inventor. His father encouraged Oswald to use his gifts to get out of Irishtown Bend, to avoid the kind of hard labor that had nearly taken his life but instead settled for his eye. Oswald tinkered and invented, tinkered and invented. This would be his escape, this would be how he would inspire awe.

When he was fifteen, he'd invented a substitute for collar buttons that could be fastened and unfastened with one hand. Then he learned they'd already been invented. This was the first of many such failures. After a time, Oswald needed money, needed to live, and, when he married at seventeen, he needed to support Mary, a young woman who at first found his inventing charming, cute even, but who later found Oswald's obsession infuriating.

Within years of his first working for the railway as a teen, his temporary morphed into a Monday, Tuesday, Wednesday, Thursday, Friday, Saturday rhythm of waking, dinkey, eating, dinkey, eating, tinkering, sleeping. For years he thought the weariness of that rhythm would provoke a long-dormant consciousness into action, or at the very least bring him some goddamned luck.

A light rain mixed with sleet now began to fall. With his W. 14th layover finished, he pedaled the bell once to signal his departure, revolved the control to pick up speed, and levered open a chute that air-blasted sand over the rails to battle the icy and final runs of the evening.

The dinkey became obstreperous as it approached West 15th, old Burns Street. The weather- and time-worn track that transitioned from 15th to the bridge attempted to jolt the dinkey off line and the trolley pole swayed from side to side as Oswald's right hand, his good hand, automatically worked the braking valve to direct air to the cylinder under the car, and then, the westerly crisis averted, just as automatically revolved the controller to regain his speed during this long stopless stretch until W. 19th.

At his busiest, Oswald transported over 2000 riders a day. The passengers he ferried this evening—two men drunkenly japed about a chicken in every garage and a car in every pot, and a couple who, Oswald knew, were married to other people but for some reason found his dinkey romantic—faced across from each other on the two wooden benches that ran lengthwise along the inside of the car. They abruptly lurched forward with the initial jolt, then skidded backward with the acceleration. One of the men said, "Oi, watch it," then tossed an empty milk bottle in Oswald's direction. Oswald stopped the dinkey, dropped his head back, and counted the gold-painted flowers that trimmed the olive-green ceiling, flowers he had counted millions of times, probably. When he reached thirty, he opened the doors, pointed without turning around, and the drunks departed as they muttered lackluster threats about reporting Oswald to management.

Oswald lived and lost his life in tiny increments along Abbey Avenue. The Market at Lorain, Gehring, bridge, Columbus, 20th, 19th, bridge, 15th, 14th, 14th, 15th, bridge, 19th, 20th, Columbus, bridge, Gehring, the Market at Lorain. Fifty, sixty, seventy times a day, six days a week. Abbey, Abbey, Abbey. His useless mantra washed over him. His shoulders slumped.

He knew his routine was wearying and maddeningly repetitive. He had tried. Many times he had tried. In 1865, he had somehow felt destined for greatness. Now, he knew the laudanum that tonight awaited him seemed a lifelong *fait accompli*. How had he gotten here?

Oswald expertly worked the controller and the dinkey smoothly slipped off the bridge and headed toward 19th. Helen stood outside her mother's Hungarian restaurant, a restaurant she now owned, and waved at Oswald. Older now, she was still beautiful, and Oswald wondered what would've happened had he pursued her all those years ago instead of Mary, his father's choice. He put his two-fingered left hand into his pocket as he opened the door with his right, and Helen boarded.

He heard her Hungarian curse begin before he'd even opened the door. "*Úgy pofon csaplak hogy kiesik a fogad, te*, it's about time." She paid her fare and sat near the front, away from the love birds. "I've more customers in there than I've food, Ozzie."

Oswald pedaled the bell once and started toward the West Side Market. He thought about being polite, making conversation, asking her whom she left in charge, but he knew the answer and stayed silent. So maybe his life wouldn't be that much different. He'd still be on Abbey every day, it and the Bend his only worlds, but at least he'd be without the shame. No, blast, there'd still be the shame, just different. Rather than Mary's leaving him over the grasshopper incident, her saying, "You're just Shanty Irish and that's all you'll ever be"—that failure comical if it wasn't for that—he'd still have the shame of never escaping, never expanding, never exploring, never living.

Now, crossing the new Abbey Avenue bridge, the excavating crews underneath knocking off for the day, their work on the western approach nearing completion, Oswald thought how unfair it was that even as Cleveland's landscape changed—renamed streets, new construction, buildings razed, bridges built—his did not. He looked north and, in the haze, could make out the looming silhouette of what had recently become, according to the newspapers, Cleveland Union Terminal, the CUT. A bone of contention of his, all of this change. The city, she was transforming before his eyes, yet here he was, the same as he'd ever been, ever would be.

At the Lorain stop, the couple departed and Helen bustled through the door. "Back soon, Ozzie?" She was the only one who called him that. "I always am," he said as Helen was off to the soon-to-be-closing West Side Market, perhaps intent on imploring a Hungarian vendor or two to sell her the last of their delicacies.

Before he'd finished resetting the trolley pole to return east, Zero Zalewski boarded with his wife, a live turkey tucked under his arm. The clank of six cents hit the hollow of Oswald's chest. It was a sound he should be used to, but even after thirty years it echoed and reverberated within him.

Being a part of the early horse-drawn carriage lines in Cleveland, Oswald saw drivers fumble with fares, saw riders pass off metal as coins, and his inventor's mind saw a need. His see-through glass farebox would fill that need. If only he'd done his research, listened to Mary even, he'd have learned one had already been invented and patented, the inventor a rich man and, ultimately, mayor of Cleveland.

The introduction of the farebox angered many motormen, though, so perhaps Oswald was lucky with this miss. For years others had lived by the motto "one for the company, one for me" and skimmed fares. A few on the busiest trolley runs reached levels of affluence motormen weren't supposed to reach. It never occurred to Oswald to cheat and steal until he saw a chance to mollify his angry thirty-two-cents-an-hour brethren. By happenstance he discovered grasshoppers would clutch at anything—when he'd attempted to remove one from his makeshift workbench a few nails on which it sat came right along with it.

The next morning at the car barn, a crowd of curious and befuddled motormen watched Oswald tie a string to a grasshopper. When he dropped it through the farebox's coin slot and then pulled it out with a coin secured to its limbs, the motormen's cheers assaulted Oswald's ears and their slaps peppered his back. Oswald beamed. This felt good, Oswald thought. His heroism, however, lasted only two weeks. Management introduced modified fareboxes with slanted saw-toothed dividers that deterred any sane grasshopper from pilfering any more fares. And when Oswald's pay was docked as punishment, Mary couldn't take him or his inventions any longer.

Years later, utterly alone, Oswald watched from his dinkey the early and rapid rise of the automobile, the chaos it created on the streets. After witnessing a collision between a horse-drawn carriage and an automobile, he devised a lighting system to efficiently and safely control the flow of traffic. When he finally got it working, in late 1923, he knew this was it. Finally. All those years of tinkering failure would drift away, would be replaced by a Renaissance of wealth and contentment. Maybe Mary would even take him back, apologize, and *recognize*. But his patent was rejected. He'd missed again, this time by a single day.

Those misses buried him, destined him to this unillustrious life.

The turkey broke free. Feathers floated in the dinkey as Zero chased and his wife cowered. "Get—Get—Get it!"

It was the third loose bird of the day for Oswald, fifteenth of the week. He sometimes found feathers in his pants as he undressed for the night. Over the decades, he'd collected enough feathers in his tiny Irishtown Bend room to build soaring thirty-foot wings.

He sighed, pedaled the bell, whispered "This is only temporary," and headed back the way he'd come. Sleet and dirt caked the windows, his vision obscured.

Irishtown Bend once consisted of twenty-two streets of tiny hovels on the west bank of the Cuyahoga. Fifteen years earlier, the warehouses encroached on his family's and friend's shacks. Where most had moved in the aughts and teens—a lucky few to Franklin Boulevard, a luckier few to Euclid Avenue, the majority simply away—the warehouses were really all that remained. And Oswald.

His room, a one-hundred square-foot windowless space tacked onto the unfinished rafters of a warehouse, sat in disrepair atop a flight of skeletal stairs that Oswald thought might collapse at any time. Accessible from the outside, the warehouse often used his landing as storage for rotting pallets, discarded boxes, rusting buckets. As he climbed over the rubbish, his foot cracked through a pallet's slat that momentarily trapped him before he shouldered the door open. An industrial haze greeted him, filled his lungs and eyes. Despite the lack of windows, despite Oswald shoving wet towels into the gap at the base of the door, the haze always penetrated. He shut the door. He didn't bother to replace the wet towels tonight.

It was right where he'd left it, the laudanum. The liquid contained in the short amber-hued and cork-stoppered bottle seemed to fill the room and freight it with potential. He felt the bottle challenge him and Oswald skirted past the uneven table on which it sat.

He removed his cap, dusted the white stitched-in "11-017" on his badge with his two fingers, then dropped it on the floor. He removed his coat and eased the coat's collar onto a single crooked nail. A feather wafted to the floor. He stamped his feet repeatedly and if someone were to see this act from afar it would have been taken as a warming action, of increasing the circulation to work out a deep-boned chill, but Oswald merely acted out a childlike tantrum.

On his workbench—an old door propped up on sawhorses— various inventions in progress, old and new, rocked with each stamp of the foot: a small star-shaped phonograph needle; a miniature gated barrier designed to impel automobile drivers to stop, look and listen before crossing a track; an elaborate iron cowcatcher with separate grates that would swivel upward to hold the struck person or animal from being rolled over. Oswald's tantrum over, his feet still, the vibration that afflicted the inventions ceased. Nailed to the wall above the workbench, a yellowed newspaper ad: "How to obtain a patent in three easy steps. Clarence C. Malloy, registered patent lawyer: Directly across the street from the patent office!"

He washed his hands in the bucket that still held the morning's water, dried them on his coat, slid the single chair out and sat beside the table.

This morning he was so certain: today would be his last ride, he had thought. But tonight, like almost every night, he faced doubt.

Earlier, after his last run to the Market, Bernie the barn-hand joked with Oswald that he was moving like it was his last day on earth. Funny, Oswald had replied. Bernie had been taking Oswald's dinkey to the Brooklyn Station car barn for over a decade. It was one of the few favors anyone did for him. Hell, Oswald thought, Bernie even locked up his padded stool for him in his locker, brought it back to him each morning.

"You coming tonight?" Bernie had asked as he switched the dinkey from Abbey to 25th for its nighttime southerly journey.

Oswald and Bernie played this game every night, just part of the ritual. Bernie invited him somewhere, Oswald asked him where, and Bernie made up some damned fool thing: to clean up his mess of a yard, to reroll and hide dollar bills into rolls of toilet paper, to wash the cars at the barn, to sleep with Bernie's wife. A few hours ago Bernie had said, "Forget my wife, Oswald. Listen to this: tonight, we're setting all the cars free. Gonna let 'em run *wild*. All *over* this here city." Oswald gave his expected response: "I'm inventing." Bernie laughed, shook his head, and left Oswald to his walk home.

He sometimes wished Bernie was serious, that he *did* want to do something, anything, those nights. Oswald, hundreds of failed inventions later, had still expected to create that one big thing that would expel him from this life to the next. All he had was this single bottle. His two-fingered hand scissored the bottle and he rolled it into his palm. He gripped it tight, squeezed his eyes shut, thought of Mary, of Helen, of his father, of Bernie, of Lincoln, of turkeys and ducks, of collar buttons and glass boxes and traffic lights, of cars running wild.

"Me arse on yez," he said to the empty room. "Me arse on all of yez."

He grabbed his coat, shoved the bottle of laudanum into his pocket, and headed toward the car barn.

At midnight, the five arched mouths of the car barn, track-tongued, awaited Oswald behind the fenced yard. Years ago, when he delivered his dinkey here himself, he had keys to the gates. Most of Cleveland had changed. Oswald hadn't. These locks hadn't. The gates opened wide. He'd delivered his dinkey a little late to Bernie—Helen needed one more run to the Market—and his car was the last one in.

He reversed the trolley pole to effect his escape, climbed aboard, and exited the barn, following the track up W. 25th. Habit automatically directed the dinkey north toward Abbey. But instinct and habit had taken three of his fingers in the streetcar strike of 1899 and instinct and habit had kept him bound to the six-tenth-of-a-mile Abbey for thirty years. No, this night required invention, demanded exploration. Four hundred miles awaited.

Oswald whisked past Abbey and slowed at Franklin, its famed circle a few blocks away. He was disappointed he couldn't travel west to the stone and redbrick mansions—the tracks rarely traveled near the wealthy; the affluent didn't want the noise of trolleys or the eyes of rubberneck riders on their streets. Abbey's residences were small-frame, shotgun-style homes, old as soon as they were built, but he'd heard of heavy Italianate- and Victorian-style homes on Franklin that, though historically styled, retained a fashionable newness that never waned. He could, behind the leafy trees, make out a few in the distance—even from here they were stately, wondrous.

Oswald's foot habitually pedaled the bell. Lights in nearby homes flickered on. Illumined faces peered from behind lace-curtained windows.

He followed the tracks a short distance to Detroit, then braked to a halt near the entrance of the Detroit-Superior Bridge. In front of him stood the stone steeple of St. Malichi's, its gas-lit cross shining, beckoning Lake Erie mariners, beckoning him. He crossed himself with his right hand while the left hand held the bottle in his pocket, as if he could hide its presence from God's omniscience, and he felt ashamed. Ashamed for what he'd done, ashamed for what he hadn't done, ashamed for what he wanted to do.

The tracks split: he could go west or east. The CUT loomed in the distance to the east. The CUT and Public Square. He hadn't been there more than a few times since he was a boy, since before he'd become "One Track" O'Malley.

Accelerating, he dropped the dinkey down toward the lower

deck of the bridge. As he made the underground turn east, the clatter of steel on steel and the screech of the wheels digging into the tracks deafened. He was going too fast, he realized, and he couldn't see—he'd kept the headlight beam off, traveling the empty streets in the dark, keeping himself in seclusion. The brake blasts of compressed air echoed off the cement and tile walls. He flicked on the beam, cut the darkness. Accelerating again, he heard a crackling hum overhead, smelled burnt electricity mixed with a musty dampness as he approached the hump of the center steel span. The outer arches of the bridge whipped by, a black collage against the night sky. Visions of the river one hundred feet below shuttered through the span's gaps, the remote chance of falling enhancing Oswald's mood. Maybe he'd be like Motorman Huff all those years ago: he had skidded through the open swing draw of the old Superior Viaduct, his forty-ton trolley plunging into the cold Cuyahoga waters. People within earshot of the calamity talked of panicked screams as the car slipped over the edge, the screams swallowed by a cacophonous splash and then the river itself. Oswald silently recited lines from a poem written to commemorate Huff's last ride: "No warning given / And the car with eighteen persons with human shrieks was riven."

Alas, Oswald made it across the span alive. He emerged up the long incline on the Superior side of the bridge and soon found himself approaching the Square, its four quadrants ahead of him, the late hour and the temperature leaving it rather deserted. He slowed. Even here, he thought. Even here, change. Several tracks had been torn up, large swaths of street gouged out, and oddly placed oriental-style pagodas ringed the quadrants at equal intervals. Tracks were limited here, allowing only passage in one direction. The CUT's fifty-two stories towered over him, its thousands of lights washing out the stars and prickling Oswald's skin. He shook his two-fingered fist. He spit an approximation of Helen's Hungarian curse into the ether.

But the CUT was only one of many symptoms, he knew, and he worked the controls and accelerated toward the switch that would take him around the north side of the Square. East of the city, that's where the millionaires lived. He would see their houses, breathe their air, walk their streets, and be one of them.

(An irony lost on Oswald: He didn't know that even Millionaire's Row had changed, the wealthiest abandoning their mansions, their estates swallowed up by the eastward commercialization of the city and an exodus to the Heights.)

Just as Oswald rounded the square, a rough bit of track forced the dinkey to jerk first left, then right, and the trolley pole broke free. The dinkey rolled to a stop. Oswald hung his head, shoved his hands in his pockets.

He stepped off the dinkey. Almost automatically, absent-mindedly, he found himself brushing aside some snow and creating a small grassy spot on which he lay. He stared up at the Soldiers' and Sailors' Monument, an homage to those better and more remembered than he. The moon, a slivered fingernail, seemed to point at him. He lay on the approximate spot where Lincoln's catafalque once stood, where throngs of people once paid their respects.

Oswald closed his eyes, imagined a floral "O.O." on his chest, could feel the weight of the arrangement, could smell the scent, and he imagined person after person filing by on either side of him, weeping for him, marveling at his passing, awed by his life's work, by his riches, by his generosity, by his contributions to not only Cleveland but to the country. "The greatest," these ghosts said. "Unparalleled." He could feel the presence of the entire city understanding the significance of his, Oswald O'Malley's, life.

In his mind, hours passed, hundreds of thousands passed. It was glorious.

"Hey," a voice said.

Oswald ignored it. This wasn't what someone would say at his celebration.

"Hey." The voice was closer now. And a foot tapped Oswald's shoulder.

Oswald reluctantly opened one eye. A young boy stood above him. His pants and coat appeared worn, a socked toe poked out of one shoe, he held his hat in his hands, and his face expressed both contrition and anger.

"That yours?" He pointed toward the dinkey.

Oswald managed a nod, closed his eye.

"Can I take it? For a ride?"

Oswald hoped to recapture his imagined glory, but that's all it was: imagined. He sat upright; the dampness of the grass had soaked through his coat and he felt cold. He opened his eyes.

"Come on, mister. I've always wanted to drive one of—"

"It's broken," Oswald said. "It jumped." His fingers picked glistening blades of grass off of his sleeve. He stood. "Shouldn't you be home, in bed?"

"Yeh."

"Well," Oswald said, "why aren't ye?"

The boy looked at his shoes, looked at the dinkey, then back at Oswald. He shut his eyes, squeezed his hat. "I sassed."

Oswald got into a crouch, his knees cracking, his face level with the boy's.

"Doesn't want me anyway, grandma. She told me. So I sassed. Cussed."

"You shouldn't sass your grandma, son." Oswald stood up straight, tugged at his jacket. "But tonight's— " Oswald sighed. "Tonight's a bad night." Oswald walked in the direction of Euclid, the east side, Millionaire's Row.

"I could cut you," the boy said behind him.

When Oswald turned, a butter knife shone in the boy's hand, the surface reflecting the CUT's lights.

"Ay, *póg mo thóin*, yez."

And the boy crumpled to the grass, lay where minutes before Oswald had lain, and cried.

Oswald puffed his cheeks, held his breath a moment, exhaled a thick cloud that enveloped his face then dissolved. He took in the Square—the monuments, the CUT, the Old Stone Church, this boy—and saw himself in this place sixty-three years before, a young lad awed, filled with hope, welled with promise. "You have to help," he said.

The boy wiped his nose.

Oswald moved closer. "You have to help."

Oswald showed him how to use a step to climb on to the car's top and reattach the trolley pole, showed him how to work the controls. The boy tentatively urged the dinkey into motion.

"Where to?" Oswald stood slightly behind the boy. The four open doors ushered in a chilly breeze.

The boy grinned, his foot worked the bell. "Over there." He

pointed in the direction of the bridge, the Bend, St. Malichi's, Abbey.

The dinkey slowly circled the Square and headed back the way it had come. Oswald taught the boy how to work the brake, made him test it and show him. His first few attempts nearly threw Oswald through the window. "Easy, easy," Oswald said and before long the boy worked the brake like an old motorman. Oswald told him about the bridge and where he would need to slow down and speed up, made him repeat the instructions back to him three times, told him about a car barn filled with dinkeys and trolleys that in the morning could take him anywhere he wanted.

"Thanks, mister, you're the greatest." The bell clanged once, twice. "Just the greatest."

The words felt like a soft punch. Oswald stepped out the open door of the slow-moving dinkey, watched it carry the boy down the entrance to the lower deck of the bridge, felt himself transported.

Oswald shut his eyes and his mind closed around the boy's last words. His hand searched his pocket for the bottle of laudanum but did not find it.

He hurried back to the site of his imagined catafalque and, hands sifting the grass, discovered the bottle, its top off, its contents already having soaked the earth.

His body and mind exhausted, he lay down, tried to conjure the visions of his earlier phantom memorial. His eyes closed, he smiled. Maybe he'd be out of a job tomorrow, maybe not. He knew this moment, this foreign feeling of contentment, was temporary, that it didn't make up for his life, that he'd soon walk back across the bridge to his room in the Bend. And when he returned, he knew, he would continue inventing that which had already been invented.

But for now, right now, this moment seemed enough.

Up in the Sky, 1938

Jerry was the youngest in the hobo shantytown of Kingsbury Run. The older men, the forty or fifty other homeless piled together like cordwood, treated him as an equal, mostly, called him Pint-Size.

And even though his grandma was long gone (the loss of the farm caused first a stroke then a fatal heart attack) and his father was long ago institutionalized (the loss of both farm and his mother caused first depression then mania), Jerry enjoyed his limited life. He ate almost every day; he had his own shanty in the gully of the Run (constructed from wood slats, cardboard scraps, and a tarpaper roof held in place by fragments of broken concrete); he had his drawings of men performing feats of derring-do covering one wall of his shack; and he had his own dog he called Shuster that, while it wasn't really his, was his enough.

Jerry lay on his cot, an old cut-down barrel that no longer fit him, and read his worn copy of *Action Comics* for, likely, the seventieth time—and, truly, he only reread the first thirteen pages featuring Superman. The other stories, what with their cowboys and magicians and boxers, were interesting, but they just didn't hold a candle to the sensational Superman. Come on, in those thirteen pages, Superman saved a woman from the electric chair, saved another woman from a wife beater, rescued Lois Lane from some rude gangsters, and revealed a corrupt lobbyist and senator. What'd that cowboy do? He was plenty rugged, but he got himself shot and thrown in a cell.

Jerry tapped the cover of *Action Comics* and smiled. Boys

had created Superman. Boys! And one of the boys, the artist, was named Jerome, too! They were only a few years older than he, graduates of an East Side high school. OK, so he hadn't graduated high school, nor, likely, would he ever, but his drawings weren't half bad, Jerry thought. Even a few of the other 'bos, those who hadn't laughed when he'd let them read his comic book, told Jerry his drawings were a sight to behold. That meant "good," right?

Jerry's dreams were simple: create and draw heroes who could overcome this Depression, who could demonstrate the best humanity had to offer, who could celebrate the human potential and, as it said in his comic book, "reshape the destiny of the world." He already had a good start: he'd submitted a colored page of Chuck Dawson to the *Action* Color-Page Contest. It hurt a little to tear a page out, but Chuck Dawson was that silly cowboy who got himself shot.

Shuster growled and then slipped through the hole Jerry'd created for him in their shanty. Jerry tucked his comic between some newspaper blankets and peered out one of the many cracks where board and cardboard sometimes failed to meet.

Firefly-like flickers of light popped up and down the ravine of Kingsbury Run. Odd, he thought. He was used to some light this late at night—the glow from the nearby steel mill furnaces often lit the black sky—but this was something different. Near the top of the ravine he thought he saw the silhouette of a large truck, but he hadn't heard anything, not since the last Rapid Transit train roared by an hour or so ago. Then he was blinded. A large light shone from that silhouette, caused him to pull back sharply from the crack, to rub his eyes. For a few seconds he could only see the afterimage of the light and the side of the hill, the shanties and lean-tos and jungleland huts that dotted its surface. Dogs barked—Shuster?—and men shouted.

Jerry thought of the criminals scattering on the cover of *Action Comics*, thought maybe the Mayfield Road Mob descended upon them all. Hadn't Shimmy, that old gray-haired hobo who lived in a shack at the far end of the Run, bragged that he'd put one over on one of the bookie joints in the Flats? Jerry had heard they killed for less.

Jerry scanned his belongings, his drawings. He couldn't allow what little he had to be filched.

27

He wished Shuster was here for comfort, for protection. But he had his traps.

They were simple. Short sticks, no more than a foot long, with rubber bands stretched end to end. One end secured in a notch he'd carved with his fingernail, the other end set as near to its edge as possible. He'd set the traps in three places: inside the thin piece of rotted wood that served as a door, under his cut-down-barrel cot, and next to Shuster's bed (a pile of newspapers that, the smell suggested, served as more than a bed, although given the smell of the Run in general, who could tell?). If anyone that wasn't him or Shuster entered their shanty or approached their beds, the traps would fire and cripple feet and ankles and knees. The impracticality of these traps doing anything other than, maybe, briefly startling an intruder wasn't lost on him. But a man who was super could lift cars over his head and smash them against boulders as criminals fled in terror. If there could be a Superman anything could happen, anything was possible, yeah?

Jerry checked his traps. Each was set, poised to spring. When he peered through the crack again, he saw men with flash-lights—twenty or thirty of them—pouring down the hill, moving between the shacks. He thought he saw the outlines of guns in many of their hands, backlit by that bright beam that shone above. One man who appeared to be the leader—he kept yelling at the others, pointing them around the camp—held an axe. The Butcher? All the 'bos talked about him, how he cut up his victims, left their torsos and other body parts scattered about. But the Butcher was one man, not an army, an alligator who hunted the swamps alone. It had to be the mob; Shimmy had doomed them all.

The sound of doors and walls being bashed in, followed by violent and slurred curses, filled the night air. Jerry saw the leader use the axe handle to bust through one door—Gina's, the camp's mother figure who'd given him the stamp to send in his colored contest page—saw her dragged out, lashing kicks at any of the men she could reach. One man used handcuffs on her ankles. Not the mob. The police? Jerry's heart pounded, sweat surfaced on his face and arms and legs. What had we done? Jerry thought. Where was Shuster?

Jerry lay in his barrel bed, pulled newspapers over him, hid as best he could. Even held his breath for ten, then twenty, then thirty seconds at a time. To keep the papers from moving up and down, giving him away.

Footsteps came closer. Jerry let out a huge breath, sucked in, held it. There was a hammering at his door. He thought he heard a rubber band snap mere moments before his door was hit, hard. The door fell in against the empty bottles he'd collected earlier that morning and the noise caused him to let out a small shriek, but it must have been lost in the bottles' clinking and clanking. The papers weren't ripped off of him, a flashlight wasn't shone directly in his face, handcuffs weren't slipped over his too-thin wrists, and no one shouted, "Got a kid here." His breath held again, his composure recovered, he hid. Amid the 'bos shouting, amid the commotion and chaos, a voice that sounded like the man Jerry figured to be the axe-wielding leader could be heard shouting: "Take them to Central. All fingerprinted, no exceptions."

After many minutes, the noise drifted up the ravine, away from Jerry. Trucks started and departed above him. Jerry peeked. The uniformed men were gone, replaced by men in shiny over-coats and oversized helmets. A few of these firemen swung large containers toward the shanties of Jerry's friends, sprays of liquid spattering the homes of Thornton and Will and Clyde and Shimmy. They moved away from Jerry and he realized he'd been holding his breath. He exhaled. The other 'bos had been taken away, yet here he was. His traps had worked. He wondered if Shuster was OK.

Jerry propped up and repositioned his door, rearranged the fallen bottles, and pulled the papers over himself. Dark thoughts of what he had escaped filled his mind. Soon, Jerry's thoughts turned warm, to thoughts of Superman and his pencil-and-charcoal drawings, to winning one dollar.

The sound of the fire woke him before the smoke, before the heat. It crackled and popped, caused metal to scream. Before he knew what was happening, his shanty was filled with smoke; he couldn't breathe. Shuster came darting in, tail between his legs, and slinked into Jerry's bed. The dog was hot.

Jerry peered out through one of the cracks. His eyes burned and watered. The entire Run was in flames. "No," he shouted. "No! Stop! Stop!" But who could hear him over the din?

29

He rushed to the door but the fire was too close. He tried to knock down the wall nearest Shuster's bed, but he slipped on a pile of shit and lost his footing and he went down with a *whump.* Above him, seemingly staring down at him, were his drawings. Men of barrel chest and iron arms, men of exceeding strength and limitless power.

Jerry plucked each drawing off the now-smoking wall. He got back into his bed, gathered the drawings to his chest with one arm, held Shuster tightly with the other. He closed his eyes, pictured a caped man striding through the five-story flames and putting out the fire with one long extended breath, turning the bright orange night sky to black. He pictured his traps springing with such force that their explosive wind whispered the fire into nothingness. Jerry felt Shuster shudder beside him.

Jerry lost consciousness. He wasn't aware when the flames licked at his barrel bed, he didn't notice when his drawings began to smolder, he didn't hear the walls give way, nor did he feel the rock-laden roof collapse on top of him.

The papers quoted Eliot Ness as saying if you can't catch the alligator, the Butcher, drain the swamp of its victims, but they said nothing of Jerry or his Pint-Size alter-ego nickname, of the firemen unearthing him to find his clothes melted to his body, his hair burned off, one arm still clutching the body of what could only be a dog. There was no trace of his drawings, of Superman.

Days later, the front page told of two young men—Henry and Frank were their names—who caught baseballs that plummeted over 700 feet from the top of the Terminal Tower, the second-tallest building in the world. They wore steel helmets, the papers said, and they missed the first few attempts as the balls, traveling 200 feet per second, slapped the pavement of Public Square and bounced thirteen stories into the air. But, finally, they caught the baseballs, they set records.

The celebrated human potential. Glorious.

DISPOSSESSED, 1946–1947

On October 9, 1946, hundreds of meteors, remnants of the Gia-cobini-Zinner comet that had passed the earth eight days prior, scraped the Cleveland sky. Also on that day, a Cleveland minister was arrested in Grand Rapids during a vice-squad raid at a licentiously bawdy house; two thirteen-year-old girls picked up by police in Cincinnati were returned to their Cleveland homes; a couple found guilty of robbing a Cleveland-area tavern to finance their wedding were sentenced to prison; the G.I. musical show "Call Me Mister," with its series of sketches capturing the absurdities of war, began touring the country and would ultimately visit Cleveland's Hanna Stage; the War Services Center, a twenty-by-fifty rectangular structure built on the northwest quadrant of Public Square—a structure that at one time housed recruitment offices, war bond sellers, and the Red Cross, a structure built using donated materials, a structure on whose walls were the painted names of hundreds of Cleveland war dead—was to be dismantled.

And Johannes Sykora, Purple Heart recipient, twisted and shifted and pivoted in a kitchen chair across from his Eileen's Aunt Betty. Not his aunt, though. His wife's. Correction: his ex-wife's. Correction: his dead ex-wife's. Yet when he was married, when he was whole, he'd made a solemn promise to Eileen: find her Aunt Betty a man. Johannes grunted with each maneuver. "Hip?" she said.

Of course the hip. The unrecovered shrapnel that resided

inside Johannes caused either pointed pain or blessed numbness. On most days, his hip hobbled his gait, a stuttering step that made him look wooden in his movements. On rare days, and he never knew when a rare day neared, his gait smoothed into a walk that made him appear to lightly hop as if some emotion or event had proffered him a flowing stream of happiness. When his hip hurt or numbed, massaging sometimes helped, a hot bath sometimes helped, icing sometimes helped. Sometimes nothing helped.

The small Queen Anne house awoke around them. The windows popped in the morning sun. Outside a bird chirruped uncertainly in the maple; the warm October must have the little guy confused, Johannes thought, about whether to head south or not. The framed and unframed posters and postcards of faraway destinations that surrounded them—New York, Chicago, San Francisco, Florida, Cuba, Aruba, Brazil, Spain, France, Siam, Australia—glowed as the sun pried its way into the room. A short stack of travel books boosted one leg of the kitchen table, held it level. In a nook behind Aunt Betty sat a black telephone, its slanted dial and A-to-Z letters unreasonably cockeyed, and beside the phone rested a picture of Eileen, her face vacuous and her eyes empty.

Johannes sighed. Eileen was beautiful. And as dead as Jesus.

A rustling newspaper vibrated in Aunt Betty's hands. Some ailment or other caused her head and hands to shake even at rest. Johannes wondered how she could read any words in that erratic zoetrope. And he at times wondered why he should even try to keep his promise—his promise was to Eileen, after all, and not Betty—but his wonder didn't last: Betty had taken him in when the Housing Authority had denied him a home.

Betty's shaking body and wisps of gray entwined in a tight bun belied her fifty years. Johannes realized he'd never seen that hair down, wondered how long it was, how it might look cascaded across her shoulders, down her back.

Johannes rotated his wedding band clockwise and clockwise and clockwise. He waited for Aunt Betty to finish the section of the paper she held aloft. He had thought he'd seen, in the paper's vibratory movement, news items of particular import to him. He finger-tapped a rhythm from the *Superman* radio serial for forty-seven seconds, by his count, waiting patiently, before he sighed and lifted the paper from Betty's rattling hands. She squeaked, opened her mouth to speak, seemed to think better of it, then popped a fingernail clipping in her mouth from a four-inch-tall Ball Mason jar filled with them.

A pot whistled and screamed and Aunt Betty pushed her chair away from the table, slipper-slapped to the stove, ceased the screaming. "Tea?" she said.

Johannes skimmed two articles: Bill Veeck's decision that there would be no more Indians at League Park meant Johannes was out of a job, his ushering days over (not that his hip allowed him to do the job all that well anyway); and Public Square's faux-monument with its war-dead names was finally coming down.

He realized he'd been asked a question. "No, Aunt Betty."

Aunt Betty poured hot water into a cup that displayed a faded picture of the Eiffel Tower. Her movements caused water to splash into and out of the cup, but she'd learned to stand far from the counter, arm outstretched, pot dangling from her trembling hand. The dangerous water did not touch her, merely mottled the countertop and floor in steaming droplets.

Johannes stood and gripped her hand from behind, steadied the pour. She stopped pouring and turned. He felt her breath on his neck. "I have to go out," Johannes said.

"Oh," she said. She pulled her hand from his, stepped backward and bumped the counter. She steadily set the pot on the counter, marched to the table, and tossed a nail into her mouth, swallowed. "That's fine, Johannes. Yes, that's fine."

Johannes and Betty stared at each other a moment. Out of the corner of his eye he caught Eileen's framed gaze. It no longer seemed empty. It seemed accusatory.

Johannes knew they were late. It was bad enough it had taken over a month to set up the date with Cadman, the city worker he'd met when he'd trolleyed downtown to witness the tearing down of the War Services Center, the city worker whose glass eye made him wonder if a scarred and damaged Cadman would see a mate in a fitful and fading Aunt Betty, but now various arguments kept them from leaving. Betty's combativeness initially surprised him: she knew how important this was to him, to Eileen. He'd made a promise, he'd delivered. But he understood nerves now gripped her; her shaking made it difficult to place a few half-moon nail bits on her tongue.

First she refused to go on her own; Johannes agreed to accompany her. Then she fussed with her clothes; Johannes stopped her from going to Halle's for a new outfit. Then it was the jar. Betty wanted it; Johannes didn't. They compromised: Betty could bring a small envelope containing three nails, no more, but she had to leave it in her purse.

Johannes positioned Betty on his left side and looped the woven wire latch over the gate that marked the edge of Betty's property. Betty had bought the fence from Sears, Roebuck & Co. before the war, before the steel shortage, and the crimped galvanized wire fence encircled the property, marked her garden, when it wasn't winter, as hers.

The bar was a short walk down Hough. He'd been there once before, found it a quiet place, peaceful, found the two brothers who owned it kind, although he cringed at their free use of racial epithets and slurs. Sure, they were acceptable words of sorts, but they didn't work for him. And the area, Hough, the former Little Hollywood, was changing: culture, sports, shopping, business, they were all becoming, subtly, derelict. Yet the neighborhood's slight decline had nothing to do with who was moving in.

He threaded Aunt Betty's right arm through his left and led her down the street, his limp counter-balanced by her shaking body.

Johannes imagined Cadman and Aunt Betty hitting it off, talking for hours. Who knew? Maybe—a long-shot maybe—Cadman would even partake of her nails. He pictured Cadman walking Betty home, taking his, Johannes's, place, pictured himself attending their wedding after a whirlwind courtship. His own wedding, many years ago, popped in his mind. Eileen's veil not nearly enough to hide her beauty; he relived their final argument before he left for war as she told him how she was getting a job at The Mounds Club, a place he had heard was both disreputable and dangerous; and then he imagined Eileen's bloated body floating face down in Wade Lagoon. His foot slipped into the gutter, jolted him back to the now.

They were well over an hour late when Johannes pushed open the door and held it with outstretched arm for Betty to lead the way into the dimness. The music and voices hit him first as his eyes adjusted: Perry Como's "Prisoner of Love" mixed with one of the young owners telling a customer about an old brewery wagon driver, friend of his father, who swore he'd heard ghosts rolling barrels on the upper floors of the old Cleveland Brewing Company. The sounds gave way to the sights: pictures of a lattice-like frame of the Terminal Tower in the '20s; League Park; various over-the-years' team pictures of the Cleveland Rams, the Cleveland Browns, the Cleveland Indians; the Arena; and, surprisingly, a tiny photo of Sam Jethroe, centerfielder for the Negro Leagues' Cleveland Buckeyes.

And then Johannes saw Cadman. His head was down, folded into his arms, half a dozen mostly empty C.B.C. beer bottles in front of him. Cadman raised his head and scanned the room but didn't seem to see Johannes. Cadman put on and took off his hat several times, even once turning it over and tapping the crown as if something useful might drop out. He placed the hat, crown down, on the table and upended and finished another beer. Cadman's fingers rubbed his temple and then found the scar and followed it through his beard and into his collar. When they'd met, Cadman, a three-foot-long piece of the wooden war memorial in his hands, told Johannes about that scar—"I had fists, he had a knife"—and Johannes had trusted Cadman when he'd said, fingernail clicking his left eye, that he'd since reformed his ways. Johannes now felt stupid, naïve.

Johannes now, in this moment, saw self-loathing in Cadman's expression. He'd misread him in the Square. He made ready to escort Betty home, abort the mission, but heard Cadman call: "Over here, your highness."

Aunt Betty released herself from Johannes and removed a glove. "I like his scar," she said.

"Sorry we're—"

"Save it." Cadman looked Betty up and down, his lone eye widening and narrowing until he reached her face, her shaking face. Cadman's head momentarily wobbled in imitation. "So you're Bouncing Betty, yeah?"

"Now wait just a—"

Betty said yes and extended her bare hand; it was unexpectedly steady.

Cadman ignored the gesture. He wiped his mouth, wiped the

35

same hand across his chest. A dark trail of saliva marked his shirt. "Sit." He patted the chair. "Betty, here." He pointed across the table. "You, there." When a waitress approached, he waved her off with the same hand. "Tell me, tell me."

"Tell you—?"

He tapped his watch. "Why your time is more important than mine."

Johannes studied Cadman, who studied Betty. A triangle of stares. Johannes had Cadman's glass eye in his favor, could study him unnoticed, unashamedly. The radio played "Doin' What Comes Natur'lly" and Cadman's tapping finger couldn't keep the rhythm, always a beat or two off.

Cadman said, "I should've seen this." He tapped the table, then tapped each eye. "Some told me, back in the day, that the loss of my eye would bring me insight, wisdom. 'The Oracle of Hough,' they'd call me." His hands ping-ponged a bottle back and forth, back and forth, across the table. "That sure as shit didn't happen, did it."

Aunt Betty looked to Johannes. "Should we leave?"

Johannes had served with heroes. And he'd served with unbalanced men, soldiers who disobeyed orders, who reveled in death, thrived in blood. Cadman's gaze and open and obvious contempt reminded Johannes of Gunnery Sergeant Perkins. After their 1st Marine Division had fended off scads of Japanese on Peleliu, a little volcanic island in the Pacific, Johannes didn't understand when Perkins forced eight prisoners to kneel and outstretch their arms on rocks he had placed in front of them. He didn't understand when Perkins removed a machete from his belt. He didn't understand when Perkins made a speech filled with references to Caesar and Uxellodunum. He didn't understand the eight pairs of hands that lay on the beach and the eight screaming prisoners. Yes, Johannes knew war, knew the taking of so many others' lives marked his soul, but he had never understood cruelty. He should have stopped Perkins. But the best he could manage was to shoot each prisoner in the back of the head.

"Yes," Johannes said. He kept his gaze on this Cadman, this Perkins. "We should leave." He stood, placed his hat on his head, hooked his hand under Betty's elbow.

"You're not going anywhere," Cadman said. "You're going to

36

sit, and we're going to have us a chat." Cadman held Betty's arm. She was stretched between the men, a Betty tug-of-war. "It's our chance to get to know each other."

Johannes reached across and loosened Cadman's grip. "I made a mistake."

"You're making one now." Cadman gripped the neck of an empty beer bottle, tested its weight.

Johannes arm-swept Betty behind him, positioned himself between Cadman and Betty.

Cadman said, "I am the Oracle." He slapped the fat end of the bottle in his open palm.

Johannes felt Aunt Betty shaking badly. He turned to check on her, to move them away from this. "Betty, we—" His head exploded and his vision shifted and his hip buckled and Betty and her screams dopplered sideways as he went down.

Johannes's breath, exhalations coming rapidly, pushed droplets of foam and bits of beer bottle glass in front of him. He was taken by the sight, blinked in slow rhythm to his breath and the subtle movement on the floor. A dull hum or a muted roar—it was hard to define—filled him with waves crashing into the Peleliu beach. He was, he thought, swimming in the sound. But that didn't make any sense, did it? He smiled at his nonsense. His head hurt. A wetness slid down his neck. He tried to move his head, to touch the pain, but he couldn't. A soft insistent pressure held his head still.

"Don't move, don't move, don't move." A woman's voice. What woman? "You're hurt." A face hovered erratically, sideways. Oh, that woman. She, she—. "They're calling for help, so lay still." She seemed nice. Reminded him of someone. Someone else. Nice. No. Not possible. She was dead.

"Eileen," Johannes said.

"Not now." The woman's face—he did know her, he did— disappeared. Her knees pressed into the glass bits, held the bits still. "Hurry," her knees said.

Johannes thought, Yes. Hurry.

He needed seventeen stitches—nine at the base of his skull and eight on the side of his head, the side that had struck and stained the bar's wood floor. When they rolled him onto the stretcher, he felt bits of hair and skin pull away, stick to the floor. He recalled the smell of ethanol and the odd thought that he was traveling to a hospital in a hearse. Who knew hearses served as ambulances? After an extended stay at Mt. Sinai, his head grappling with dreams of Moses receiving the laws, he learned from Betty that he took two solid knocks on the head, that he was lucky his marbles hadn't spilled out.

He slept a lot, now in Betty's bed at home, and he swore he could feel his brain, swollen, pressing on the inside of his right eye. Convalescing, he'd heard it called, back at The Hudson Boys' School. If one of the other boys wasn't on the job reforming himself through a back-to-the-land theory of farming, hunting, trapping, fishing, or one of the cottage parents was absent, Mr. Parker said they were "busy convalescing," and then added, "the layabouts."

The last thing he really remembered, the last event that tracked, was holding the door open for Betty, his hand at her back guiding her inside. He didn't remember meeting Cadman. He didn't remember Cadman's rudeness. He didn't remember Cadman's attack.

He spent weeks in bed, bored and disoriented. His vision doubled. Betty read him the *Plain Dealer*, first page to last, every morning. The susurrus paper shaking in her hands didn't bother him. And the dates sailed past.

By April, Johannes had learned of the forced resignation of the governor of Formosa after he'd slaughtered 5,000 natives; of an Illinois mine accident that killed over 100, a note above the suffocated bodies advising whoever found them to search their pockets for notes to wives and children; of a Bronx bus driver who, leaving his family behind, hopped on highway No. 1 and kept on going all the way to a Hollywood, Florida, racetrack; of an April Fool's joke advising anyone and everyone to call Shadyside-7711, the zoo, and cleverly ask for Mr. Bear, Mr. Fox, and Mr. Wolf. Currently, Betty reread an article about some guy who'd stood eggs on their ends, something to do with the vernal equinox.

He'd fought for that, Johannes thought, right? For people to do nonsensical things, to live a life of bus-stealing and egg-standing foolery? He knuckled his temples to dispel his discomfort. "Look," he said. "I'm sorry."

Betty peered at him over the paper and tsked disapproval, waved a shaking hand his way. "You tried, Johannes. *I'm* sorry. All of this on account of me."

"I try to keep my promises."

"You do, yes."

"But I don't. Not to you, not to Eileen, not to myself." Johannes stared at a spidery tree still bare from winter. Thin branches ticked against the window, the sound exceedingly loud to him. "And I see her. Often." Johannes tugged at his blankets, pulled them to his chin. "Saw her the day I met Cadman. Could swear it was her, this woman, who bumped into me, knocked me down."

"But it wasn't, Johannes. Euphemisms aside, and not to put too fine a point on it, but she, Eileen, is dead. Gone."

"My head, it plays tricks on me." He pushed the blankets off of him, suddenly too hot. "You look like her, I think. Sometimes." He wiped his face with his hand, up and down, up and down. "But you're kinder. I may have promised Eileen, but I did it for you."

Betty smiled, shuffled and reshuffled the paper. Johannes couldn't be sure, but it seemed that Betty held still.

"If I could do this one thing. For you. It might—"

"Stop, Johannes. I am not yours to fix." She sighed. "I'm just not. And your promise? I'm freeing you from it."

Johannes continued to wrestle with the blankets. He couldn't get his temperature right. His head ached. "You know I killed?"

Betty re-folded the paper, set it on the nightstand peppered with pill bottles for his pain and half-empty water glasses for his thirst. "I imagine you did."

"Violence, it follows me."

"Nonsense."

"Getting worse."

"Nonsense." But Betty's head nodded, contradicted her claim. Johannes nodded back, but not in mockery: he agreed with her body not her words. The body always knows the truth before the mind. The branches ticked again, pulled his attention.

"You know, my grandma—I don't think I or Eileen ever told you," Johannes said, "she terrorized me. Some of my earliest memories, her furious heels hitting tiled hallway. Just like that." Johannes pointed at the window, the ticking branches. "She'd sweep in mad as hell and, if I was lucky, scream and yell. If I was unlucky, she'd throw the nearest, heaviest object at me. Hell, if I walked in the snow-covered front yard, marred it with my footprints, I'd get it. A kid, you know? I was bad, I guess. I was bad."

Betty closed her eyes.

Johannes tried running away. The first try, he got as far as the corner before a neighbor, an ally of his grandmother's, escorted him home. The fifth time, he escaped school during lunch, made it to the Pick-N-Pay, when a policeman approached, questioned why he wasn't in school. He initially tried to explain, pulled up his sleeve to show the marks on his right arm, but the officer only talked about familial loyalty and educational responsibility. As soon as the officer was out of sight, Johannes's grandmother lit into him.

For weeks and months after his eighth attempt, he had witnessed at a distance a new building growing skeletally. A classmate's father worked on the building, welded beam to beam, built the skeleton into a body that would house at its center a vast train station, arterial tracks snaking out of the city. A young Johannes had pictured those tracks ferrying him across the Cuyahoga, moving him away from his present self to a safer and truer one. But his youthful ideas were just that. The rails of his freedom ran parallel to one another, mirrored what came before, what must come after.

His eleventh escape—he notched each attempt on the wooden windowsill with a tiny pair of scissors—brought him to Public Square. He couldn't watch the Union Terminal from afar any longer. And then that man opened up his world, gave him a trolley with which to run wild. He felt free. Until the troller jumped off the wiring above and the trolley stopped. A young boy cursing loudly on the roof of an empty trolley draws attention, especially near Franklin Circle in the middle of the night. When the policeman took him home, his grandmother said she was done with him.

"Hudson wasn't much better," Johannes now said.

"I know."

"Then the war—what I saw, what I did. Eileen's death. You. This." He touched the bandage at his temple.

"That man," Betty said, "that man was no good. Nothing to

do with you." She apparently hadn't liked how she'd arranged the newspaper on the nightstand, took it back, re-tidied it in her lap. "You cannot control others, the world around you."

Johannes nodded absently, his eyes heavy. Within moments he slept.

After finishing the paper, Betty would read to him from her travel books. Odd, he thought, how she so desperately wanted to escape and he so desperately wanted to settle.

Other times she'd sift through a shoebox of seashells and rocks. The shells came from a trip Eileen had taken to Florida, the rocks from Betty's own garden. Occasionally Betty's hands would emerge with an almost matched set of shells. With surprising steadiness she'd glue them together. Add a spiral shell, small obsidian pebbles, and before Johannes's eyes a bird—or two birds, depending on his head—would come to life, perched on a piece of granite. In time, Johannes found himself surrounded by shell birds, shell gators, shell horses, shell snails. And in time he made slow and mobile progress and occasionally unmoored himself from his bed in ways his seashell pets could not.

On good days, the pressure and the headaches eased; on bad days they were relentless. He remembered a Greek myth, taught to him by one of the cottage parents at Hudson, that Athena sprang full-grown and armored from Zeus' head, the birth the result of an intense headache that only the smithy's hammer could cure. Johannes wished for a hammer. He wished that the epitome of wisdom would spring forth. And if not, that the strike of the hammer would end him.

Betty compelled Johannes to attend Easter service at The Old Stone Church. She said it would do him good. Johannes doubted.

She wore a beige suit, the shadow striping giving both the straight skirt and the long jacket a lengthened emphasis. With her calfskin pumps and blue sailor hat finished with beige moiré bows, Betty appeared taller, as if she had a far-reaching significance that Johannes couldn't discern. Johannes pulled a thin box from between the mattress and the box spring, presented it to Betty. A thank you, he said, for caring for me the last few months.

Betty's hands shakily unwrapped and opened it.

41

"It's hand-painted," Johannes said. "The artist, Edith Gohr? At May Company last week. That day I slept all day? That morning took a lot out of me."

A hand spasmodically wiped a tear off course, created a zig-zag trail that glistened on her cheek. "It's beautiful." The scarf's image, which Johannes had requested of the artist, was a bright field of morning glories, Betty's favorites. "Too much, it's too much," she said.

Johannes expected this, had prepared a lie. "Eagle Stamps paid for most of it."

Betty's head jerked from the glories to Johannes. He couldn't tell if she believed him. She studied his old gray suit. It hung on him loosely, too big for his slight frame—he'd lost weight since the assault. "You wisp of a man, you should have used them to get yourself a new suit." Her fingers worked the scarf around her neck. "But this, this is lovely."

"It's becoming," Johannes said. And it was. Very. In that moment, to Johannes, Betty was both older and younger, at once mature and unripe.

Johannes removed his hat as they entered the Old Stone Church. Betty sat beside him in a pew and silently prayed. The stained-glass Tiffany window, "The Sower," caused Johannes to wonder, not for the first time, at its significance. But now it seemed to blast a sunny aura around Betty.

The church was full to overflowing. The aisles on either side held the standing and the standing spilled into the vestibule behind them. After war or tragedy or heartache, people always seemed to become a more spiritual lot. Fur coats made a final appearance today, summer storage and preservation in Engel-Fetzer sawdust their after-service fate. The pews, recently polished to a gleam, filled Johannes's nose with smells of saints.

The reverend entered and the Easter service began. Betty held Johannes's hand and did not shake. Johannes's attention drifted, became held by the mass of people, the men in navy or black suits, purchased from Zucker's most likely, the women in beige and white and flower-laden hats. One woman, in a pew across the center aisle, removed her hat, adjusted a runaway strand of hair, and pinned the hat back in place. Johannes squeezed Betty's hand and studied the woman, waited for her to turn.

The service followed a familiar flow: prayer, song, scripture, sermon. Johannes simply stared. It wasn't until Betty whispered in his ear that he should pay attention, that the reverend was speaking directly to him, that Johannes moved his attention away from the woman, the woman that he was certain, no matter how unlikely, was Eileen.

The reverend, the pulpit holding him aloft, began with a chastisement for those not attending more regularly before moving on to the crucifixion, Jesus' time on the cross, and the world he'd left behind. He said, "God is not aloof from human suffering."

Johannes removed his hand from Betty's, rubbed his head. He tried to focus.

"On Calvary God obtained scars far worse than ours and there are no sorrows He has not sounded."

The words pinged inside Johannes. The reverend, he was wrong, Johannes thought. He rubbed his head harder. He felt sick.

Johannes looked for her again. He couldn't find her, couldn't find her, couldn't find her. Faces blurred. He pulled at his collar. Betty touched his arm, looked at him expectantly. Her hands twitched back to life. Her head nodded and Johannes couldn't tell if she were agreeing with his assessment of the woman or not.

The Sacrament of the Lord's Supper sealed the congregants' promise of faith. Johannes felt as if a transformation should have completed, that his pains should have eased, that his head should have cleared.

"Stay," Johannes said. He patted Betty's arm, kissed her cheek, rose and pushed his limping self through the throng and out into Public Square.

In May, Betty and Johannes returned home after having seen the G.I. musical "Call Me Mister" at the Hanna. Betty clicked a lamp and the bulb burst sending the room from light to dark.

She said she had a new bulb somewhere, stepped into the kitchen.

They had walked home in silence, the stars hanging in the sky like a grand chandelier. The play, in turn maudlin and absurd, featured some of Betty's favorites—Betty Kean, Carl Reiner, Bob Fosse—and it began humorously enough: a sketch playfully mocked the Air Force from the view of the infantrymen. In all he'd seen, in all he'd experienced, the island invasion the most brutal, Johannes tended to agree with the sketch. It had seemed like the flyers were far removed from the violent world, lived a life of Sybaritic luxury. Johannes had laughed. He had relaxed for the first time in months. He leaned his body closer to Betty; their shoulders touched. Betty ate fingernails like popcorn.

Then the final sketch. It was a simple story: a soldier, Carl Reiner, returns home in perfect health, but his family, alarmed by articles they've read regarding the horrors of war, assume he must be a lunatic. One extreme overreaction after another reveals the soldier as the only sane member in the house.

Johannes felt removed: from Betty, from Eileen, from himself.

Certainly Johannes's hip and head did not equal perfect health. But he couldn't help but wonder if his magnetism to violence, or at least his hyperawareness of it, meant something deeper. Or was the world changing, itself becoming more violent? The preoccupation with such distractions as baseball and football and bird clubs—Betty had gone to one bird club at the spring salon in the Higbee's lounge just last week—allowed a naïve clinging to that which no longer held fast. Amidst the advertisements and the radio programs, the movies and the sports scores, the comics and the puzzles, the news was peopled with men doing terrible things. And while occasionally there'd be an article exhorting the instilling of love and peace into the youth, making them "lamplighters of the world," Johannes couldn't get over the fact that many of them, too many, had, like him, been taught to lie, encouraged to cheat, forced to steal, tempted to kill. The world was different, he was different, and maybe it was time to accept that.

All of this flashed through Johannes in the time it took Betty to return with a new bulb.

"Let me," he said.

"That's sweet." Betty pulled off her gloves and laid them over the armrest of Johannes's couch. "Tea?"

Johannes held the bulb in his fingertips. He felt, for a moment, that his anxious energy, triggered by that last sketch, would course through his heart, his arm, his hand, his fingers, and bring light. His other hand rubbed his hip. "Tea? Yes. Please."

Betty disappeared into the kitchen again while Johannes worked the broken bulb out of the lamp's socket. He pulled his hand back quickly, sucked at his fingers, copper in his mouth. A rivulet of blood slid toward his chin. Betty, tea cups in hand, found him like this.

"Damn bulb." He spoke around his fingers.

Betty grabbed at Johannes's elbow. "Let me—"

He pulled away, but then relented to her shaking touch.

"Stupid," Johannes said as Betty pressed the edges of the wound together.

"Potato," Betty said.

"What?"

"Potato. Slice it in half, slide it over the broken shards of the bulb. Twist."

"Now you tell me."

She laughed. "Always hurting yourself."

Her laugh reminded Johannes of Eileen. He'd liked that laugh. He looked at the lamp, thought of halved potatoes.

"Hold it like this." Betty disappeared upstairs. Johannes closed his eyes, pictured Eileen, felt Betty's touch at the play, heard their laughs blur together. He jumped when Betty pressed a damp towel to his hand.

"How on earth did you survive the war?" Betty placed several bandages between her lips.

"You're older, of course, but you're a lot like her, you know."

"Hmm?"

"Eileen."

"Hmm." A slight frown creased the bandages. She took them from her mouth, wrapped two fingers together tightly, scissors and tape finishing the job. "That should do it." She picked up the damp and pink-stained towel, the bandage scraps, the scissors.

As she turned away, Johannes reached out, turned her to face him. "I'm sorry," he said. And he kissed her. Her left hand dropped the towel and slapped at his chest, his hip. Johannes held tight. He pressed his forehead to Betty's. "I've missed you so much."

Betty continued to slap at him, softer. "Johannes. I'm not, listen to me, I'm not—"

"Stop." He shook his head, his forehead rolling back and forth on hers. "I promised you a man."

"Dead. Eileen's dead." A tear hit Betty's cheek, rolled into her mouth. She did not cry.

"I need—"

"I know."

"I need to—" He moved to kiss her again. Betty turned her face away. "Please." Johannes's grip tightened on her arms.

Betty's hand still held the scissors. She repositioned them in her hand.

Johannes's fingers ached. His hip throbbed. He slid down Betty's body, hands gliding over her curves, until he sat on the floor, legs bowed around Betty, arms stretched palms up in front of him, head bent. His body shook as he cried. Betty placed a hand on his head. They stayed like that for minutes, in the muted darkness.

She bent over and pressed her head against his. "Johannes." She set the scissors on the floor and cupped her hands under his arms, tugged.

Johannes got on one knee, paused, then stood. Betty ushered him to the couch. He fell to his seat; the springs groaned. She sat beside him, placed a pillow between them.

"I could never," Johannes said, "understand the why."

"The—?"

"Her need to work there, The Mounds. With those men. We were OK. We were doing OK." Johannes lowered his head. His chin touched his chest; a speck of blood spotted his shirt. "Her dying? It just doesn't—"

Betty looked away.

"I keep seeing her," Johannes said. "Have I told you that?" He couldn't remember if he had or not, his memories of late uncertain. His palms rubbed his eyes.

"I'm not her, Johannes." She slapped his knee. "What you just—"

"I'm so sorry." Johannes picked at the edges of the bandages. "I get, I'm just, confused. Can you understand?" Johannes closed his eyes. The words of Carl Reiner resonated: "I'm not crazy."

In Betty's house, the lingering and dying smells of Erigenia and toothwort swam through the open window of the kitchen. The golden-hot but humidity-free days loosened his hip and the aroma lessened the ache in his never-quite-healed head.

His summer had been filled with picnics and music in the

park, with small block parties and meetings of the Polish Legion of American Veterans, with reading Betty's travel books (when his head didn't hurt), and with occasional films at the Lowe's or the RKO Palace (when his hip allowed him to stay seated). Today, a cloudy day in early September, he was going to his first baseball game in years. Not as an usher, but as a fan.

He suited up in a hybrid uniform. The Indians were honoring his veteran's group, yet he wanted to honor both his service to country and his service to Cleveland so he sported his military dress shirt and cap but wore the blue and gold pants and jacket from his ushering days at the now little-used League Park.

"You look," Betty said, "nice." It was the best word she could come up with for the odd combination he presented. She returned to studying a travel book of Peru.

Johannes smoothed his coat, adjusted his cap, and smiled as the screen door slapped shut behind him.

It was a fast game, done in two hours. The Indians beat the St. Louis Browns 2-1. The Indians struck twice in the first inning and Feller pitched all nine, striking out eight; his fastballs traveled from mound to plate faster than a policeman's motorcycle. The win was nice, and while he was disappointed not to see Larry Doby take a few swings, it was the recognition of his group during the seventh inning that made Johannes's day. The crowd of 10,000 or so in the cavernous stadium offered sincere applause and gratefulness. It filled Johannes's heart, as did the knowing looks from stadium ushers. He felt himself stand straighter, more upright, than he had in many, many months.

He considered going out after the game with some of the others but while he liked their company at times, and while their support had helped him greatly, he opted to walk home alone, his hip loose and his head free.

The walk took him down Chester, toward Hough, toward home. Toward, well, Betty's home. It wasn't his. It hadn't been his. He'd never had a home, a true home. Not with his grandmother, not at Hudson, not even with Eileen, the time cut short by the war. The ease he'd felt during the game and for a short time after began to dissolve in the air along with the sprinkles of soft conversations, clinking dishes, and snippets of songs that came from living room radios and open windows.

He considered guys in the veteran's group as potential Betty suitors—Otto Szalankiewicz seemed pleasant, Alfred White seemed nice—but his promise seemed less and less important. And since he'd taken down the various pictures of Eileen, placed some of her belongings in the hall closet, threw out the tiny lock of hair that had accompanied him in the Pacific, that, to his belief, had insulated him from death, his link to Eileen had waned and so had his link to Betty. He wondered what his life would've been like without Eileen, without violence, without promises. Or maybe all of it brought him here. Regret and rumination, they were for the promise keepers.

He jockeyed up E. 55th, across Lexington, peered through a locked gate at League Park. This place, this was a sacred place. Historically, Cy Young pitched his first game here in 1891. And legends like Ty Cobb, Babe Ruth, Satchel Paige, Lou Gehrig all played here. Personally, Johannes witnessed firsthand the Cleveland Rams' march toward an NFL Championship, witnessed the Cleveland Buckeyes' title in 1945. Even if the latter was the Negro World Series, it was a world series and the Negroes never bothered him, could play some damn fine baseball, in his opinion, and certainly served admirably alongside him in the war as part of the most heroic black units in the Pacific: the 11th Marine Depot Company and the 7th Marine Ammunition Company.

What pulled at Johannes now, though, was one of his first post-marriage dates with Eileen. He'd had to usher, but he'd escorted her to her seat, right across from first base, and checked on her obsessively to the detriment of other fans' needs. The hat she wore that day caught and held the sunlight, refracted it into a soft shadow on her smiling face. After the game, near the spot where Johannes now stood, she'd told him about a job at The Mounds Club, how a man named Moe would drive her there each day, how she expected to make enough money for the both of them, enough money for Betty to take a trip, maybe. Johannes had protested. Eileen insisted. Then while he was eight thousand miles away struggling for life he learned of her death.

That night, Betty and Johannes ate dinner on the front porch, sun setting on their right, plates held delicately in laps, cups balanced on the window's open frame behind them. Johannes told Betty about the game, Betty told Johannes of her latest travelogue, Twain's *Innocents Abroad*. Betty told him of a newfound desire to see the Old World and the Holy Land.

"The hepaticas." Betty gestured toward a large beech tree and a family of plants with heart-shaped leaves and colorful flowers on the lawn beside the street. The tree's roots raised the sidewalk unevenly. "Autumn's almost here." She washed a small piece of bread down with a trembling sip of water.

Johannes watched the hepaticas, flowers partly closed. At Betty's words, their heads seemed to curve downward like the crook of a shepherd's staff. "I'm thinking of going."

Johannes thought he saw a brightness in her eyes, a hopefulness, perhaps. He'd done a horrible job of reading people in the past, though, knew he was likely misreading Betty now, likely far too often misread himself. He was surprised when she said, "Jerusalem?" as if it was an invitation.

Johannes set his empty plate on the porch. "The Mounds."

Betty's head nodded even as she said no.

"I," Johannes said, "need to see."

"There's nothing to see."

The sun fully departed and the *chik-chik-chik-chik* of a hoard of crickets surrounded them.

Betty stood unsteadily. Johannes reached to her but she waved him away. Whatever he'd thought he'd seen in her had vanished. "Let the past, Johannes, be the past." She went inside, catching the screen door with her hand before it had a chance to bang the frame.

Johannes pried himself up. The relief he felt in his hip after the game had since doubled down on the pain. He was now twenty-nine, but his body and spirit felt twice that. He liked to tell Betty he'd gone to pot, that he was beyond repair. But Betty informed him that he misunderstood that phrase, that it instead alluded to a melting pot where scrap metal pieces were converted back into their original state. A smelted rebirth.

Johannes wanted to pick a few flowers, vase them for Betty. But on the second step he lost his footing and went down. His hip banged into the steps and he slid-skipped to the bottom, collapsing waves of pain swallowing him. He cursed and cursed, punched his fist into the pavement until his knuckles bled. His breath was ragged but in time with the *chik-chik-chik-chik* of the crickets, a sound that Johannes believed sounded like laughter.

When Johannes attended a Polish Legion meeting a month later, he learned The Mounds Club had been robbed. Otto told what he'd heard from a friend of a friend who was somehow related to the comedian Peter Lind Hayes, on stage at the time of the strong-arm robbery.

"There were, maybe, twelve of them. Each about the same size. Same suits. Masked. Same masks. Same submachine guns." Otto positioned his arms and hands like a gun. "And guess what they called themselves? Guess. Just guess." He looked in turn to each of the twenty veterans gathered around him. He smacked the table. A sprig of dust shrouded his hand. Gabe coughed. "Numbers. Goddamn numbers. No names. 'Three, take that side.' 'Six, watch him.' 'Ten, get the bags.' Like that. It was a military operation. Precise. Hayes says there were two, three hundred patrons there. Made off with a half-million dollars. At least."

Louis whistled. Michael wondered aloud what he'd do with that much money. Gabe asked if anyone was hurt.

"Scrapes, bruises. A few shots fired. But I don't know. I don't know."

Johannes said, "Serves them right."

"Serves them right?"

"The Club. Them that own it."

"My guy says the owners didn't lose nearly as much as the patrons. Hell, Hayes and his wife lost over a thousand in jewelry, cash. And they were just performers. The rest, the gamblers? *They* had the cash." Otto wiped dust from his hand. "I tell you what, those are some dead men."

"Who?" Johannes said.

"The numbers. The owners, they're putting out the word."

Johannes felt a sense of justice. He pulled on his trench, belted it around his waist, readied to leave. He wasn't sure why he stopped and asked what he asked; he'd truly given up long ago, he felt. But: "Otto, you maybe someday going to come and meet Betty?"

Several of the guys shook their bodies and laughed. And then Johannes remembered.

A week passed. With The Mounds Club fresh in his mind, both Johannes's desire to visit the place and his visions of Eileen increased. He could swear he saw her at Chandler & Rudd grocers, on the corner of Chester and E. 105th, at the RKO Palace during a showing of *The Best Years of Our Lives*. It wasn't until he and Betty wandered into Wade Park one evening, only the second time he'd been there since meeting Eileen all those years ago, that he felt maybe, just maybe, he could at last let her go.

"This is where we met," Johannes said.

"I know," Betty said. "She told me."

Before the war, Johannes had found a job collecting trash and corralling stray swans around the Museum of Art. After Johannes had finished working a long-handled net to skim the leaves and garbage from the Lagoon, after he had collected the detritus into his shoulder-slung bag, after he'd laid the net in the grass, dried his legs, shoed his feet, after he'd made the mistake of swiping his net at several flies that circled a woman lounging languidly on a sun-dappled blanket, after he'd sprinkled her with droplets of cold water, that, as Johannes had said, was that.

Betty and Johannes now stood beside the bronze sculpture of *Night Passing the Earth to Day*. In the distance, the neoclassic white marble façade of the art museum; directly before them, the Lagoon in which Eileen's body had been found.

"The things that happen in this world, they don't make sense. To me."

"Johannes." Betty moved her bare hand, the hand that had been resting on one of the bronze figures—Night or Day, Johannes couldn't tell—and touched his cheek. Her hand felt cold. "When something, some event, is fixed to happen, it's fixed to happen. We can hope it won't, but that's about it. So we learn. We learn who we are, even at our worst." Betty removed her hand, patted and rubbed Johannes's shoulder. It was a gesture an aunt would make. "The world doesn't define us, doesn't end us, Johannes. Do you see?"

"There's a single moment, a, a, a lightning bug spark of a

moment, when I first open my eyes in the morning, that I think, Today's a good—I feel good. Then Eileen comes. The war comes. The dead come. The weight of it all—" Johannes raised a hand and tapped the metal world. "It crushes. Waves of it come and come and come." Betty nodded but Johannes couldn't be sure she understood, truly.

"Coming here was a bad idea," Betty said.

"No, listen." Johannes grabbed Betty's shoulders, lowered his body so his eyes were even with hers.

Betty tried to step back, couldn't.

"I'm not—" Johannes said. "I'm not—I just need you to listen."

"OK."

"I met her here. She died here." Johannes's head ached. "Parts of me, they're everywhere: Grandma, Hudson, League Park, Pacific, Peleliu, Eileen. This place. It all—" He released her shoulders and stood straighter. He laughed. "Eileen used to say I chewed with my mouth open. I didn't, I don't think, but she said she loved me, she told me once, because, despite my childhood, I took in everything in great mouthfuls. Work. Baseball. Life. Love. All of it. I breathed in, my mouth wide, and swallowed it all. But that openness? Loss, grief, suffering, they all find their way in, too, yeah?"

"I don't think this is helping you."

"I'm trying to say I'm done. With her." It had begun to rain. Drops fell from Johannes's head as he nodded toward the rippling Lagoon. He heel-rubbed his eyes. "I won't see her anymore."

Johannes had been working in the attic, ridding it of as much of the final remnants of Eileen as Betty would allow. He worked up a sweat even though a crisp October evening reigned outside. When he grabbed several stacked boxes and descended downstairs, he found two men sitting on his couch and Betty in a chair across from them. One, his felt fedora hooked on his knee, held a teacup featuring a picture overlooking Rio. The other held his hat in his hand, spinning it from hand to hand. Over and over. The dim lamplight beside Betty skittered across a badge on his belt. A closed notebook rested on his thigh.

Teacup rose, his hat falling to the floor. "Johannes?" He

looked at Shiny Badge who opened his notebook, double-checked something.

Betty said, "They're here to offer, to ask, I mean—"

"We've some questions, Mr. Sykora." Teacup extended his hand.

Johannes set the boxes on the last step, wiped his hand on his shirt, and reached to shake Teacup's hand but realized he, Teacup, was merely gesturing toward the chair beside Betty. On the low table between Johannes's chair and Betty sat a jar of clipped and torn nails. Johannes wondered if she'd offered them to the policemen.

Betty grabbed the Mason jar and screwed and unscrewed the lid. "It's about time. You police, you never—"

"What do you know," Teacup said to Johannes, "about that robbery a few weeks back?"

The dust from the attic had holed up in Johannes's lungs. He coughed. "The Mounds? What the papers say, what fellas at the Legion say."

"Legion."

"Polish Legion of American Veterans."

Betty opened the jar, removed the lid. Her fingers fished.

"You Polish?" Shiny Badge spun his hat around.

"Slavic."

"Huh," Shiny Badge said. "My mother's Polish." He shrugged. "Do you know what happened?"

"Gambling. Drinking. Shows."

"No, the night of—"

"I wasn't there."

"It seems one or two people you know were," Teacup said.

"Cadman Collins," Shiny Badge said. "Scar. Glass eye."

Johannes nodded, wiped a streak of sweat from his forehead.

"This Cadman, he was found murdered in Toledo two nights ago."

Betty smiled at Johannes. Johannes ignored it. It's like she sought a new connection with him. But Johannes felt any connection he'd felt with her—whether it be during his time spent convalescing, she his caretaker, that past Easter service, that night during and after the play, that day at the Museum—those connections, he felt, were dying, dead. Johannes looked from Shiny

53

Badge to Betty. She had one finger in the jar scrambling for an elusive nail, rattling them all. She felt it, too, he thought. She felt it, too.

Behind Shiny Badge, through the window, lightning bugs glowed then turned dark. Johannes remembered as a kid at Hudson Farms hunting lightning bugs with a thick stick. He'd step carefully through the tall grass behind his cottage and wait. A glow. A swing. A shower of sparks raining softly then blackening before hitting the earth. Johannes reached across the table, gripped Betty's hand, ended her search.

"Eileen McGinty, neé Sykora, neé Hannigen, her body was found this morning in a dump out in Lake County," Shiny Badge said.

"I don't under—" Johannes reached for the mantle to help him stand. He instead knocked off a small figurine of a primly dressed man presenting a bouquet of flowers to a woman holding an umbrella. It bounced once, twice, shattered. Johannes fell back into the chair.

"Mr. Sykora, we need you to—"

"I'm sorry." Betty's eyes were rheumy. Johannes wasn't sure what she was sorry for.

"You need—?" The room felt small. Johannes's clothes felt tight.

Teacup said, "She might've been, not sure, but she might've been their person. Inside. Electrified fence had been shut down, allowed them access."

Shiny Badge checked his notes again. "A witness reported a Number Eleven—"

"It doesn't matter." Johannes leaned over the arm of the chair, picked up pieces of the man. Betty reached a shaking hand to help Johannes. "Leave it," Johannes said. Betty was now on her hands and knees, helping. Johannes gently pushed her back into her seat, handed her the Mason jar. Betty had said that once a thing's fixed, it's fixed. That the world doesn't end us. Not true, Johannes thought, not true. "Can I—?"

Teacup, who had set the empty Rio cup on the table minutes ago, pulled out a picture.

"She looks different." Betty finger-scooped several crescent-shaped nails from the jar into her mouth. She cried, inhalations and exhalations coming quickly.

"Is it her?"

"I thought she was—"

"Is it her?" Shiny Badge said.

A small delicate hand, lit by the lamp between Betty and Johannes, fluttered to Betty's throat, captured the three men's attention. Betty's hand looked transparent, touched her throat, pawed at it softly. Johannes shifted forward in his chair but Teacup was already on his feet, a hand on Betty's shoulder. "Can you breathe?"

Johannes watched what happened next as behind a veil or a caul. The thought of Eileen alive all this time, unknown to him, she not even contacting him since his Pacific return, the memory of seeing her or thinking he saw her—in the church, at the play, at the movies—made his vision falter as the slowed-down movement of Teacup pulling Betty upright, laying her on the floor, sticking a finger in her mouth and digging, then taking a fist and practically punching her solar plexus, forcing bursts of air up up up, punching once, twice—*chik-chik*—a bone? a rib? cracking, the voice of Shiny Badge on the phone requesting a somnambulant, no, no, an ambulance, or a hearse like before, and a distant roar of breath rushing into Betty's lungs, a roar like that of the surf at Peleliu but not that roar, not really, not possible, for he was in Cleveland and Eileen was alive, Betty was alive, he was alive, and Eileen was dead.

For days, Johannes wandered Betty's empty house. In her room, he sat on the bed where he'd spent so many prolonged days recovering himself. Once she was released from Mt. Sinai, Betty would be here, too. He wondered if he would be here, then. If he *should* be here, then. He had proclaimed he wouldn't see her anymore. He wasn't sure to whom he'd referred.

Books and maps lay on the nightstand. Dog-eared pages told of sin-filled Sodoms in Nevada, restive Edens in the Caribbean, olive-treed Gethsemanes in the Middle East. Johannes replaced the books, hobbled downstairs, and outside. He hadn't intended to walk anywhere, but found himself walking nonetheless. The wheel of stars above him turned slowly, imperceptibly. Johannes wondered about comets, of falling stars, of fleeting lives. His mind rolled backward to the beaches of Peleliu and those hand-less deaths, to Cadman's assault and the effect on his brain, to Eileen's death and resurrection and death, to the beatings he took at Hudson, to the trolley ride that started it all.

He found himself inside the Old Stone Church again, seated in the same pew as the earlier Easter. The Amasa Stone stained glass window glowed softly and watched over him from behind. Johannes thought it odd that the industrialist and Old Stone Church savior would be honored so grandly. Stone had killed him-self after his negligence led to the bridge-collapsing death of 92 people. We honor others in strange ways and for strange reasons, Johannes thought. And sometimes we don't honor them at all.

OUR LADY OF CLEVELAND, 1954

I heard the cracks of .22's echo through the Stockyards, the other knockers finishing their early day with final shots. I trusted, had always trusted, the steel face of my great hammer. I needed the physicality of the stroke, had to feel my large hands and swollen forearms, my tensing shoulders and my thick legs, had to feel each and every part of my body vibrate with exertion and with the impact of hammer against skull. And it's how I spent my anger and loss. A .22 felt weak and empty, and even those knockers who'd switched to the rifle sometimes missed and the beast would crash into the sides of the chute, exciting the others, causing the brief panic that we would all be overrun, until a second report finished the job.

The white- and brown-headed steer in front of me was the last before the game, the game the reason we were released early today, the game I hoped would be a sign. Its large eyes stared at me blankly, accepting its fate. The ancient blisters rasped against the wood handle as I reloaded the sledge. I cocked my arms: batter up. I felt like Wertz digging in; early word was he was having a helluva day.

I inhaled as I brought the sledge first low and then behind, my lungs filled with a mix of dirt and manure and blood and sweat, and I swung for the last time today, felt my muscles tense and then explode in unison as I released my breath, a loud "Paahhhh!" escaping my puffed cheeks as the hammer's hard steel connected forcefully with the steer's hard-then-hammer-softened forehead, the contact sending a rattling up the handle, through my arms, to my shoulders. I loved that feeling. I loved my job.

Usually a steer dropped immediately, easily stunned, often dead. This steer stayed standing, shook its head and blinked, bored with me.

Jozef, a Czechoslovakian like me—he had lived two towns over, married my cousin Edita, knew my grief over Isabel—returned from chaining and dragging the previous steer to the cutter and the bloodletting. "Finish, Mart. David says it's 2-2." David was one of the urban cowboys who led the steers into their pens and from their pens down the chutes to me and the other knockers. We'd watch the rest of the game at Jozef's, thirty of us gathered tightly on his porch. He and six of his neighbors had gone in together to buy a television set, passed it around on a daily basis, each getting a turn to have the outside world brought inside his home. And today was the first game of the World Series. "I—"

"Let's go," Jozef said. "Eighth inning's about to start."

"I already—" But I didn't know what to say.

I heard other knockers locking their rifles away in the other room, heard gates opening and closing, heard the sounds of the abattoir shutting down, heard the talk of the Indians winding up. At this job for twenty-plus years, never had a steer withstand my assault. Maybe my swings were weaker, maybe I couldn't last the whole day, maybe I'd have to switch to the .22. I nodded dumbly at Jozef, grasped the handle, swung again, hard enough to shatter brick. Nothing. The steer shook its head again, blinked, waited for more. I breathed nervously, felt a pinch in my chest.

Jozef gasped and as I readied another swing he grasped the handle and stopped me. He pointed. "Look." His finger traced the outline of a brown patch that wound its way over the face of the steer, around its right eye.

"I don't—" I said.

"Look." Jozef pointed again, traced again. "Don't you see?"

The Cleveland *Press* had been running versions of Rorschach-like inkblots in its pages, inviting readers to submit their interpretations. It was entertaining, what people saw. Butterflies, trees, wolves, flowers, bats, spread animal hides. Jozef was testing me.

I sat the sledge's head on the ground, my hand resting on the handle's end, and I studied the steer's face, followed the pattern's outline with my eyes, searching. On the nose, a bit off-center, what appeared to be a mouth, lips spread in a simple smile; slightly up from that, the tip of a delicate nose; on the forehead, where twice I'd struck, the outline of an eye mirrored the steer's own right eye; surrounding the face, the soft female face, and running down below to the dewlap, what appeared to be either long hair or a veil. It was the very likeness of the Virgin Mary.

I came to Cleveland in '39 from the old country, Czechoslovakia, although I'm partial to the Slovak side of that equation. I had lived in the High Tatras region, near Prešov. My mother had worked in the garment industry until a factory fire killed her and several others in 1922. My father had worked in the salt mines, but when Hungary invaded Ubl'a he fought for the Slovak Army, helped stay Hungary's advance. He died in battle, one of only a handful of deaths in the short-lived war. Jozef suggested I move with him and Edita, leave everything behind, start over.

I had just walked in off the streets, hands out, palms out, a question on my face. Foreman took one look at my thick forearms and hands, my broad shoulders, my wide back, told me to swing a sledgehammer. I hadn't learned much English yet—"hello," "thank you," "shit"—but his tossing the handle of the giant hammer toward me was talk enough.

He pointed at an old wood fence that leaned against the red brick building, the fence obviously in disuse, made an "x" with his fingers on one wood slat, and I swung, gave it all I had. Smashed through fence, smashed through brick. From the other side a worker stuck his head through the wall, screamed words I didn't understand. I dropped the sledge, afraid I was in trouble, would have to pay for the wall when all I had on me were a few *koruna* jingling in my pocket, but the foreman patted me on the shoulder, shook my hand, gave me the sledgehammer and walked me inside The Cleveland Union Stockyards.

I worked the second or third stage of the process, depending how you looked at it. Steers—and hogs and sheep—came in by train. The steers, with my ability to drop the great beasts with a single stroke, were my specialty.

I had started at Hotel de la Hoof—guests checked in on their four legs, checked out as steaks and sausages—at the height of its rise, the height of the city's rise. Being a part of it made me feel special, blessed even. I didn't get rich, but I lived. I didn't get weaker as I aged, I got stronger.

And at the peak of my strength, I met Isabel.

I first saw her on a passing trolley, watched her tuck a loose strand of dark hair behind her ear, a gentle sweeping of her hand that highlighted her delicate beauty. Each day for two weeks I stood at the same spot on the street, watched her pass, waved to catch her eye, wondered how, exactly, I could meet her. One morning she sat near the back, the wind of the open-air car pushing her hair around, and I ran behind the trolley, jumped onto the coupler and as the conductor yelled at me to get off, I smiled, extended my hand, introduced myself to her. "Bronislav Martincak." She laughed then shushed the conductor, took my hand in hers—my large rough hand fully enclosed her small soft one—and told me her name. The music of her Spanish accent—the "i" an "ee" sound, the "l" held just a split second longer—rang in my ears for hours, and the lightness of her touch caused my swing that day to be smoother, more elegant, even more powerful. The next day she stepped off the trolley and approached me where I waited.

There was always a nervousness about her, but I figured it likely her steel mill-working father didn't want his daughter to be with a foreigner. He'd taken her from Puerto Rico to find prosperity, not love and a forty-year-old Slovakian knocker. He eventually saw my devotion, understood our happiness, but her nervousness sustained.

Within months we planned to marry, Jozef my best man, Isabel's friend Asunción her maid of honor. Isabel lived on the east side, her church the newly established Our Lady of Fatima Catholic Church.

As final preparations were made, as we discussed our future, our family-to-be, Isabel confessed the cause of her prolonged nervousness: she'd had *la operación* in Puerto Rico. She'd been sterilized. She cried when she told me, said she'd understand if I wanted to cancel the wedding, end our relationship. The more I declared my love, assured her it would be fine, the more upset she became. I'd talked about kids too much, she'd said, it would not be fine. Shortly after that, in the fall of 1950, she leaped in front of a speeding trolley and died two days later.

My swing may have altered, become rougher, without Isabel in my life, but it was fiercer. "Like Mart" became a common phrase in the Yards. It meant violent strength, the ability to mow through steer after steer, a single swing for each, without letup. "You, you're like Mart," an urban cowboy would say of a new knocker who landed a solid blow, the steer letting out a low moan before dropping.

I longed for something to explain the reason for the loss of my parents, of Isabel. During my walks to the Yards each morning, electric street lamps would flicker off as I passed them. This, assuredly, was a sign, I thought. Until Jozef told me the lights worked according to a set timer, had nothing to do with me.

I didn't attend church, but my daily practice consisted of translating my mother's tattered Slovak Bible into English, verse by verse, page by page. Perhaps the truth would reveal itself to me one morning before I prepared my *hemendex*, sunny side eggs over slices of fried ham. It was an old-country breakfast Isabel had adored.

When I walked to the Yards the morning of the signified steer, it was a cold September day filled with crackling hope. The sun shone through the grayness of the sky, heated my face, quickened the smell of the shit and slaughter. The Indians—winners of a record 111 games!—were about to begin their rightful and inevitable World Series title and we'd watch the last few sacred innings, our pilgrimage to Jozef's congregation in abject contrast to the steers who over the last two and a half decades met the steel face of my hammer. My hands throbbed and trembled inside my jacket pockets, perhaps in wonderment at the morning's translated verse—"And you shall be secure, because there is hope; you shall dig about you, and you shall take your rest in safety." Or perhaps in anticipation of Game 1— Lemon pitching, Avila, Doby, and Wertz batting, and that young kid for the Giants, Mays. Perhaps it was both.

The Virgin Mary stared at me.

I almost swung the hammer again, aiming to knock the image squarely off of the creature, but Jozef stayed my hands.

"What does it mean?" I said.

"The Lady of Fatima." Jozef rubbed the image with his thumb. The steer's eyes closed and I swear it smiled.

I thought of Isabel's church at first, then understood.

"Jozef, not the same. That, that was a real thing. Mary *appeared* to them. In *person*. This is a *cow*."

"So, so." He rubbed his hands together. "But she's shown herself, and Jesus, too, on walls, on stained glass, in water stains. Always a message, always a meaning."

"What do we do?" I said.

"I … see if it speaks."

I stared dumbly at Jozef.

"It must be here, to us, for a reason." He crossed himself.

I had waited for something like this, but now, confronted by the Virgin Mary or her likeness, confronted by an apparent miracle, my anger flowed. "I have to kill it."

"You can't," Jozef said. "It's a sign. A, a—" He leaped to Slovak, an old proverb, one my mother used to say, one I had taught Isabel. "*Tvár: duše obraz.*" The face: the picture of the soul.

I released the hammer. It fell to the dirt-and-shit-covered floor with a soft thud.

I approached. Jozef stopped rubbing its head. It opened its eyes. If it did so because Jozef stopped rubbing its head or because it sensed me near, I wasn't sure.

I leaned into the steer's face, felt its breath against my skin. I listened. I wasn't sure if I expected the mouth to move, to speak, or if the image of Mary would take charge.

"We should free it," I said.

"Is that what it—is that what *she*—said?" Jozef crossed himself again.

"No no no. I just—"

"We should call the *Press*. The *Plain Dealer*. Call the church."

We were alone in the yards, I knew. All had gone to watch the end.

"No, it's for us. We're like those three girls. We're to be trusted, no one else. It—she—would not be happy with us."

"How do you know?"

"A feeling," I said. "A guess."

"And do what? When it's free?"

I hadn't thought that far, but I was working to turn it around, head it back up the chute. "It could stay with me." I walked it up and out toward the holding pens. Jozef followed. "Until it does … what it's here to do."

"Which is?"

"I don't know, Jozef. Just help me."

Outside, the yard was empty. It felt odd, this emptiness. Back in the heyday of the yards, when the business knew no limits, its propensity for death—almost two million a year in the 1920s—was only matched by the city's propensity for growth, and even in death the yards were constantly busy. A fear of mine, this decline. I worried I'd lose my job someday soon, worried my anger would have no outlet. But lately, even in the face of decline, there lived a hope of sorts, a hope not unassociated with the Indians resurgence. I saw in the paper the other day a picture of the world's largest tomahawk on display at E. 9th and Euclid. I think it was meant to tell the Giants that they were about to get scalped, but to me it said more, that the city itself was poised to take on all comers.

Jozef unlatched the main gate as I took a loose scrap of rope and looped it around the steer's neck. I felt humbled.

Jozef closed the gate behind us. Mary's eyes changed and, as if it recognized its own exodus, pulled and broke free, ran across the railroad tracks, across 65th, causing the light traffic to brake and skid and honk, the sounds spooking Mary as it darted first north, then south, then north again.

The alarm raised, stock hands, game-watching drinks in hand, emerged from the bar across from the abattoir, and a few gave immediate chase. It wasn't the first time a steer had escaped. More than once a good citizen had escorted a wayward steer back to the yards, earned a small reward, and more than once a steer on the rampage, chasing stock hands and citizens alike, had been shot by officers from the second precinct.

As the steer panicked, ran away from those giving chase, I half expected it to ascend, rise up above the yards, disappear into the sky, the Miracle of Cleveland witnessed by many, the miracle bringing hundreds of thousands of pilgrims a year here, to this hallowed place, their days spent in prayer, awaiting another sign.

Patrolman Roskovensky emerged from the bar. I ran to Mary, tried to get between it and the stock hands, between it and Roskovensky's raised gun.

"No no no no no," I said. "You can't." I held up my hand as if I was directing traffic to stop, as if I could catch the bullet soon to be coming my way.

Mary veered away from me, out into the open, back toward the pens.

Patrolmen Roskovensky said, "Mart, what're you doing?"

"Look, look at its face," I said.

Jozef moved beside Roskovensky. "It's a miracle. It's the Virgin Mary."

Roskovensky looked at Jozef, lowered his gun. "What?"

"Mart couldn't even drop it. Hit it two times between the eyes. *Mart*." He moved his arms around with an imaginary sledgehammer, twice hitting Roskovenskey's forehead.

"You two been drinking? It's a menace. It needs to be caught. Or killed."

"You can't kill it," I shouted over my shoulder as I ran back across the street, hoping to corner the steer, calm it down, hear its message.

Its hooves crunched the gravel as it slowed and approached the tracks. I held up both hands, willing it to come with me, to let me learn from it.

A sharp crack echoed in the yards. A second. I looked back at Roskovensky. He still talked to Jozef, his gun still lowered.

Two red dots bloomed from the steer's forehead, from the Virgin Mary's face. The steer's expression was unsurprised, almost apologetic. It knelt on its forelegs, tilted, then dropped. Gravel cascaded around its heavy and fallen body as if it had hit water.

A stock hand, one I didn't know, a .22 held at port arms, smoke still billowing from its barrel, approached. "Darndest thing," he said. "I'd heard of escapees. Never thought I'd see one. Gun's the way to go." He held the gun out to me. "Did I hear you call it Mary?"

I turned, walked away. Jozef, having crossed the street to me and with tears streaking his begrimed face, said, "*Ked Pán boh nechce, môže človek robiť, čo chece.*"

I nodded. "If God be unwilling, man can do nothing."

Back at Jozef's house, our bodies resting in rusted metal chairs, we watched numbly as a pinch-hitter, Dusty Rhodes, blooped a lame home run down the right field line to win Game 1. The loss barely registered. Until the replay.

In the eighth, two on, Wertz boomed a ball 460 feet to dead center. The thwack of his bat rang inside the wood-frame porch. That kid Mays, his back to the Polo Grounds infield, sprinted straight toward the center field wall. Jack Brickhouse yelled. "A long drive waaay back in center field," he said, "waaay back." There was no possible way, with Brickhouse's long-winded and time-consuming call, that this was anything but a home run. Mays stuck his glove up, speared it out of the air with his back to the ball—"It's caught by Willie *Mays!*"—he turned, fired the ball back to the infield, his hat floating off his head. The throw's finish wasn't visible, only a stunned fan's hand slapping his forehead.

The second time they showed it, I didn't see Wertz, or Mays, or the catch, or that fan. With the crack of the bat I saw my sledge's swing uselessly strike that steer; with the ball landing in Mays's glove I saw the first bloody bullet strike Mary; the fan's head slap became the second. And when Mays and his hat hit the ground I saw Mary's crash. I stood and flicked off the television set, mumbled a goodbye to Jozef, walked home under an increasingly gray and darkening sky.

It felt like the beginning of an end. Or the end of a beginning. The Indians were swept, the underdog Giants the World Series champions.

The morning after Mitchell fouled out to third to end the game, I awoke early and sat on the edge of my bed, my arms hanging loosely and limply between my legs. On the dresser, my mother's Slovakian Bible and my translated pages waited for me. I ignored them, slowly got dressed for work.

Cleveland was numb. The city still slept, the Yards remained quiet. I took my sledge, slid my hands up and down its handle, the sound of my calloused hands on the wood slipping into my ears for the last time. I set the great hammer outside, leaned it against a fence post. I removed a .22 from a locker and practiced my aim.

When Jozef and the others arrived, saw me with the .22, they understood very well what it was all about.

The train arrived, the steers were ushered single file down the chutes. I lifted my rifle, took aim at the first one's forehead, fired. The butt kicked into my shoulder, the sound shocked my ears, and the steer, the steer dropped immediately.

Butterflies on Fire, 1969

Dominic finds himself retching as he settles into his spot along-side the Cuyahoga River, a spot hes marked as his with well-read mimeos of *Marrahwannah Quarterly*, cigarette butts, various brands, beer bottles, empty & otherwise, several coffee cans of cat litter, fresh & not-so-fresh, a tiny green ceramic Buddha, seated, skin magazines, not as well read as *Marrahwannah Quarterly*, or, perhaps that well-read & more, he didnt like to count, cigarette butts or beer bottles or things well read, & aniway, he is here to count his breath, his breathing, here, now, & the last thing he wants to do is count the riffles & crimples of pieces of paper to see wat warranted worn, wat warranted well worn, & the differences thereof, therein, thereby, therewith.

He knows for a fact, as far as he knows facts, that, even money, the skin mag was less well-worn, still, than *Marrah-wannah Quarterly*. Maybe, 2-1 or, hell, 5-1. Against. Its a good skin mag, Dominic thinks. Here he is counting again. Enuf, you fuck-off, get it together.

The river's strong. The sewer of the city, it is, flows right through Cleveland, acts as its putrid, acrid, infected, chemical-and-shit-filled aorta. Its a challenge, here, sitting here, doing his breathing & counting thing. But if Dominic can raise his consciousness here, he thinks, in this place, with this smell, if he can do away with words and melt into experience, if he can somehow replace, rework, revise, revisit his broken parts, he could—

So the retching. First the retching. Then the counting, altho, yeah, he hates counting, but counting is kind of the thing, when it comes rite down to it. Alwaiz. Usually. He means, at least, thats how it went. Counting could come first, but why not cut to the retch? Ha! "Cut to the retch." Hed have to remember that, after, write it down. For posterity, posterior, postage, postwar. Hed have to look that up. The difference. After. After retching, after smoking, after drinking, after breathing, after counting, after enlightening. Dominic has grown tired of flunking this here life—hed even nearly flunked death but Sarah had only caught him nodding—& hed heard the hallucinogens, the psychedelics, the LSDs, the grass, mite not be the third-eye-opening key of, of, of …

Dominic swigs from his beer. That alwaiz happens, doesnt it? he thinks. So close to having it, you know? Capital I. Capital T. But it goes, poof, flies downwind into the air, flows downstream into the river, & the sneering sun gives him a whatre-you-gonna-do-about-it? glare. As near as he can tell. A sun's facial expressions arent alwaiz clear.

A boat, the *Putzfrau*, motors by Dominic's meditative platform. German, I know German, he thinks. *Nein, bitte, guten tag, sprechen, Götterdämmerung.* Now theres a word! he thinks. Where on earth—? "Frau," Dominic says. "Lady. Putz lady. Putz lady?" Tubes snaking out from the boat scoop and suck at the river's surface. Cleaning lady? Dominic thinks. Ha. Yeah, good luck, *fraulein*, this here crack runs right through the middle of Death City.

Dominic spits up a few thick chunks of phlegm, washes down wats left in his mouth with another swig.

You remember, he thinks. I know you do, Sarah. When we were kids, & even tho we were kids, you my neighbor opposite Lincoln Park, you of the pigtails or pony tail or braids—you could of been cue ball bald, for all I cared—I knew I liked you in that its-more-than-like kind of tune, & I thot you liked me similar. Aniway, we used to play Sick Hand Tag, you remember? Id dip my hand in this chocolate-brown Cuyahoga goo, this goo that smelled everithing-but-chocolate, & Id chase yr ass all the way bak to Lincoln Park, you screaming yr head off, thinking my touching you with my tainted mitt would stain you, & Id first laugh but then Id scream becuz that shit, it fucking alwaiz burned until I rinsed it into the pool, creating weird rainbow eddies that shooed the other kids & gave us our own private part of the pool. Dominic rubs his hands together, feels a long-ago tingle rise up in his Sick Hand hand. You have to remember when my mom would take steel wool to me, scrape layers of skin, peel me open. Worth it, Sarah, worth it all the way.

Dominic stands, opens the lid of one of the cat litter cans, the new one he brought with him, & takes a piss. The litter sucks it in, turns a charcoal gray. Dominic used to piss in the river when he first started coming here to meditate, to practice meditating, altho, to be honest, practicing was not making perfect, in his mind, &, in fact, as far as he knew facts, he likely wasnt meditating proper aniway, at least as he compares himself to the Little Green Buddha he bought for reference, but pissing in the river would cause it, the river, to bubble & river-sewers were not supposed to bubble, Dominic had figured, at least he knew his toilet, which *led* to the sewers didnt piss-bubble, so hed stopped pissing in the river. He means, hed thot one exquisitely long piss ago, Wat if that bubbling flowed upward? His dick, he & his dick were attached, baby, & he didnt want it burning like his Sick Hand, no sir, & he wasnt about to take steel wool to it, not with his Sarah waiting in the wings, well, truly, he was waiting in *her* wings, waiting for her to ditch that ultra-cool Mr. Natural poet, waiting for her to see him, Dominic, for all that he was, &, that being the case, his dick was essential equipment. Hed thot about the grass & the bushes here near the side of the river possibly being safe but why take chances? Thus entereth the cat litter coffee cans. Dozens of them pepper the area around him, almost a Fort Knox of piss-&-cat-litter-filled cans of weirdly petrified versions of himself. He dies today? They could rebuild him with rock-hard miniature silos of litter, build an igloo-like-construct, just like him & Sarah had done back in the day, using snow-filled coffee cans & creating Eskimo hideaways to do secret things together.

Dominic shakes the last drops—good to the last drop, his piss, rite? Ha. Hed have to remember that one too. Tell Russel, tell Catherine. Tell them that & that other one, that other bit of Deep Dominic Deliverance. They sed they alwaiz loved his bits. Alwaiz looked forward to hearing the latest, the greatest. Wat was that other one? It had to do with, it had to do with … & there it goes: wind, river, sneer, & not alwaiz in that order.

Dominic zips up, arranges his well-worn copy of *Marrah-wannah Quarterly*, & sits in a lotus position he thinks mirrors the Little Green Buddha that rests in front of him, restfully, in perfect rest, in perfect stillness, a stillness of still rest.

Dominic breathes in. Dominic breathes out. This is wat hes been taught. Breathe & count. One-in, two-out, three-in, four—Sick Hand. Dominic chuckles. That wasnt as funny as Got a Light. You remember, Im sure, he thinks. Id dip an old button-down shirt into the muckish river, put it on over a trash bag I'd poked head- and arm-holes in—I learned my burning lesson the hard way!—& youd chase me, flick lit cigs at me, & yell, Got a light? Got a light? Got a light? Dominic smiles but hes lost track of his breath, his count. He shifts his spine a bit, realigns. One-in, two-out, three—

Got a Light was fucking funny. Til that monk. You remember, rite, baby? That night in '63, when you were over for dinner? Phoosh! Just fucking phoosh! Thick oily flames, thick black smoke, just alive & electric coming off of that stone-still robed monk. Not sure if that gasoline hed had poured over him was as potent as my Got a Light shirt, maybe those robes were some kind of extra-flammable material, but after seeing that monk burn, Got a Light got banned.

Dominic hits his knee. Concentrate, he thinks. Hes got to make good, hes got to repent, no, not repent, repenting's for the Christians, not him, he just wants to be reborn not here, not as Dominic, maybe not even on this creepy planet or in this creepy city or at this creepy time. He needs to be someone else. One-in, two—

Chessus K. Reist, he thinks, this river reeks. Hed thot meditation, breathing by this swamp of a river, would be helpful to practice. Force his focus. That protesting monk, the burning was bad enuf, but smelling burning flesh? & that little bald fucker nev moved a muscle. Nothing. Keeled over, only time he moved. So if he can do that? I mean, Im not on fire, Dominic thinks, so I got that going for me. But I have to be smelling smells smellier than—

One-in, two-out. Not just smells, he thinks. Its the whole sensory experience. Flickering of lights behind closed eyes. The hairs on head, face, arms, pushing this way & that. Mill sounds, truck sounds, foundry sounds, train sounds, the 11:45, most like.

Accept & absorb them all. Even the heat of the sun. Suck in the heat. Heats good & the wind, it cools me aniway, Dominic thinks. Being cool, thats me. I'm Mr. Natural too, Sarah.

She calls them the UTP, the Underground Thought Patrol, out there, with their mimeo revolution, their opening closed minds, their getting people, including those dying in their TV-addled suburban homes of close-mindedness, pumped full of fresh views of trust & compassion & awareness. The UTP, they with their bookstores & coffee houses & benefit concerts & poetry readings & article rantings & collages & montages &—

Dominic yells. No, thats most definitely not being still, peaceful, he thinks, but his thots keep committing random acts of psychic violence on himself & maybe a yell, totally contrary to the meditative practice, he figures, certainly contrary to that flaming monk, that brilliant orange-&-charred flaming monk, he didnt yell, well, maybe he did, who could tell, he wasnt there, but maybe a yell to expel the old views? Purify the mind? Dominic yells. Thots, he reminds himself. The deal is not about stopping thot. Its about not paying attention to them. Thats the thing. Dominic decides theres lots of things now, the things keep grow-ing: retching, smoking, drinking, breathing, counting, enlighten-ing. Altho, that last bit, enlightening, thats been elusive thus far, thusly, theretofore.

Dominic winks open one eye. The Little Green Buddha is definitely not yelling. Dominic sighs, unwinks. One-in, two-out, three-in, four-out, five—. There it is. Now Im hitting it, baby. You seeing this? There it is. Maybe not I-T it, but, aw, fuck, Dominic thinks, wat number was I on? His shoulders droop. One-in—

You, Sarah, I just wanted you to notice. Me. Like you did. Before. I mean, I tried to write poetry too. I patrolled thots too. I became a boo hoo of the Neo-American Church for you, Sarah. I dispensed the truth of, of, of the True Host of the Church to my congregants, Sarah. I mean, yeah, I was the only congregant of my branch, but I mattered, Sarah, I could be both boo hoo & congregant, you know, people can be multi-dimensional, multi-faceted, multi-lingual, multi-dexterous. You know? I downed the saturated sugar cubes, I smoked pot, & I huffed & I toked & I could not could not could not get high. Not high enuf, anihow. I sealed dime-slots on parking meters, Sarah. I plastered police cars with BOMB CLEVELAND NOT HANOI stickers. I was subversive, trying to live my life at speed brutal. See? "Speed brutal." That's fucking poetic, Sarah. Or bad grammar. No no no no no, its poetry, thats wat it is. Wild words of poetic genius blowing out of me like the truth of oneness drawn like a bow. Poetry, baby.

Thots. Thinking. Thots. That's wat Dominic thinks. One-in, two-out, three-in. Open mind. Spacious mind. Wind, air, smell, trains, foundries, breath, experience, urge to piss. Out of dry cans, baby, youve got to hold it, Dominic thinks. So let that go, let that go.

You & me, Sarah, we let the worms go, remember? See it so clearly, Im sure you could too. Yr dad, The Fisherman, The Weekend Angler, would have us go earthworm digging. Wed deliver our bounty of wriggling wonder to him as proud as proud can be, I mean, not as proud as he was of you at that sixth-grade piano recital, even tho yr *Eine Kleine Nacthmusik* sounded so off-key it couldve even killed earthworms, which I know for a fact, as far as I know facts, earthworms dont have ears, theyre hard of ear-ing— eh, that ones not a candidate for Deep Dominic Deliverance, no need to remember that one, to make a mental note, sorry, Russel & Catherine—but those worms. Then you found out wat he did with them: spearing them with a hook &, still wriggling & writhing, casting them out into the water for the fish to eat whole, Jonah-like. Fucking cruel. It was the Hough riots of earthworms, rite there in yr house. I mean, cant we all just get along? Blacks & whites, Dominic thinks, not earthworms, dont get confused, there arent any racial tensions between whites & earthworms, not that I know of. Altho before Hough? I'd of sed the same thing, again, not about the earthworms. After Hough, I mean, the shits got to stop or well have a desert of civilization.

Dominic readjusts, frowns a bit as a thorn or a nail or a some-thing-sharp nicks his butt. One-in, two-out, three-in. Calming. Relaxing. I was talking about Sarah & her father & earthworms. I wasnt talking, no, not really. Thinking. But Im not supposed to be thinking, Dominic thinks, yet here I go. So, remember? Wat we did? We liberated them. Ran an entire bowl of earthworms rite here, rite to where Im sitting, this old edge of Jefferson Bridge, & let them go, rite into the river. Freedom! I yelled that. I think. Mite of been you. Mite of been the earthworms. I didnt know earthworms could scream. I mean, I just learned they mite of had ears, rite? But those earthworms, I think, screamed. Should of known, I guess, if Sick Hand burned my hand, should of known earthworms couldn't hack it, but still, but still, still.

Stillness, Dominic thinks. You fuck-off, youre thinking about stillness. Wait, not thinking, no, just not paying attention to thinking. Counting. Counting is the thing. One of many things. A list, litany, label, lip service. One-in, two-out. Dominic shifts his hips, the urge to piss gets stronger, but he will not risk his dick, no sir. He winks his rite eye open, Little Green Buddha stares back. He doesnt have to piss, I bet.

A few butterflies have become interested in him, the Little Green Buddha, the coffee cans filled with Dominic, the beer bottles. A few flutter around, rest, flutter, rest. Theres about ten or twenty of them, yellow- & orange-winged candle-like flickers that float around Dominic. One or two rest on him. Flutter, rest, flutter, rest. One-in, two-out, three-in. Dominic closes his eye. He feels the butterflies. American Lady, he knows for a fact, as far as he knows facts. Hed built one in art class. Papier-mâché. Still hangs from his childhood bedroom's ceiling, the bedroom his mom loves to keep untouched especially after hed gone all boo hoo & subversive on her, hoping hed come back & be the Dominic she knows he can be. She kicked me out, Sarah, Dominic thinks, thats when it was set to work for us. We could of moved in together, Sarah. But.

Dominic tried reading poetry, he remembers, before he tried, impotently, writing it. He didnt get it. Then that concrete shit? Wat the fuck was that all about? Word pictures for peace poets & beat poets & meat poets that Dominic, Deep Dominic Deliverance, felt too dumb to understand. Give him a papier-mâché American Lady any day. But Sarah, you dug them, baby, so I tried. I tried poetry. Speed brutal, you dig? I searched for something that could be us, just us. Establish, re-establish, re-educate a connection. Between us. Don Marquis, I found him, his stuff. Loved his poetry. Shocked I could find any poetry I liked, much less loved. Shared him. Thot youd like how a typing cockroach & a talking re-incarnated cat could cut through the illusions of the world. Thats wat youd sed appealed to you. "Illusions, Dominic. Its all illusions. The city, it sleeps, it pretends. So stop fooling yrself." You sed that. Well, wrote it. Now *thats* a well-worn piece of paper, that note you left me, that note Ive kept pocketed for the last years plus.

One-in, two-out, three-in—. I understand nothing, Dominic thinks. Im trying. Im reaching. Trying to work through the puzzle of consciousness, enlightenment, trying to electroshock my mind into awareness to keep up with you, Sarah. Instead you called me a lowercase radical, whose liquid emotions were as thick & dense & murky as the Cuyahoga's.

Dominic feels his arm hairs move but theres no wind. He keeps his eyes closed, imagines more & more butterflies alighting on him, sensing hes gaining such peace that hes magnetic, or whatever it is that mite attract butterflies for, surely, he knows for a fact, as far as he knows facts, that butterflies do not include metal. How could they fly, rite? Wat did attract them? It wasnt art class or a kid's ceiling or earthworms. Maybe needles. Pins & needles. Dominic had seen a brown briefcase, one side glass, that held butterflies pinned to the inside. Maybe we could of freed them, Dominic thinks, but we would of not murdered them. Not like those earthworms. Serial earthworm murderers, we were, letting them into this river.

One-in, two-out, three—. I became subversive to get yr attention, Sarah, plugging dime-slots, plastering stickers, dropping acid, & they made me become a subversive infiltrator. Of you. If only I could of wrote poetry, Dominic thinks. Maybe you wouldnt be gon. But its when I saw you last week in that coffee house, I couldnt have been happier. Itd been so damn long, Sarah. Didnt even say hello, didnt even look at me. All we had? Sure sure sure, I hear you, Sarah. We had childhood moments, but they were some kind of moments. Moments of living poetry. Poetry living. Yeah yeah yeah, that's good, Dominic thinks. I get it, you just jumble words around, poetry. See? I've got some poetry in me. A poetic meter. A yard. Iambs, I learned about iambs, I tell you that?

But you didnt even look at me. All yr attention, all yr words, they were for them, the thot patrol, the ones who had such ideas, such good ideas, ideas of simply wanting the world, of wanting Cleveland, to just grow up, to end suffering, to, wat was it, turn everione on like a cosmical—comical?— light bulb.

A train whistles in the distance, the noon o'clock, he knows. Then: phoosh! Or maybe Pah-phoosh! Or PHOOSH! He swears he hears it, that PHOOSH, far off, but hes concentrating. You know his heart, that monks heart, didnt burn? Even after they re-cremated him? Thats fucked up shit, Sarah. It became holy, that heart relic, worshipped as a symbol of compassion unending. Dominic thinks, wonders, ponders: his piss-cans could be symbols too. He smiles. He likes that idea. Its portentous, portraying, pornographic, poetical.

Its hotter. Its like hes covered in a thin blanket. Linen. Tulle. Gossamer. Silk. One-in, two-in, three-in, four—. Yr yelling, I try not to imagine. Even tho, Dominic thinks, its my fault. Jail, they told me theyd throw me in jail, Sarah, unless I gave them some names. Unless I gave them tapes. I recorded you. Not you, actually. Catherine. She played you. Read a poem of yours, that one with motherfucker in it, that one with praise for the Hough riots. She sounded like you, she did. I just told the pigs it was you, aniway. But Im not a narko. Im not. Not. No. One.

One-in—. Dominic feels hes missing something, something big, something heavy, something epic, epicurean, epicentric, epicardium. He opens both eyes, Little Green Buddha opens its eyes, it seems to Dominic, but thats not possible, he has no eyelids. Its the butterflies, the American Ladies, floating off Little Green Buddha. Dominic moves his eyes, not his head, his head feels stiff, his neck feels stiff, even tho hes supposed to be relaxed, calm, peaceful. Hes still, tho, he knows that. Stillness. His body feels held-in-place even tho his mind keeps racing racing racing. But his eyes move, the sun sneering, but its not the sun, its fire. Five, six, seven—one-in, two-out, one-in, two-out—five, six, seven stories high, the fire, just south of him, maybe where the river bends, maybe, hes here not there, but he thinks he sees, he knows for a fact, as far as he knows facts, that the rivers on fire—again, for its burned before, many times—just south of him where the river bends. Hes on fire. Hes the monk, that flaming monk, that monk aflaming, flames licking off of him, Dominic. But its really the butterflies. Hes covered in butterflies. American Ladies. Fifty, sixty, seventy— one-in, two-out, three—one hundred, its more than one hundred butterflies.

And theyve lifted off of him, spinning away from him, floating & lifting, not resting, floating & lifting, fluttering & lifting,
& its like the butterflies are flames & Dominic is the monk &
the sun isnt sneering, not this time, not this time, becuz the suns
ruffly behind him, his shadow in front of him, the shadows of
the butterflies are in front of him, shadows only. It wasnt a poem,
Dominic knows, hes not that dumb, he knows for a fact, but
hes in a cave, his minds a cave, & the shadows hes seeing arent
anithing, just shadows. He thinks he knows & understands but
the shadows, theyre just a reflection, & he needs to turn & see,
to turn & see—one-in, two-out, one-in, two-out—to turn & see
wats true, that Marquis and his anarchic cockroach are rite, &
this poem Dominic knows, this one hes memorized, memorial-
ized, Mirandized, for he thot hed share it with Sarah, share it
with Russel, Catherine, Cleveland, becuz its important, impo-
tent, impolite: "it wont be long now it wont be long / man is
making deserts of the earth" & Dominic sees only shadows, cant
face the sun, cant see the flames.

FLOOD, 1975

Derek was a helluva shortstop. A seeming pipsqueak of a boy, he played full seasons at both the Pee Wee and Tee Ball divisions of the Beaverdale Little League. At seven, he played partial seasons in the Minor and Intermediate divisions. At ten, he skipped over the last two years of Intermediate and jumped straight to the Little League Majors where he competed with and against kids two and three years older. I was one of those kids and I got to witness his greatness up close.

Derek's range at short was incredible. He could move left or right, fill the holes and gaps, dive behind second to save a hit, leap high to save a run. His arm impressed, too, in both its unorthodoxy and its strength. He threw submarine style, his sidearm motion flicking the ball to first base so quickly it was hard to pinpoint its release. He threw so hard it stung Matty's hand, caused Matty to bounce up and down as he shook out the pain.

And then there was his bat. Ten years old, mind you, and, boy, could he hit. Fastballs, curveballs, change-ups, the pitches didn't matter. He might let a ball or two go and slap into the catcher's mitt, might miss once or twice, but those were elements of his strategy; he was measuring, gauging, judging, lining up his single to right, or his double to the gap in left-center, or his triple down the line. Derek told me he'd once read that Babe Ruth could read the label on a spinning record. Inspired, he would spend hours in his bedroom shuffling his albums, blindly placing them on the turntable one at a time—first at 45 then at 78—and he'd stare and follow and track until he could read every single word of every single spinning record. He owned over one hundred, purchased most of them at The 'Vous on Prospect with money he'd saved delivering newspapers. The practice took him almost a year to complete. But he said it allowed him to see the seams of the baseball spin his way at the plate, allowed him to accurately guess the pitch a split second before he needed to swing, told him where he'd need the fat of the bat to enter the plate's plane.

Of course, he didn't hit 1.000 or anything. He wasn't perfect. But I sometimes wondered if those rare occasions when he struck out or grounded into a double play or flied out to center were intentional, as if he wanted to keep things interesting—not to himself, but to the growing mass of people who gathered for each one of his games.

When Derek first came into the majors at Beaverdale Little League Park, vaulting past two additional years of intermediates, there was a curiosity among the other teams' players and coaches, among the parents who had heard but not seen Derek's talent.

In his first at-bat, anticipation ran high. Everyone expected him to knock the cover off the ball or something equally Herculean. He struck out on three pitches, swinging wildly at the third pitch, a ball high and away. I saw a few of the parents who had gathered fall away from the fences, shaking their heads and smiling, as if they knew all along this kid was nothing worth noting.

I later figured Derek intentionally struck out. In his next four at-bats, he hit four solid singles; he seemed to command both their speed and their placement.

After the game I overheard my mom talking to other parents, some of whom had been the head-shaking smilers who left in the first inning, and she marveled at Derek's prowess. The parents who missed Derek mourned their absence. "Don't worry," mom said, "he'll be doing this all season."

And she was right. Mostly.

For two months, Derek racked up three and four hits a game. There was a brief period when opposing coaches intentionally walked him. But it wasn't long before the screams and beratings from the crowd, and eventually the intervention of the Beaverdale board, forced the coaches to have their pitchers pitch to him. Derek logged putout after putout in the field, his whip-like submarine throw beating runners by six, seven steps and causing more than one coach to throw his hat and yell at his team to stop hitting to "that damned kid."

And for those two months, the crowd grew. The bleachers were fuller than I'd ever seen, and people gathered four deep behind the home plate fencing and down the short fences that lined first and third. Parents whose children played at other fields abandoned watching their own children—their limp swings and ball-between-the-legs errors devastated them—to watch Derek play.

As a team, we could have been jealous of Derek, the attention he drew. But we were as caught up in his gift as everyone else. From left field, I watched his preternatural anticipation, his effortless movement, his errorless fielding. Before Derek, I'd fielded lots of grounders and liners in left. With Derek, I spectated. He cut off every grounder, stabbed every liner. He was marvelous to watch. Plus, winning feels good, and we won. Often.

And then Derek disappeared.

He had never missed a practice, so when he didn't show we figured he was sick. A few nights later, he missed a game. Afterwards, my dad, our coach, got a call from Derek's uncle. My dad repeated each question—Has he been at practice? The game? Have you seen him? What about your son?—and dad responded no to each one. When he hung up, he instructed my mother to get over to Derek's, help his aunt. He then shoved a flashlight in my hand and pulled me along to the car.

We joined Derek's uncle and searched along what his uncle said was Derek's usual bike route to practice. When we found nothing, we headed to the ball fields. Outside the barred gate, we met up with Matty (first baseman), Ted (catcher), and Oscar (center fielder). We climbed over the gate and our flashlights scanned the gravel drive and the woods that surrounded the eleven fields.

Beaverdale sat in a flat depression about two miles from our neighborhood. Adjacent to Big Creek, a large, and largely cleaner, tributary of the lower Cuyahoga River, I later learned parts of it used to be a small trading port, catching traffic from the man-made canals and Lake Erie during the 1800s. Trains made the port obsolete by the early 1900s and in the 1960s a portion of the land was repurposed as baseball fields, a generous donation by the relatives of Marcus Hanna. There was one other reason it failed as a port: it flooded several times a year. The depression, bound by a natural levee, would fill to the brim during a heavy and sustained rain. If a mid-season flood occurred, players, coaches, and parents of the affiliated thirty-six teams converged on Beaverdale when the waters receded and they'd clean the fields of the debris and the detritus left behind by the retreating creek. Once, Derek and I had found three arrowheads embedded in Field 6's second base. Mr. Regan, Pee Wee coach and history teacher, said we'd made the find of the century. "Boys, you might very well be holding equipment once belonging to Blue Jacket himself."

On the night of our search, the fields dry from a months-long drought, there were no arrowheads. And no Derek.

Police became involved. Searches continued every day for two weeks, news bulletins ran nightly and signs were posted in every storefront, restaurant, gas station, and school.

But Derek was gone.

We'd canceled six games over those two weeks. The opposing coaches could've demanded our forfeiture, the rules stated, but out of an understanding of our deep loss, they merely asked we reschedule.

In practices, we were listless. Originally, dad asked me to take over at short, but after four straight errors he tried out Oscar, then Matty, then Doug, then Ted, but none could make the right moves, could capture the ball in their mitts, or capture the weight of their duty.

I remembered once watching an air show at Lakefront. Five planes flew overhead, then one peeled away, leaving a gap in the formation where it had once flown. When Ted walked away from short, leaving only Matty at first, Doug at second, and Robbie at third, from my vantage in left field the gap made sense.

Dad brought the team together and pitched my idea: we would play the last eighteen games with an honorary opening for Derek, ready for him when he returned.

The league said we had to field nine, but my dad could be persuasive when he needed to be, and by the end of the board meeting he even had the other coaches agreeing how fine an idea this was, how it showed respect for one of its own players, perhaps the best player the league had ever seen.

We shifted, of course. You can't leave shortstop empty, not

completely. Robbie eased a little away from third, Doug edged a little closer to second, and I played up a little.

But it wasn't the same. And we lost. Game after game after game. At first, scores were close, whether because we competed beyond our ability or because the other teams showed sympathy and uncertainty, I never knew. Maybe we lost because we had loss, that loss made clearer whenever Derek would have been on deck or up to bat; we'd leave the on-deck circle empty for him, hoping he'd emerge from out of the woods—his quirky grin on his face, flipping a ball up from his right hand into his mitt—and he'd grab a bat, step into the box and will us to victory. But as each at-bat and each game went by, his spot remained untenanted.

The season ended—we didn't even make the playoffs—and two years passed. In that span I moved from middle school to high school, I quit baseball, and the city suffered one of its worst droughts in its history.

Derek and his disappearance never went away. The anniversary led to two-page articles reliving his on-the-field antics and of expert and not-so-expert guesses as to what had happened to him. Some said he ran away, tired of the spotlight, and lived on the streets in downtown Cleveland; others said his father returned and took him to exploit his talents for personal gain; and students in Ms. Krolokowski's tenth grade English class, after reading *The Natural*, didn't doubt that the temptress who killed athletes at the top of their game emerged, whole cloth, out of the book to strike Derek down as punishment for holding beyond-his-years talent.

When the rains finally came, they were unrelenting. It rained for seven days. First, the poorly drained streets flooded, then the dryness and hardness of the ground and dirt couldn't absorb the fast-accumulating water and eventually caused citywide flooding. Every neighborhood, every open field, every park, and every yard disappeared under the deluge. To make matters worse, Big Creek eased up to and then rushed over its embankment. Some neighbors found it simpler to use canoes and rafts to get around, but there wasn't much to get around to—everything was closed as first the mayor and then the governor declared states of emergency.

It took a week for the waters to lower, the ground and the creek and the river reclaiming what belonged, ultimately, to them. For weeks, families dealt with their flooded basements and first floor family rooms, dining rooms, and kitchens whose walls were now, seemingly permanently, marked with a moist black line that ran at a steady height two feet off the floor.

Matty called. He and a few ballplayers were heading to Beaverdale to begin the work of cleaning up the fields; even though I hadn't played since that season, even though I'd drifted away from my former teammates, lost touch, Matty hoped I would help.

Only nine of us were able to come—many were still dealing with their own personal losses and they just couldn't be tasked with cleaning up Beaverdale—so we split up, each of us given a handful of garbage bags and assigned to a particular field. I got Field 8, the field on which Derek awed hundreds, the field to which he'd never returned.

Floods of years ago had taught me garbage bags filled quickly: Pepsi cups, napkins, chip bags, score sheets, straws and straw wrappers, wax paper, half-eaten hot dogs, baseball hats, lost homerun balls, lost foul balls (although who could tell the difference?), popsicle sticks, candy wrappers, shirts, socks, gloves, tires, and the occasional historical artifact.

Before I'd even got to my field I'd filled two garbage bags. A few fields away, Matty had left several bulging bags in his wake. It looked like a discordant cemetery, haphazardly placed and poorly designed tombstones poking through the earth.

I made my way behind the home plate fence and picked up papers and cups that had plastered against it, pulling a few loose sheets through the chain link, and moved to the right, into my old dugout, duck walking to snatch each and every scrap of trash and shoving them in the bag.

It was hard work and the week of rain had given way to a thick humidity that caused sweat to pop on my brow, my arms, my legs, my chest, my back. I sat on our dugout's bench, took my hat off, and wiped my arm across my eyes and forehead. As I replaced my hat I saw through the dugout fence a rumpled pile of garbage, and its size, larger than any scrap I'd picked up so far, caused an odd feeling in my stomach and a catch in my throat.

It was Derek, I knew. He had floated, perhaps from out of Big Creek or from out of the Cuyahoga River, bobbed from field to field during the flood, and as the waters receded, he had found his way here, to this field, his body looking like it had attempted to slide head first into the pitcher's mound. I would have thought, if he'd ever come back, that he'd end up on deck or at home or at short, reclaiming what was once his. Or maybe his ending up at the pitcher's mound was a final, lost claim to how he had owned all who had pitched from that particular piece of land.

Police investigated, coroners came, news trucks arrived, journalists reported, and gawkers gathered behind the yellow tape that now surrounded the field.

I was the center of attention for a few weeks (The Boy Who Found the Star), as was Derek's uncle (a suspect two years ago, a suspect again). But, as before, it all died down. And once the funeral was over—a real one this time, with an actual body in a casket—life returned to normal. Speculative certainty gave way to misguided guessing which gave way to insoluble mystery.

Thirty years passed. I now tended to these very same fields— mowing, raking, sodding, fertilizing, watering, lining, preparing. It was therapeutic, what I did, especially after my son's accident.

I often reflected on that magical half-season where Derek's talent propelled him to stardom and where, perhaps, his talent contributed to his death. His virtuosity sometimes made him wink at his own perfection, made him incautious. After one game he'd journeyed into the woods, drank from a six-pack he'd lifted from the neighborhood's EZ Shop, shared it with older boys who idolized him. Another time he threw match-lit sticks into the Cuyahoga. It had only been a few years since the infamous fire of '69, and I think he hoped he'd catch the river again, but the oozing river had lost some of its chocolate brown and rainbow-slicked flammability. The burning sticks landed in the river with ineffective whispers. Over the years I convinced myself, perhaps unfairly, that Derek brought what happened to him on himself, that people with untainted talent often think they are invincible, that no sin and no ill luck can befall them.

But I learned then, and I know now, that there is no insulation from tragedy, that perhaps it is that very excess of skill that calls tragedy down upon the innocent and the not-so-innocent alike.

I finished lining first and third. I repacked the front of Field 8's pitcher's mound, the mound where I had found Derek those many years ago. Clouds passed overhead, glided over the fields and the city equally. They ignored no one.

AND THE MOON SHIMMERED, 1984

Lawrence's mom opened the door and faced two figures. The female wore shiny black leather pants, a black hard-plastic chest plate, a black wig pulled into a bunch on top, and makeup. Her face was painted white, her lips and eyes were black, the black rising from her eyes to her forehead to form two black flames. The male wore only a diaper on his bottom and tiny white angel wings on his back. He puffed clouds of chalky sugar out of a candy cigarette. Both figures carried empty pillowcases.

"Look at you two," Lawrence's mom said. "Great." She looked at her feet a moment, looked up. "You look just great."

Behind her, in the darkness of the hallway, Chas, the Van Halen angel-baby, saw what he thought was a crippled dog. It moved slowly on all fours, but its movements were awkward. He heard a high-pitched growl. "You get a new dog?" he said.

She stepped one foot back to see what Chas saw and almost stepped on its paw. It crept around her foot, out the door, between Chas and Kelly, nearly tripped on its tail, and loped toward the street. "It's Lawrence. I made it. For him."

Chas and Kelly watched the creature head in the direction of the park entrance a few houses down. Chas didn't know what to say. Kelly said, "You *made* that?" She was awed by the fur, the movement, the way other costumed kids gave it a wide berth.

Lawrence's mom said, "Thank you for taking him out with you. We never see you anymore, not since—"

"Yeah, sure," Chas said. He felt uncomfortable being in front of Lawrence's mom, of Leo's mom. She was right, it had been a while. The funeral, maybe. He shifted his weight from foot to foot, saying nothing, before calling out, "Lawrence, wait up."

Away from the house, following Lawrence, Kelly said, "Always told you." She double-checked to make sure Lawrence's mom wasn't in earshot. "Kid's a freak."

It was unsure of its new form, but it was growing to enjoy it.

Its escape, its transformation, had started in the bathroom. No, earlier than that, it knew, but the bathroom is where things really took hold.

His mom had placed the box between him and the TV. "You ready?" Lawrence ignored her, continued to push the joystick buttons, battled the invaders from space on his Atari even though he couldn't see the screen.

When he put the joystick down, he opened the box and found hair. A lot of hair. Or was it fur? And, oh, did it smell. He'd had a dog, once, for a few weeks after Leo, his parents, he thought, thinking taking care of something else, showing him love, would help him. It tore up the house, pooped and peed everywhere, seemed to always have a wet dog smell, and was finally taken away when it was clear Lawrence lacked any attachment to it. Lawrence covered his nose and asked, "What is it?"

"A werewolf," his mom said.

The costume was in one piece, like the pajamas he wore when he was five. But it had paws, a snout and—

"I made it," she said.

—the head which would flip over to cover his head and face. The eyeholes didn't seem like they'd line up correctly.

"The hair, the fur, it's real. I've been saving it at the shop."

Lawrence touched one tooth with his finger. It was sharp.

"The teeth? Those are real, too. From the vet's. Next door?" Lawrence's mom sighed. "Leo always wanted to be a werewolf."

Lawrence didn't want to wear this thing. It smelled, it was hot outside, hotter than normal for October, he'd look ridiculous, he wasn't Leo. "I wanted to be The Fonz." He raised his thumb, began a prolonged, "Aaaaaay—"

She snatched the costume. "Lawrence, I knew you'd find a

way to—" She squeezed her eyes shut. "You just can't do this one thing, can you." It wasn't a question.

Lawrence found himself grabbing the costume, saying how Leo would've loved it, how the fangs were scary, and he watched himself, as if separate from the situation, move upstairs and into the bathroom to change. He always did this, it seemed. He always gave in. He gave in to his mom now, he gave in to Leo then. Mostly. And now Kelly and Chas were coming, perhaps to make things right, perhaps to include him, finally, perhaps to forgive him, even though he wasn't sure he did anything wrong. He needed a costume, he decided, or Kelly and Chas would certainly not let him come along. This, this, this *thing*, he thought, was better than further isolation.

In a few minutes, in the dim lights of the bathroom, the black-grey fur replaced Lawrence's skin: first his legs, then his back, arms and chest. For a final moment, he had two heads: his and an eyeless one dangling down his back. He felt different, secure, maybe, or was it a sense of freedom? Finally, Lawrence merged the two heads into one. It twisted its head, fastened its neck, pawed at its fur.

For a short time, it stood still, uncertain what to do next. It moved its head back and forth, as if testing out its new body, or maybe it was lining up its once separate eyes —old and new did not merge easily, it seemed. It silently jerked its head: first left, then right, as if it was snapping at something just out of reach. A growl coalesced around its snapping teeth, first low and thin, then gaining strength. It tested its legs and paws, padded back and forth in the confined bathroom, paced, snarled. When it was ready it pawed open its cage.

In the street now, among the sheeted ghosts, gunless cowboys, and green-hatted Peter Pans, Chas moved up behind it, and it twisted and turned its head around to see clearly. Chas asked a question. It responded. It felt like it asked, or wanted to ask, "Wht ahr yu gys?" but it came out, maybe, like a kind of growl. Chas stepped back, almost lost his balance, caught himself. It lost sight of him, then saw both of them pass by, the winged one on the right, the made-up one on the left. As each passed, it snapped its head, first right, then left. Missed them both.

Its fur felt tight against its skin, the two seeming to mix

together, unclear where one ended, one began. A thin sheen of sweat caused its outer layer to slip around and its breathing became ragged as they climbed the steps to the park's football field; its width separated them from their destination. It recalled that it and its brother used to come to the park all of the time, but it had never ventured to the other side, toward where Chas and Kelly walked. It snorted and growled to its right, to a trail worn over the years by kids' feet and bicycle tires, to The Path that ran its way behind the park, behind the dead end of Valdez, to the edge of The Ravine.

Walking across the park's field brought it memories, memories that now, in its present form, seemed disconnected from it: tears of a mother and a father, yelling, blaming and not-blaming, loss of its own brother, loss of its brother's friends. It cut itself off from the world, in a trance at school, barely saying words at home. For almost two years, it had been like that.

If it moved its head around just so, it could see Chas and Kelly a few yards in front of it, talking. They turned around to check it was behind them, their faces expressing something. Confusion? It hoped it was fear, but didn't know where that hope came from.

When it noticed they weren't heading toward the opposite side's stairs that led into Chas's neighborhood, it loped faster, caught up to Chas and Kelly, thought it said, "Whr ahr we ging?"

Kelly, the Kiss Demon, said, "Will you stop with the growling already?"

It repeated its question. They stopped and turned toward it. Chas looked at Kelly, Kelly at Chas—at least that's what it thought happened as it could barely make out Chas in one wolf-eye, Kelly in the other. Chas said, "Look, whatever it is you're doing, stop it. We get it. You're a wolf." He turned away, said something that may have been *Let's get this over with*, and headed toward a house whose backyard faced the edge of the park.

Kelly said, "We want you to do something."

It cocked its head to one side, might have said, Whts tht?

The sun had finally set, though its afterglow still lit the sky with a few final streaks. The moon appeared, faintly at first, then more prominently.

Most houses in this neighborhood had fenced-in yards, but

the house they approached didn't. The sliding glass doors gave way to a small patio surrounded by grass and a low line of bushes. It couldn't see for sure, but one of the sliding glass doors looked like it was slivered open. Kelly slipped through the bushes and headed toward the door.

The creature growled a question.

Chas said, "Shhh, she's checking something."

It tilted its head to get a better look. Kelly peered through the glass doors and then slowly slid the door open. She turned, waved a come here.

It thought it said, "Wayt," but it came out as a whimper. Its breathing roughened, it pawed at its neck.

Chas stopped its pawing. "No, leave it on, Lassie, case some- one sees." Chas pulled then pushed it across the yard toward the door. It initially tried to lope away, find its way home, but real- ized it needed this, it needed friends again, even if they were Leo's friends. And they were friends, right?

Once inside, Kelly thrust a pillowcase at it. "Grab everything you can."

It tried to say, "Wre robbin thous?" but no one was around to hear it. It was alone. To steal? To run? It had never done anything like this, didn't know if Leo had ever done anything like this, but if this is what it took—

It held one edge of the pillowcase in its mouth, hooked it on several teeth, loped to a shelf, used one paw to sweep VHS tapes and cassettes into its sack, loped to another shelf and looked for something valuable among the framed pictures that sat on the shelf and stared back at it. It thought it recognized something, someone. It tried to grab one picture, just pawed it aside, knocking it and another one facedown. It grabbed another one between two paws, held it close to one wolf eye. It was a picture of Kelly with adults who could only be her parents or grandparents. It dropped that picture, pawed another one. This one held Kelly, Chas, and Leo. There was no Lawrence in it. Never was. Never would be.

There was a time when it had thought differently, a time when it had still loved Leo. A time when Leo didn't make Law- rence cry, back when Lawrence *did* cry. Right? Those weren't bad times. Or maybe they were all bad.

It heard a voice yell, "What do you think you're doing?" It

didn't sound like Kelly or Chas. "I said, wolfboy, what do you think you're doing?"

It jerked its head around, tried to see who spoke. Then, right by its ear, it heard, "You know what happens to people who steal from me?"

The growl, which before had only issued from its throat, began in its stomach. It wasn't the growl of a ten-year-old in a costume, it wasn't the growl of a dog, it wasn't the growl of a wolf, even. It was the growl of loss, of pain, of sadness, of betrayal. It swatted at Kelly, although it didn't know it was Kelly, with one paw and knocked her over; it lunged at her, its sharp teeth ineffectual without a jaw's compression. The seeming savagery of the attack—it had Kelly pinned underneath it, head jabbing at Kelly's head, neck, shoulders—caused teeth to fly out of its maw. Then it felt a sharp tug at its head, heard a tearing, and it let out a final thick and heavy growl.

Lawrence's second head hung to one side. Chas yelled at him, but Lawrence couldn't hear him. Kelly lay underneath him, small cuts and long red welts popping on her face, but Lawrence didn't see her. He stood. His back ached, his knees cracked.

Lawrence pawed open the sliding door and left. Behind him, if he could have heard it, Kelly said, "You crazy fucking freak, it was just a joke."

Instead of walking home, Lawrence took The Path. It wound through a field first, then into the woods. Fallen leaves crunched underneath his paws, the head bounced against his back. He arrived at the edge of The Ravine. Kids rode their bikes on The Path all the time, nothing bad had ever happened. But Leo, riding his bike too closely behind him almost two years ago, had yelled at Lawrence: *Hurry up. Get out of the way. Move it, dammit.* And the shouts had first caused Lawrence to pedal harder, to do what his brother asked, demanded, and he felt himself become flush, felt sweat pop on his forehead, felt a wetness in his eyes as his knees pumped feverishly, and then something broke inside of him, and he had hit the brakes and scraped to an abrupt stop. Leo—he was too close, right?—had swerved and skittered over the edge.

Lawrence stood at the edge of The Ravine and for the thousandth time he pictured Leo's broken and bloody body in the creek below. He didn't mean it, he thought.

He picked up a small rock in his paw, rubbed the soft and gritty sandstone against his face. He wound up and threw it out over the ravine. In the moonlight he watched the rock arc high then drift downward, heard it brush through branches and leaves and then crack against the bare rocks below, pictured it shattering, the pieces scattering and splashing into the creek.

They had played catch a lot, in the backyard, Leo with his back to the house, Lawrence forty feet away at the base of the hill, lined up with the garage, waiting for Leo's throws.

"Throw it," Lawrence said.

"Not till we agree. You're not playing." Leo flipped the ball into the air with his glove, caught it, flipped it, caught it.

"I'm as good as you." Lawrence tugged at a loose lace with his teeth, tightened the glove on his hand.

Leo pulled the ball out of his glove and fired it, hard, at Lawrence's chest. Lawrence got his glove up and caught it, the pop in the mitt echoing off the garage into the yard. "Stop it," he said. His hand was out of the glove. He shook it, tried to massage the sting away with his other hand. He replaced the glove.

"Make me," Leo said.

Lawrence threw the ball as hard as he could. Leo caught it, smiled, whipped the ball back at Lawrence. Lawrence protected his face, jerked it away as he held his glove up to shield himself. His cap fell to the ground.

It hadn't been his fault, what happened. Leo started it. He always started it. He'd let Lawrence tag along, and Lawrence would watch Leo and Chas and Kelly play ball. Sometimes they would let him hit. It seemed nice, it seemed like a good time, but more often it ended with their throwing too hard, striking him out, sometimes throwing at him, Lawrence only able to escape getting hit by diving to the dirt. They'd laugh. He'd laugh, trying to be in on the joke. He thought they were accidents, the throws, thought they wanted him there. At least that's what he'd wanted to believe.

Lawrence picked up his cap, put it on. He licked his fingers, grabbed the ball, wound up, and threw. He put his arm, his shoulder, his whole body into it. The ball sailed a little high. Leo raised his glove. He could've caught it. Lawrence had seen Leo pluck plenty of hard liners out of the air routinely. Heck, Lawrence, in the bleachers, would proudly boast, back when he was proud, "That's my brother." But this time, the kitchen window in danger, Leo pulled his arm down, smiled, and was already in the house before the last piece of glass had fallen.

Lawrence threw another rock, then another. Each whip of the arm became faster, harder, more frantic. It started as a repeated whisper. "I didn't mean it. I didn't mean it." Soon he yelled those words, thought he could see them sail over The Ravine with each thrown rock.

Exhausted, he sat, the wolf head swayed against his back, his paws dangled over the edge. He reached behind him, pulled the head over his. The heat of its heavy breathing pushed against Lawrence's face. The wind kicked up. Dirt and leaves and cool air blew into and around it. The treetops swayed. The moon shimmered.

Its fur-wrapped body began to tremble. It pressed its head back, stretched it so far that the costume tore a little at the neck. A low and sorrow-filled sound rose from its belly, through its open throat, funneled between its remaining teeth, out its open maw. And its howl, Lawrence's howl, released into the air around him and into The Ravine until its lungs emptied.

In the Shade, 1999

"Where's the motherfuckin' shade?" Finn said.

Snowball and Finn sat at an aging picnic table in the Metroparks. Finn picked at a loose fleck of table wood with his thumb.

"The what?"

"The shade," Finn said.

"I don't under—"

"The fuck shade, Snowball." The fleck of wood flew into the leaves.

Snowball looked around. Not only was it a typically cloudy Cleveland day, but their table was under a large oak. As near as Snowball could tell, they were both, decidedly, in the shade.

"I always heard growing up, 'Finn, you'll have it made in the shade.' So?" Finn sighed hard. "I'll tell you where it ain't," Finn said, "my life."

The wind picked up and a light rain began to fall, but the tree protected them from the drops. Behind Finn, a boy in an open patch of grass by the river set a kite on the ground, played out some string, and took a running start. A strong gust kicked up and the kite shot into the air. Neither the cloudy day nor the rain affected him.

"Mine, neither," Snowball said. He lit a cigarette, took a few drags, watched the kite flyer, listened to the rustle of plastic in the breeze.

Finn saw Snowball's attention was neither on him nor his

shade problem. He threw one leg over his bench and swung his body around, leaving him in a position between staying and going. The boy and his kite caught Finn's attention. He looked back at Snowball. "Remember that?" He nodded toward the boy.

"Remember what? Kite flying? I am a black man from East Cleveland. Think I had time or money to fly one of those damn things growing up? Fuck. And remember, 'flying a kite'? Whole different thing to me."

Finn remembered. "You hit the trifecta on that one."

"Fucking A, the superfecta. Four years."

Finn looked at the boy, looked up at the kite—a diving speck now as a hard wind caught it and drove it down toward the treetops on the other side of the river. The kid yanked the string down and to the right, his move jerking the kite parallel to the trees before it caught an upward gust. "You ever see her again, you got out?"

"Nah, never," Snowball said. "She kited a few when I was in. Stopped after a year. Found someone else, I heard." Snowball pulled the hood of his sweatshirt up. "Why?"

"I remember."

"Yeah, I fucking remember, too. I was just say—"

"No, no, no. Being a kid." Finn flicked his thumb to the boy. The wind gusts had died to a breeze and the boy had control of the kite again. "No worries. You went outside, played. Life, the world, wasn't, you know—"

"Fucked."

"Yeah." Finn turned his face toward the tree, closed his eyes and felt the breeze wash over him. The rain, still only a drizzle, had finally penetrated the tree's canopy and a few drops hit his face. He opened his eyes, lowered his head, looked at Snowball. "Then, world was easy."

Snowball tamped the cigarette out on his bench, chucked the butt, still smoking, into the wet grass. "Yours, maybe. Mine, felt life-and-death every day. The streets, my house, everywhere." He gestured to the boy. "That? Never fucking happened. You had that once? Fuck, I'm jealous."

"I just—"

"Yeah, we all 'just,' Finn. World's fucking cruel. That kid, he's born, he sleeps, eats, shits, flies a kite, goes to school, learns shit, gets a job, gets laid, has a kid, dies. His kid? Same fuck thing."

"He know that?"

"Fucking hope he doesn't." Snowball took a candy bar out of his pocket, unwrapped it, took a bite. "He'd be over here sitting at this table, bitching about shade."

"Fuck you." Finn swung his other leg over the bench, gave his back to Snowball.

"It's what it is, Finn," Snowball said between chews. A few crumbs fell to the table.

"I asked a simple-as-fuck question, Snow."

"No you didn't. You want shade? You want easy? That kid's showing you easy." They both watched the boy. The kite flew high now, a red speck barely visible against the dark clouds. "You—I mean, tonight? Before that kid goes to sleep, what you think he'll be thinking about? Bullshit shade? No. You ask him what his favorite part of the day was? The best part of his life? He'd say flying that motherfuck kite right there. Today. Now. I ask you that question, know what I get? 'No shade, Snowball. No life, Snowball.' Your shade shit's the same rhymes I been hearing for years, just different words."

"Why the fuck we even friends?"

"Jesus Christ, here we—"

Finn turned and slapped Snowball across the face. "Don't."

Snowball, a drop of blood forming at the mouth, threw the last third of his candy bar at Finn's head; it exploded into bits, various sizes, and fell around Finn. Snowball stood and stepped, one leg after the other, over the picnic table's bench-like seat. "Yeah, whatever. But you know what? It sure in hell ain't Christ that's going to save you, get you out of the mess you're in, find you your shade. And it ain't me neither." He stepped backward a few feet, still facing Finn, then turned away. "Take care of this shit your damn self." He tucked his hands in his sweatshirt pockets and walked away, leaves kicking underfoot.

Ants trailed to some crumbs on the table. It took a few seconds, it seemed, before dozens lined up to take their piece. Finn turned to watch Snowball go, but the ants' activity hustled a faint memory.

Finn mumbled "fuck" to himself. "Look, I'm sorry, all right?" he shouted at Snowball's back. "I shouldn't have, you know." Snowball kept walking. "Hey!" Snowball stopped on the just-reached paved walkway. "I'm fucking apologizing." Snowball turned to face Finn. With the coming dusk and Snowball's dark clothes, Finn could barely see him. "You ever read *Hamlet*?"

"The fuck you talking about?" Snowball said, taking a few steps toward the table. He was still about fifty feet away.

"*Hamlet*. You ever read it?"

"Shakespeare? You slap me, draw blood," he said, wiping his mouth and walking toward the table, "you ask me if I fucking read motherfucking *Shake*speare?"

"Yes or no?"

"You *ever* hear—? No, I ain't read *Hamlet*." He sat on the side of the table he previously left, but he kept his back to Finn.

"I had to. High school. This one part ..." Finn stared toward the boy and his kite, but wasn't seeing him this time.

"Yeah?"

"You know the story, right?"

"No, I—a kid's father's killed, right?" Snowball said.

"Right. And the killer's the king now, is fucking his mother—"

"Some nasty shit."

"And this kid, Hamlet, he can't—he's stuck. Can't decide shit. He do nothing? Kill this guy? Yell at his mom? Go to school? What?"

"He kill him, right? That me—"

"Nah. He doesn't do shit. Until—and this is the part; I could, can, picture it—he sees this army. They're marching. Going to fight—"

"Where they marching? Who they represent?"

"I don't fucking know, Snow, just listen. He sees this army. They're going to fight for a, a tiny shitass piece of land. Not even big enough to bury all their dead asses. It's nothing, this land. Nothing. And here's Hamlet. He sees this. And he's like, 'I have a murdered father, a mother who's, who's—'"

"Fucked."

"Yeah. 'And, and I can't fucking do anything? This army's going to die for nothing and I just, just sit here?'"

"So what happen?"

"I don't know. But I know he fucking *acted*. Here's a guy, no fuck shade for him, and he made it *work*. He—"

"So, you're thinking ... what." Snowball turned to face Finn. "You got a reason? You gonna *act*?"

94

Snowball's stare weighed on Finn. Finn's life weighed on him, too. He thought he had something. Something definite. Something concrete. A chance, maybe. "I don't—"

It was colder. Finn rubbed his hands together, blew into them. The ants had cleared out. The wind picked up again, the trees blew restlessly, leaves played across the park. Behind Finn the kite jerked and fluttered higher. Finn and Snowball heard a yelp. They looked toward the noise and watched. The string had snapped. The kite was gone.

"That fucking sucks," Snowball said. "I was wrong. Ask that kid tonight about his day? Fuck, Finn. He'd say he hates flying motherfucking kites."

Finn, his realization gone, sighed. "That's what I been saying."

Mistakes by the Lake, 2013

Me and Fal, we like to call ourselves deconstructors. Others call us scrappers or termites or vultures. We pick apart the derelict and abandoned buildings that litter Cleveland. Calling ourselves deconstructors, Fal says, makes us sound respectable.

My crew—Fal, Packy, G—had just worked an empty house off Train Ave. that sat in a whole fuck block of empty houses.

"Bres," Fal says. He picked up this bres shit from a student of his, thought it fit him being in a crew. "Bres, for the birds." He reaches into his back pocket and pulls out a yellowed handkerchief. He wipes his forehead and neck. Packy and G bang wobbly-wheeled Walmart shopping carts. The carts overflow with crowbar-bent aluminum siding, wall-ripped copper, and an A/C unit we pulled out a window and thumbed S C R A P into its coils. A short piece of pipe frees itself and clangs to the street.

"Fuck, bres." He bends over, hands on knees, wheezing. "This shit's for the birds." He picks up the pipe and stares at it.

"What else we do, Fal?" G says.

Early summer, a hot day, and this is hard, hard work, deconstructing. Fal isn't used to this. He'd been a middle school teacher, *my* teacher, when The Donor had killed Sally. When he lost his job years later—pictures got his certification revoked—he dragged his ass to me. Now here he was, past 40 and nearing 300 pounds, beads of sweat dripping off his black-and-white wiry beard. What did I, a nineteen-year-old barely high-school-graduate have to offer him? Deconstruction.

We work the shopping carts down the potholed street. The houses around us look like a crackhead's grill: messed the fuck up.

It's a walk back to the scrapyards on 65th. Every week this walk gets farther and farther. Overnight, rival crews pick houses and buildings clean. Some squat in the middle of the night and stake their claim until the rest come. Fal might be right. I know when we come back to these same streets tomorrow or the next day or the day after that, we will find them already deconstructed. The mouth, it'll be absolutely toothless.

We pass a funeral home. Rusted-out cars with little flags on their hoods file behind a dusty hearse. After ten years of barely scraping by, barely helping mom and gramps, that dead guy might be the luckiest man in the Stockyards.

G's uncle owns Ca$h for $crap, one of the many junkyards and scrapyards that line 65th and whose signs scream at people to turn their scrap into cash in hundred-yard intervals. Only a few blocks from my house, Ca$h for $crap's eight-foot-high brown corrugated fencing rings the lot, protects piles of metal, used-up cars and trucks, garbage. Two giant cranes overlook it all. Every day, from my house, I can see and hear those cranes work their metal jaws around mouthfuls of metal, the noise deafening— sometimes gramps and I'll be talking, neither one of us hearing the other—and clouds of dust and metal flakes will rise up and drift and cake our windows.

We load our haul on the floor scale, weigh in, get our claim ticket, redeem it at the clerk's window. Two hundred fifty-three dollars, sixty-seven cents.

"Another day in the Yards," G says.

"OIC," says Packy. Only In Cleveland.

"Five hours' work." Fal counts on his stubby fingers. Blackened Band-Aids cover each hand. "Fuck, bres, it's like, sixty apiece." He wipes his face. "Can't live on that."

"You're the only one *trying* to live on that," Packy says. "I mean, we got other *jobs*. This scrap shit is supplementary."

"Naw, bres, naw."

"We could always go back to nicking manhole covers," G says.

This was a sore spot with Fal. We used to pull up every cover we could find—big money, those, and G's uncle, who didn't log our IDs like the law required, didn't give a shit how we got what we got. Fal fell behind, stepped right in one of the open pits. His fat saved him. Three of us couldn't pull him loose. Had to borrow a tow from the scrapyard, hook Fal up, drag him out.

Packy puffs his cheeks, sighs. He knows. "Our scrapping days," he says, "done."

G agrees. Fal breathes heavily, squeakily. Could've meant yes, no, fuck off. His handkerchief mops his face.

"Fuck." I remove my weathered baseball cap, salt-stained and faded to a light brown, the Browns helmet barely visible, and slap it against my knee, replace it. I say, "I got to get to work," and walk out the gates of the scrapyard.

I latch Sally's bike to the rack on the front of the bus, climb the steps, dig in my pockets for an old farecard or the two-and-a-quarter that will get me over to Pepe's. I don't have it. The driver shrugs, flicks his thumb in my direction. I go to sit, thankful to be floated, but he says, "No fare, no ride."

I ride this bus three, four times a week. Fucker knows me. The other passengers look out the windows. I am not their business.

His thumb points to the street. The doors close behind me and he pulls away. I smack the doors, yell, "My bike, you fuck."

I unhook the bike and start the three-mile ride. Not a huge deal, really. I deliver pizzas all over the Yards and Clark-Fulton on this bike, her bike, but I am going to be late.

It's bad enough to watch the Yards flicker by while on the bus. The big movie-screen windows play a short film of run-down houses, crumbling storefronts, boarded-up buildings, people wearing twenty-year-old clothes, the obvious hookers, the obvious users, the obvious gangs, and all the kids who'd grow up to be in one of those groups. A few churches and *iglesias* hold tight, but after the scandals even those offer little.

By bike, the same film, but solid, real, three-fucking-dimensional. On one corner, a few kids push each other while they play king-of-the-mountain on a pile of broken concrete. Dangerous game, that.

I chainlock Sally's bike to the dumpster. Inside, place is empty. Pepe yells the obvious—"You're late"—from the back office where he likely sits touching himself while watching a Victoria's Secret show. Or worse. People should not order pizza from Pepe's Pizzeria. He makes most every pie, Pepe does, unwashed hands and all.

I take my place at the stool behind the counter. The cracked edges of the fake leather dig into my leg. "Yeah, yeah." I cross my arms on the counter, fold over and rest my head. This place, man, this place.

Pepe's pizzeria's been in the same paint-flaking woodframe building for over thirty years. It was Fat Vinny's Pizza Palace before Pepe bought it, but other than the name change everything had stayed the same.

Wood-paneled walls, dark. Coupled with the one-bulb table lamps and two high windows, the room feels like a morgue. The furniture's a mash-up of a single hard plastic booth—stolen from a failed Burger King—and wobbly tables with chairs that a blind man could see don't match. On one corner table rests a deck of cards, a pen, a pad of paper, an endless game. The décor is an odd mix of old bowling and softball trophies, plastic flowers, and pictures of those who had eaten the infamous thirty-inch Pepe's Special. Numerous drop-ceiling tiles are swollen and stained with water damage, maybe hold a bloated rat or two in their bowl-like bellies. A gumball machine sits beside the counter, untouched, filled with candies that are diamond-hard. A game of chance—for a dollar, customers can move a claw around, try to grasp some shitty prize—rests in one corner. In another corner, an old TV is cabled to an older VCR; it shows old movies, the showings only interrupted if the Indians or Browns or Cavs are playing. No Indians today, just some black-and-white called *The Third Man*.

All of that's nothing compared to the carpeting. From the entrance and throughout the dining area, a thin blue-gray and heavily stained carpet covers the floor. Thirty years of dropped pizzas, spilled drinks, leaked water, bloodied cuts, mishandled diapers, and, who knows, maybe a dead body or two, gives the place both character and smell. Large floor mats cover some of the stains and gather the snow and slush and salt in the winter. The largest one, in front of the counter, holds the old Fat Vinny's name and logo. Pepe had spray-painted Pepe's Pizzeria over it, but the change has long since worn away.

After The Donor killed Sally, mom used to make decent money dancing in the Flats, but when the Flats died she got work at the front counter of The Velvet Lion making a fifth of what she used to pull dancing. Gramps doesn't work and the pills are expensive. I earn minimum wage plus delivery tips. With the deconstructing dry, this is it.

I spend a few hours folding boxes, sweeping, avoiding Pepe's office, not serving a soul. Pepe blames the economy. I blame his filthy habit. Whatever.

I worry about mom and gramps, about how we're going to keep the house, about how we're going to survive. *The Third Man* shows some fingers clawing uselessly through the underside of a manhole cover, no escape. I am taken by the one dude nodding to the other to shoot him when the phone rings, startling me. It's old Mrs. Brud. She and her husband live over on Dearborn, near our first house, the one The Donor had torched. Mom likes her. I think she's fucking nuts. She always wears a tinfoil hat; if she doesn't, she says, she'll hear voices, do things. Don't know how her husband puts up with it.

I want to do something right, for once, at least feel like I can, like I'm capable. I make a pretty awesome pizza for Mrs. Brud. Washed hands, plenty of cheese, a freshly opened pack of pepperoni, a crust cooked through, the cheese with hints of bubbly crispness. Even the box is perfectly constructed.

I slide the pizza in the warmer, go outside, and strap the package onto Sally's bike. A homemade board and bungee hold it above the front tire.

It's late and with the traffic thinned it doesn't take me long to get to her house. She opens the door a crack, the chain strangling the door. Her tinfoil hat is crooked; strands of white hair poke out like a scattered nest. She hands me two bills then theatrically drops two quarters into my hand. My tip.

Cheap nutjob. I clench the quarters. The edges dig into my palm, hard. But I am distracted.

I don't know many words, but I think even if I knew all— *all*—words, there aren't enough to describe the smell coming out that door. Imagine leaving the garbage out too long. Imagine a squirrel crawling in and dying. Imagine that squirrel rotting for three or four weeks. Imagine a few dogs taking shits in that same bag. Imagine letting *that* sit for three or four weeks. This smell, that came out of Mrs. Brud's house? Not even close.

I hold the pizza up high, near my nose, eyeing her eyeing me. Not only do I not know how to get the pizza to her through a two-inch gap—what was I going to do, slant it to her?—now I need the pizza smell to mask the *other* smell. I don't want to part from it. We are at a standoff, me and Mrs. Brud.

"My pizza?"

The box muffles my response. "I don't—" want to smell—"know how to." I push the pizza toward the door, show her the problem.

She sighs, closes the door, works the chain, opens the door wide, takes the pizza, and bathes me in the smell of worse-than-old-garbage-rotten-squirrel-dog-shit.

I throw up. On her slippers. Which are on her feet.

I wipe my mouth, give her the money back and head to Pepe's. I think about what will happen if I lose this job. Think about deconstructing more, squaring off against other crews, talking to G's uncle, maybe, negotiate a higher payout, think about other jobs me and the guys can pull. Think about mom and gramps. I stop twice to throw up on the side of the road.

But Mrs. Brud didn't call.

A few days later, a UPS guy pukes on her shoes—the slippers must've been done—and calls the cops.

I think Mrs. Brud will be arrested—her not reporting a long-dead husband sounded illegal. But she is simply left alone.

A week later, me, Packy, G and Fal are inside Brud's house, mid-day, robbing from the doornail dead and the insane alive.

It started the night of Mr. Brud's discovery. We were hanging at The Hoof. Tavern de la Hoof, officially, a dive near the west edge of the Yards. A skeletal, hook-handed friend of The Donor's owned and worked it. Country flags covered the walls. Some repped the old Yards—Irish, German, Czech, Slovak, Pole—some the new—Puerto Rican, Dominican, Mexican. Captain Hook repped the old. He'd moved here young, worked the slaughterhouses for forty years. At one point he lost his hand. The company, in a rare moment of sensitivity, gifted the captain with a small portion of one of its dying buildings. The whole industry in Cleveland collapsed shortly thereafter, but the captain, who drew beer with his two-pronged hook-hand working the tap, never left. The Yards might have claimed a hundred million cows but it would not claim him.

The captain, out of some remaining respect for The Donor—this was the place where he'd hold court, spin his stories—let me and mine hang at damn near any hour.

We had sat at the end of the bar. The tip of the Slovak flag ticked my shoulder as a nearby fan labored. Their beers mostly empty, mine mostly full. I hadn't told them about delivering to Mrs. Brud, the smell. But when I heard what they found inside—Mr. Brud was stuck to his recliner—I told them the whole story.

Packy and G had given the proper responses: "Goddamn," "That is some sick shit," "You threw up on her *slippers?*" But Fal had just stroked his gray-flecked beard, stone silent.

"Fal," I had said. "Nothing?" Fal stared off. I took a long pull from my beer, gave him a chance to spout his Fal-type wisdom. An ancient German clock with dangling weights and chains hung over the bar. When it chimed three, Fal finally spoke.

"Bres, check it." He had leaned forward on his stool, tapped each one of us on the knee to get our attention. "What happens when someone dies, bres?"

Packy: "Heaven?"

G: "Hell?"

Fal rolled his eyes. Packy said, "OK, OK." He had tapped his hand nervously on the bar, like he was taking a real test or something. "The *soul*, yeah, the soul it—"

"Funerals, bres."

Packy and G had nodded like they'd been a second away from the answer.

"So?" I'd said.

"Bres, listen. When I was a kid, when my mom died? During the *wake?* Some asshole broke into a bunch of the cars. Took purses, stereos, whatever. People couldn't believe the *balls*. Who the fuck *robs* someone while they're fucking *mourning?*"

"Yo, I know this one," G said. He'd slapped my chest.

"But why settle for cars, bres? These houses, no one's around for *miles*. And we're not talking copper and siding and shit. Deconstructing. Look, someone dies, they run a notice in the paper. Tell you about the person, family, their life, when the wakes and funerals will be. All the family, friends, neighbors—all the people who *might* be home? Gone."

It wasn't good, but it wasn't bad. Stealing from the dead, pretty low. More or less victimless. They're fucking dead.

Our first one had a dog. Dogs don't go to funerals. Her dog, a big dog, bit Packy on the ass as he grabbed some jewelry. We fled. Only made twenty-six bucks. Our second one, same day, after first checking for dogs, made 400. Not bad. Lot easier than working in the heat for five hours, manual fucking labor. In a half hour, on one of these funeral jobs? Same money. Greater potential. No rivals.

Fal and the others had insisted on doing Mrs. Brud's. I was reluctant, but it didn't take long for the three of them to make me cave.

We wear rags over our mouths and noses, but the smell, man, that smell gets through anyway. Mr. Brud's body print still burns the chair.

Mrs. Brud has money hidden everywhere. Mattress. Books. DVDs. Coffee cans. Photo albums. We already have about five grand, cash. The jewelry, once we sell it, will net another grand. A photo of Mr. and Mrs. Brud and a little girl watch us, me.

Fal, huffing and grunting, works a chain with a closed locket over his head.

"What the fuck," I say.

"Something to remember her by, bres."

"Put it back."

G and Packy stop tossing the kitchen. "What's going on?" one of them says.

"I—" Don't want to do this. And it fucking pisses me off that I don't want to do this. "We need to go," I say.

"Yo, we're almost done," G says.

"Let's go." I head for the back door. "Fal, put it back."

"Shit, man." G follows me out. Packy and Fal are close behind.

Later, in the brick-walled basement of The Hoof, among a world of Indians, old and new, we count what we have. Our best take ever.

G says, "We could've had more, you hadn't—"

"Shut the fuck up." I shove the take into a pillowcase. "Fal, give."

Fal shuffles around the felt-worn pool table while eating a chicken wing. "Bres, I'll hold it."

"*I'll* hold it," I say. I go to Fal, snap off the necklace, and head home.

I carry my sister's bike up three stairs to the sagging porch. A few more winters, I predict it'll detach completely from the wood-frame house. The ice cream trucks park in the lot across the street and cut their engines, each truck's song a winding-down death as the sun slips lower over the Yards. Sally would've loved that we live across from the Land of the Ice Cream Trucks. I love that she would've loved it. But that same fucking Mr. Softee song, over and over, amazing I haven't killed anyone.

I grab the sack containing Mrs. Brud, lock up the bike. I lock it up everywhere. This bike, it's all I got left of her.

Inside the two-bedroom shotgun, I kick off my shoes, close the door, bump into gramps. A naked sixty-eight-year-old gramps, some parts hanging, flapping. But my gramps has a little something extra: titties. I'm not talking about the oh-he's-old-and-the-man-boobs-sag titties. I'm talking real fucking titties.

"Gramps, damn, put some clothes on."

Gramps says he should've been a grand*ma*, that he had tried to hide his inner-womanly feelings, but after years and years and years of wrestling with that, of denying, he came clean to himself, to his family. I had tried calling him grandma but it got confusing. I simply call him—*her*—gramps.

For years, gramps has been going through HRT, the estrogen, the anti-androgens. She longs for a trachea shave, an invisible Adam's apple and a higher voice, and she wants, more than anything, reassignment surgery. To be authentic, as she likes to say. She'd told me she knew she didn't need that to be part of her transition, that the biology didn't determine her identity, but she was who she was and it's just what she wanted. "And wants aren't so bad, Hal," she'd said. I sometimes excuse my crimes by telling myself that she's why I do them.

"This frees me." She holds her arms out from her sides.

I turn away. "I feel you, gramps, but—"

I am wrong. Gramps isn't naked. She wears high heels and she clicks herself up the stairs to her room.

I sit on my couch, the sack on the floor between my feet. "Mom?"

"Working." Gramps reappears in a robe and sits beside me. Her robe opens. "Sorry," she says and closes up shop. "You know, someday I won't have one of them dickiemahickies." She looks out the window behind her as the last driver slides the barbwire-topped gate closed, corralling the trucks for the night. "Least I got these." She grabs her chest.

I laugh. I love this man, this lady. Doesn't matter to me. But, as amazing as she is, she struggles, too. She lives as a woman in this house, but she rarely leaves this house as a woman. She's started going to meetings recently, and those are good for her, gets her out once every other month or so, but truly being out there as herself? Hasn't really happened since I got in a fight in middle school over some asshole talking shit about her. She is brave, I know that. But she's scared, I know that, too. And she isn't, not really, free.

"It's hard, you know. She made more as a lingerie model when she met your father. More as a dancer after he left."

"I got money coming in."

Her eyes drop to the bag at my feet and she winces. She worries about my extra income, its origins.

I foot the sack under the couch. "It's all good, gramps. It's legit."

Gramps shakes her head, frowns. Her robe starts to slide off her knee. I reach over and catch it.

"You're a good kid. You help support us. You help pay for my pills. I appreci—"

"I need some sleep." Gramps is in my bedroom. "Got the ten-to-close shift."

"Here." Gramps slips a postcard onto the table. The return address says Lorain Correctional and my name, Hal Boland, is written in The Donor's all-caps block lettering.

"Sleep, gramps," I say.

"Consider it?"

I stare at the postcard.

"Say no more." She gives me an open-robed hug, heads upstairs to paint. Her hobby. Canvas after canvas stacked one on top of the other on the floor of her bedroom.

I pick up the postcard and flick it like a razor across the room. An edge sticks in a soft, damp spot in the drywall. It hangs for a moment, flutters to the floor.

I pull sheets from under the couch cushions, a pillow from under the coffee table, and set up my bed. I swear I smell Sally on the pillow, the little-girl perfume my mom gave her one birthday. Every time I think I'm past it, something blindsides.

I dream a thin memory. Sally just a barely walking thing, The Donor talking to mom about the future, about how he was going to be a big deal, how he just needed money. Sally giggles like she knows something the rest of us don't. Then the dream shifts: through fog or smoke, a burned-out house. Mr. Brud stands on the porch between two smoldering pillars that once supported a second-floor deck; he tries to speak, but no words, only smoke. The smoke turns into The Donor, handcuffed, his plan a big fuck failure. Buzzards circle. A one-legged, wheelchair-bound man rolls out of the house right through Mr. Brud, Sally's tiny body smoking in his lap.

I come awake quick, feel the tear-damp pillow under my cheek. It is dark; the clock says I have time, but I need out. I go to the bathroom, splash some water on my face, get my shit together, and pedal to Pepe's.

In a short time, we pull a little over sixteen grand from the funeral jobs. Split four ways, we're not doing half bad. But word is out—police are looking for some lowlifes who steal from the dead—so we ease up, haven't pulled a single job in a month.

The Indians are on. I don't watch, can't watch, not since The Donor. And if I change the channel, Pepe senses it somehow, comes out, yells at me to turn it back on.

My back's to the TV. I'm fucking around with the game of chance. I try for and miss a miniature Browns helmet several times, the crane's claws hooking the facemask on the last try before slipping free. Behind the counter, I put my head down and wait for someone to call, something to deliver. Our recent successes have allowed me to consider quitting the pizza business, but I just don't feel secure yet. In fact, I'm straight-up unsettled for reasons I can't explain. Maybe a rich fuck will walk in, leave me a ten-thousand-dollar tip. I hear that kind of shit happens. Not to me, but it happens. So, I wait. For something, someone, anything, anyone to deliver me.

All I get is Fal.

"Bres." He steps back and forth through the doorway, ringing and re-ringing the bell of a customer's entrance.

Pepe yells from his office. "Hal, if that's your fat *comemierda* friend, you get him the fuck out my restaurant."

Fal stops dead in the middle of the doorway.

"Fuck you want?" I am more than a little mad at Fal.

He steps through all the way, rings the bell one last time. "Bres, relax. Just stopping. To say, you know, hi. And shit." He glances at the TV, checks the score. Game's been in rain delay, just getting going again. But Fal's eyes keep moving, never settle on anything. He makes a short air-escaping-from-a-bike-tire sound. Pepe comes out, glares at Fal, announces he's leaving, that I have to close.

Fal sits at a table in a tiny alcove in the front. He barely fits, looks like squeezing a pig into a mouse hole. He somehow manages to put his foot up. A toe pokes through the sole of his light blue-trimmed J's. He tries to look relaxed, fails, takes his foot down. He keeps looking from the door to the kitchen and back to the door. He clears his throat. "Bres."

"Well?"

"C'mon, bres, this ain't about, you know, *Ti*na. It's—" He checks the door again. "I saved you." His eyes sweep to the game. "From her."

I come around the counter, the stool crashing to the floor in my wake. He covers his face, his wounded eye. "Wait, wait, wait." I grab his arms, try to pull him up, but he's wedged tight. "Look, bres, look. Help. I need help." His crotch bears a faded stain. He smells like piss.

I push him one last time, turn away, fumble a dollar to the crane. "Kidding, right?"

"My life, bres."

"Your life." I work the joystick, angling for the helmet. Miss.

"Please, bres. Icepick is coming. For me. If I don't come up with seven. Large."

Fal tells me about the last week, how he'd tried to become a

107

pimp. He'd started with Tina, but she'd walked before turning a single trick. Then he'd decided the best way wasn't to develop his own stable, no, but to recruit someone else's, start small, just win over one. Then two. Icepick, their actual pimp, caught up with Fal a few hours ago. Pressed him. Fal in a panic—an icepick to the throat will cause panic—said he'd get Icepick seven to make nice, just don't hurt him. Fal didn't have seven.

"You—why would you say that?"

"Bres, bres, it's not like that. I stood up to—"

"Kneeled, more like. Sucked his—"

"I'm no coward, bres. But when that, that, icepick came out ..."

"*Seven?*"

"The, the, the icepick!" He wipes a drop of saliva from the corner of his mouth. "Look, if he doesn't get the money by midnight, he'll kill my sis."

"You don't have a sister."

"So? It's my *fictional* sis. She always—" Fal checks the door again. "I mean, I had to give up someone."

I laugh. A funny man even when he isn't trying. "He's coming here, isn't he."

"I told him I'd buy him dinner, bres, a pizza."

"You fat fuck." I take out what little I have on me and slap it into his chest.

"What about the rest?"

"You're on your own."

"Bres. *Hal.* Me. Please." Then, "My sis."

"You don't—! I'm *working*, Fal." I go behind the counter, set up the stool, sit. I start assembling boxes.

"Working?" He looks around the restaurant, holds his arms out wide. "All these people, bres?"

"You're killing me, Fal."

He checks the game. "Fuckers are blowing it." The Indians are tied, the Royals have the bases loaded, two outs. A few pitches miss the zone. Then the batter gets beaned, losing run crosses the plate, a walk-off hit-by-pitch.

I pick up the phone, call G, tell him what's what. It takes some convincing, but they each give what they have. On his way over, Packy stops by my house, picks up the rest of mine.

"G's pissed," Packy says.

"He ain't the only one," I say.

Packy and Fal get into a shouting match. Fal loses. He knows he's wrong, knows he just knocked us all back to square one.

A few minutes before midnight, a scrawny big-nosed guy rolls in. He can't weigh more than 120. Fal could've sat on him, ended his life in eight seconds flat. His oversized Cleveland State shorts hang below his waist, the bottoms hitting him mid-shin. He wears a white T-shirt under an unbuttoned short-sleeved dress shirt. It opens and floats behind him when he walks. Tucked in one hip of his underwear's waistband is the wood handle of what could only be the icepick; the handle of a gun pokes out of the other hip. He sees Fal in that tiny alcove, laughs. He nods in my direction. "You da man?"

I put a pizza box on the counter. Icepick opens it, sees the cash, closes it. "You are da man," he says. "I trust you'll keep your fat man on a leash, meng? Now on?"

Icepick grabs the box, heads for the door. I wait for Fal to say something stupid, but Packy appears ready to kick him if he tries. Instead, Icepick turns back, his eyes narrow. "I know you."

"I don't—" I say.

"Yeah, yeah," he says. "Give me a sec." He sits, the pizza box of money in his lap. He puts one hand over his eyes like a psychic, like he can conjure me up in front of him.

None of us knows what the fuck he's talking about. I didn't know *him*.

"You're dat, you're dat *Bo*land kid, right?" He stands, comes to the counter. "Yeah, yeah, I thought I knew you. Saw your ass on da *news.*" His right hand smacks the counter as if to emphasize his memory. "You haven't fucking changed, meng."

I nod, uncomprehending.

He laughs. It starts low, ends high. Ha-ha-ha-*HA*. "Yeah, *meng*. I *knew* it." He takes a toothpick from the dispenser on the counter, sticks it in his mouth. He looks over at Fal, at Packy. "What you—? Naw, naw. You know, I felt *sorry* for you. Meng, your *sister* and all? I gave my girls the night off when we saw it. Shit. Dat was, what, four, five years ago?"

"Eight."

"*Eight?*" He shakes his head. "Your father, meng." He sets

the box on the counter, turns to the others, takes them into his confidence. "This guy's *father*? He makes *you*," he points at Fal, "look like a fucking genius." With his back to me, he casts another look at Fal who squirms a little in his tight seat. Icepick shakes his head again.

I think about taking some of the money back but can't figure how to open the box even an inch without him knowing.

He turns back, his tongue flicks the toothpick from right to left, left to right. He squeezes his eyes shut, waves his hand toward himself. I lean in. Icepick says, low, "What you doing, meng, with these *clowns*? I mean, I don't even *know* dat other one, but if he's anything, *any*thing, like da big one? Fuck, meng. *This* your crew?"

I am getting lectured by a scrawny-ass pimp. "Who said I had a 'crew'?"

Icepick scoffs. "With what *your* father was into? You got a crew, you're doing shit. I know." He pulls the toothpick out of his mouth, sets it on the counter. "It's da natural fucking order. My dad? Numbers. Dat's how I started, working for him. Then I graduated. *You*?" He holds his arms out, takes in all of Pepe's.

I move around the counter, brush past Icepick. I click the flashing O-P-E-N window sign, the one above Fal, to off. I flip the door sign, hold the door open. "Time to go."

"Look, look, all I'm *say*ing, meng," Icepick says, "is you *need* to get your shit *straight*. Moving in on me?" He pulls the icepick from his waistband, runs his thumb up one side, pricks a small drop of blood with the tip, sticks the thumb in his mouth and sucks.

Even with the door held open the room feels airless. The nighttime summer breeze kicks through the door and, redistributed by the rattling and rotating fan that stood beneath the TV, becomes stale. I see Packy exhale deeply; he takes a few steps toward the counter, toward Icepick. I shake my head. He stops.

The pick still in his hand, Icepick grabs the box. "And if you can't do it on your own," he says, "there's always Ed. Even I pay tribute to ol' Early." Icepick moves past me and out the door. "Pleasure doing business, meng."

I close and lock the door behind him, run a shaking hand through my hair. I try to slow my breathing, get a hold of myself.

"Bres, that went well."

"Shut the fuck up," Packy says.

"I could've been a good pimp." Fal rubs his beard, tries to stand, discovers he's still stuck. He holds his arms up. "Bres?"

I swipe Icepick's toothpick off the counter. "Enough's enough." My fingers tattoo the counter. "No more deconstructing, no more funeral jobs. No more small time."

The Donor was once known as King of the Yards, the Stockyards his domain. The town loved him.

Part of his power was his history. He was homegrown. Standout outfielder and hitter in high school over at LW.

Being a part of the Indians organization solidified his place in the Yards. Not only did it look like he was making it, but he was going to make it for his hometown team's glory. The Donor, drafted right out of high school, knocked around Class A Waterloo and Double A Williamsport. He loved to brag that he played with future Indians Greg Swindell and Albert "Joey" Belle. And for one game at Triple A Buffalo, his only game in Triple A, he faced Len Barker. *That* fucking Len Barker, one of only two Cleveland pitchers to ever throw a perfect game. Barker was on the downside, coming back from an injury or something, but it only took three pitches to strike The Donor out.

He loved to talk about his almost-Indian days—as far as most people in the Yards were concerned, they were whole-Indian days—and he'd tell people about the games, the bus rides, the pranks, the ladies. He'd hold court for hours, neighborhood suckups drooling over every word spoken, every name dropped.

He'd try to impress me when I was little, tell me the stories. But mom had told me the full story, how he'd ruined a good thing, got mixed up in cocaine, violence. He fought everyone. Mom. Gramps. Neighbors. Opponents. His own team. Albert-Don't-Call-Me-Joey fucked him up more than once.

Then the sorry end. At an exhibition game somewhere in Central America, he got stabbed, lung punctured. He claimed it was a crazed fan. My guess? He was buying, didn't like the price, got stabbed. He was forever pissed about it, but not for the getting stabbed part. What pissed him off? The "fan" only got fined the equivalent of a buck or two for the attack.

Between the injury, which fucked his timing, the drugs,

which only got worse, and the bad press, which the Indians couldn't handle, his ass was dropped. He said he'd retired.

He came back to the Yards a hero. He was, after all, the one who almost made it, the guy who hung with the city's future heroes. People loved him. Even threw a parade. It was actually St. Patrick's Day, so a parade was a guarantee, but he had his own float: a big red, white, and blue baseball, streamers, The Donor in his uniform throwing green miniature baseball candies to the crowd. His big fuck day, he'd said, his start to bigger things.

In the days after his failed baseball career, he initially tried to ally himself with Early Ed, collecting Ed's bookmaking and loan-sharking debts door to door. The problem? Ed had never asked him to. The Donor said he had showed initiative, something he would later say I never did, and Ed instructed him, with a gun, to step off, do something useful.

He married mom—"I rescued your mother from lingerie modeling and a destined life of prostitution"—but soon attempted to steal some of Joe Loose's territory. Joe Loose had him brought to his office. With spit flicking The Donor's face, Joe Loose said, "Who the fuck you think you are, another Danny-fucking-Greene Irishman? You stop or end up like him, you potato-eating fuck." Or something like that. That's what The Donor'd said.

After he had me, had the perfect-looking family, he opted for legitimate power, ran for city council. "His people," as he liked to call them, elected him to the 15th Ward. They got what they deserved.

He thought meetings could be handled like he handled his baseball career. He broke up one meeting by leaping across the table and punching an opponent in the nose. A highly publicized night of shared beers at The Hoof and a newborn daughter rescued him from assault charges.

The 15th was part of Early Ed's domain. He controlled all of Clark-Fulton, most of the Yards, other pockets east and west, and councilmen. A lot of the Cleveland mafia bought councilmen, but given The Donor's checkered history it was hard to know who exactly sent Councilman Donor his first briefcase of money. Joe Loose? Doubtful. Early Ed? Maybe. Didn't matter. That money and more bought the house The Donor would later burn.

A do-gooder eventually blew the whistle on the bribes and

Councilman Donor resigned. He always thought Early Ed had set him up, upset he wouldn't back some shit project or another.

The Donor lost it. He'd storm around the house, yelling about getting back in the game. But all his backers, all those that loved him, that hung on every exaggerated story, they felt he was used-the-fuck-up done.

But The Donor had one more comeback play.

Me and Fal sit on an old couch shoved in one corner of The Hoof. Two Hook-poured beers, half empty, sweat on the low table in front of us. A paper towel holds the bones from a dozen hot wings Fal brought in from the outside. The Hoof doesn't do food. In the basement, Packy and G play pool on the uneven table.

It'd been a few days since Fal's short career as a pimp ended, a few days since I'd told my crew to come up with something. Anything. G had a plan, but it felt far too bold.

Fal says, "What time is it, bres?"

I check the clock over the bar. It is clearly visible. "Beer and food make you so slow you avoid the issue?"

"What's that, bres?" He slurs the last "s." He unsteadily carries his trash to a garbage can next to the bar. When he returns, crushed cushions and springs echo inside the empty bar.

I down the rest of my beer. "Ask me what you want to ask."

No answer. Fal is slumped low on the couch, his fingers locked over his stomach. He snores. I punch him in the chest. He jerks awake, his hands balled into fists. "What happened?" he says. He turns and throws a leftover bone; it bounces harmlessly off the brick wall behind me.

"Ask me."

"Bres, you don't have to—"

I sigh. "Say it."

"I mean, I always wondered what kind of leader you'd make, bres. Your father, Icepick was right, he—"

"Don't."

"And you?" Fal chuckles. "Deconstructing? Thieving the dead?"

I want to get the fuck out of here.

"Here's the question," Fal says. "I just wonder if you'd, you know, end up like him."

"I'm not—"

"Whatever."

I can't tell if he's tired or stupid. I run it down for him. "You ask me what time it is, I tell you that that's not what you want, then you—"

"Oh, right right right right *right*," he says, caught up. "G! Packy!" They come up the stairs, close the low gate behind them, order a couple of beers from Hook, and sit on the table in front of us.

"*My* plan, bres, *my* idea: we jack that truck, sell it, make mad money."

"Fucking hell, Fal." That's G's plan. Fal's original idea is one I'd already shot down. "We're not—"

"They've worked it out." Fal points at Packy and G.

"They've worked it out," I say.

"Yo," G says, "it's a plan." He drums his hands on his knees, a habit of his whenever he gets excited.

Packy says, "And I'm out of money. G's out of money. You're out of money." He glares at Fal who is clueless to the blame. He licks his fingers, brings some dried sauce back to life. "Damn, Fal, you'd sell your soul to the devil for beers and wings."

"Give the devil his due," I say. It was a phrase of The Donor's. I can't believe I'd just used it.

Both Packy and Fal make air-escaping sounds. Fal's likely means "blow me." Packy's means "move on."

Packy says, "I know the problem, your worry, cameras and shit. But—"

G drums his knees. "But we'll take it, yo, not at the de*livery* point. On the *road*."

I roll my eyes. "This isn't an empty house."

"Do you know how much we can sell a truckload of cigarettes for?" Packy says.

"We don't even know who we can sell to."

"G does. His uncle does. Sell the whole load for forty, fifty grand."

"You—"

"Shhh, shhh," Fal says. "This is the good part."

I don't expect any of this to have a "good part."

Packy says, "I have the truck's route. One of those Google

maps, a line tracing its path. We work backwards from the time of delivery, estimate the time it'll hit a spot that works best for us. Take it down."

"Right," I say. "And what? How we gonna get it? None of us have cars. We gonna ride up alongside on my sister's bike, yell at it to pull over or we'll give 'em one of Pepe's pizzas?"

"Shit, bres, now I'm hungry."

They'd really thought this through. I stand to leave.

"All right, bres." Fal pulls me back to the couch. "Yes, right, we'll use your bike."

The cigarette Packy had just placed in his mouth falls when his mouth opens wide at this latest gem. He picks up his cigarette, brushes at the ash in his lap. "What?"

"The bike."

"You're not using Sally's bike."

Escaping air. This time I guess it means "whatever." Fal says, "It'll be fine. It's good. A good idea."

"You and 'good idea' do not go together."

"Trust me."

"Really, Fal? If we were talking about you eating a bucket of chicken or a whole turkey or five of Pepe's pizzas—"

"Dang, bres, stop."

"—then I'd trust you. This? Trust you? Fuck you."

"No, the bike," Packy says. "It's, it's not bad."

Great, Packy and Fal thinking alike. "Use your own damn bike."

"I don't own a bike, only you," Packy says. "Trust me. Not Fal. Me."

I nod. "Count me out."

"Bres, if you don't come I'll, I'll, I'll hang myself. You have to—"

"You?" Packy says. "Hang yourself?" He chuckles, mimics putting his head through a noose, tightening it. "What rope could hold you?" Packy falls to the ground, his imaginary rope broken.

"Nothing good can come of this," I say.

"You're not a friend, you're not a man," Fal says, "if you don't stand with us." He holds his hand over his heart, stares off into the distance, poses like some kind of inspirational painting or statue or some shit.

Goddamn, the drama of him. "Since you put it like that, Fal, I guess I'm not—"

Fal stands, which seems to take a while. His feet firmly under him, Fal farts. "Sorry." He waves a hand behind him. "I will be who I be, bres."

I start to protest again, but what's the use? Fal only hears what he wants to hear, and sometimes not even then.

Packy says, "Fal, leave us alone. I'll give enough reasons to make him—and not just Sally's bike—go with us."

Fal blows a "pshht." This one either means "good luck" or "never gonna happen." To clarify, he says, "I hope persuasion is with you, bres, that Hal hears the profit. Money, bres, money. This shit's deconstructing and funerals times a million." Fal offers to Packy, "Remind him of his grandma?" Fal turns away. "Whatever. I'll be at Pepe's."

"Fal, you know he hates it when—"

But Fal has already left the building. G trails behind him, cracking jokes about pizzas and hangings.

Packy moves from the table to the couch, punches my thigh. "Hal, I have something I can't do alone. You, I swear, you're gonna love it."

"The truck?"

"Still happen. We just do something else. After. You don't even have to be a part of the main job."

Still pissed about Tina, about Icepick, I say, "Tell me."

"Fal and G rob the truck. And when they have it? *We* rob *them*. We don't? Cut my fucking heart out, Hal." Packy takes his thumb, runs it across his chest. "Telling you, it'll be a riot."

This I like. The thieving Fal bit, not the heart-cutting part. I lean back in the chair, thinking. "What about us?" I point at my face, at Packy's face.

"Covered. Masks, clothes, dis*guises*."

"They'll fight back."

"Bro, who we talking about? They'll *run*." He's right. "But the real enjoyment in this," Packy says, "is the lies the big fuck will tell. How hundreds attacked him, how he fought all of them single-handedly, how he saved G's life, carried him to safety." Packy laughs. "Funny, funny shit."

Packy loves his pranks. Loves to target Fal. Started years ago, back in the seventh grade, Packy put liquid soap in Fal's coffee. Fal blew bubbles the entire class, thought he had rabies.

"Set it up."

Pepe's in back, the perverted fuck. His pinstriped sweats make it easier to do what he does. The TV in the corner shows a movie The Donor loved: *One Flew Over the Cuckoo's Nest*. The scene: some dude with glasses yells over and over that he wants his cigarettes, flips out until that Jack Nicholson McMurphy guy—The Donor loved him, too—punches through the glass, grabs a carton.

I've heard nothing of the truck, the plan, in days. The radio fucking silence baffles me since they were all jonesing so bad for this job. Any minute, I expect Packy to come in, give an update. Or Fal. But me and McMurphy are alone.

Worry and hope keep me awake most nights, and I doze in the Burger King booth. When the phone rings, McMurphy's brainless and Mrs. Brud's on the phone.

Pepe comes out of his office, washes his hands for once, makes her pizza. I strap it on Sally's bike and pedal off.

At Mrs. Brud's, all the lights are off. I lean the bike against a tree, unclip the pizza, go to the door, knock. Nothing. I set the pizza on a chair, cup my hands to my face, lean against the window, try to see. A girl comes around the side of the house, the driveway side, says, "We're in back," and walks behind the house. I pick up the pizza and follow. Maybe it's the lack of sleep, but it feels like I'm following Sally. Same hair. Same style clothes. She looks the same age as Sally when—

The back of the house. Small kiddie pool beside a tiny one-car garage. The water in the pool green and brown. The girl sits on the grass beside the pool, one hand tracing a finger through the muck. Tinfoil-hatted Mrs. Brud reclines in a worn lounge chair. Her ass pokes through the bottom; vinyl multi-colored straps dangle beneath her. I think the chair might give up any second. It was an odd scene.

I can't find the ticket, blank on the cost. Being here makes me nervous. Fuck it, make it up. "Twelve ninety-five," I say to Mrs. Brud.

"Hal, Alexis. My granddaughter."

Granddaughter? I didn't even know Brud had kids, much less—I remember that picture in the house, the night we robbed it.

I set the pizza in the grass, say hello without looking at either one.

"She goes to school over there." Mrs. Brud points vaguely toward the Stockyards. "Don't you, dear?"

I don't look at her directly, but I catch a nod, a smile.

Mrs. Brud says, "Sit, Hal, stay a minute."

No fuck way, lady. "Fourteen fifty," I say. Is that what I said the first time? Alexis opens a picture book; it looks like a book I once read to Sally, but my brain must be playing tricks.

"Hal," Mrs. Brud says, "my husband knew you, watched you, *watches* you. Knew your father, too." She reaches over the arm of her lounge, grabs her purse. "We still talk about you, he and I."

"Uh huh." I edge toward Alexis, try to see a page as she flips through.

"You like kids, Hal." She isn't asking. I don't know what I like. Standing here—weird Mrs. Brud digging in her purse telling me she still talks to her dead husband, this Sally lookalike reading a Sally bookalike—I know what I don't like. That's clear as fucking day.

"You like this neighborhood, Hal?"

"No."

Alexis looks up from her book. Her hand hovers over a picture. The art looks the same as Sally's, but hers went with her in the fire. Can't be the same.

"You do, you—"

"Thirteen. I mean, sixteen. Please."

"You know, my husband worked with a redevelopment group. Trying to bring these neighborhoods back."

Good luck, I think.

"We both agreed. It starts with the people here, the kids. So he helped open Alexis's school."

She holds out a piece of paper. It isn't money. A business card.

"I told my husband you'll likely end up a good-for-nothing, Hal—truly, I believe that—but he insisted. And he can be persuasive." She taps the card. "See this woman. She could use your help. You, you could—"

118

I take the card, ask for the money again. Mrs. Brud doesn't move. Alexis has moved on from the book; she's humming while she chalks the garage door in rainbow colors, adds pupils and eyelashes to the two round windows.

"Fuck it." I head down the driveway and grab my bike. As I pedal away, Alexis's humming seems to be louder, following me. Damned if I don't feel like McMurphy, wishing someone would hold a pillow over my face.

When I get back to Pepe's, Fal's jammed into his usual seat. A pizza's on the carpeted floor. Pepe points and yells, points and yells. "Get your *comemierda* friend out of here before I use his fat to clean the floor."

I step over the pizza and grab Fal's collar, drag him through the door, reenter to Pepe demanding I clean up the mess then cursing his way to the back. I throw the pizza out, wipe the floor with some paper towels, only managing to work everything deeper into the carpet, add to the history of stains. Through the window, I watch Fal looking over the bike. I finish cleaning—a fairly shitty job, I admit—and head outside.

"Thought it was pink," he says.

"What did you do?"

"I told him his pizza was shit, knocked it on the floor." He burps. "I'm stuffed."

"Asshole."

"Yeah," Fal says. "Thought it was pink."

"Always purple."

"Hmmm." He rubs a patch of facial hair that never fills in completely.

"Problem?"

"Purple's good, won't work as well as pink. Not as visible."

"Not as visible."

"Not as visible. Girl's bike, girl's bright color. Needs to be *seen*, bres, for the truck to stop."

"An actual girl might help, too. You planning on dressing up, being in the road with that thing?" He looks surprised. "And what you gonna do once it stops?"

"I got this." I'm shitty at guns, but it looks like a .38.

"Jesus," I say. "Put that away." I maneuver myself between Fal and a couple who walk past on the sidewalk. "You out your mind?"

"Tonight's the night, bres. Our break."

"No one told me."

"Packy just worked it out, bres. Told me to tell you. He'll be by at one." Fal pulls at the bike, rattles the chain.

"You're not gonna use it, are you?"

"If an icepick can make me piss myself, bres, then flashing a gun? It's cigarettes. Nobody hauling cigs is gonna stand up with a gun in their face." He pulls out what looks like a leather testicle. "I got this, too. It's a sap. Hit someone over the head? They ain't be getting up for a while. G comes up from behind while the driver's checking on me and—" He whips the sap at my chest.

I drop to one knee. "Fuck!"

"Yeah, lead's in there. Lights out."

My chest burns. I feel a lump forming. I pop up and smack Fal in the back of his head. "Where?"

He rubs his head while I massage my chest. "Behind that pawn shop next to the Dollar Store. Packy says low traffic, easy target." Fal slaps the sap into his palm. "So." He scans the bike. "I need it."

"What the hell am I supposed to use—?"

"Tell people Pepe whacks off in the pizza."

Fal's on to something with that. He tugs at the lock and chain.

"Christ, hold on." I undo the lock and Fal rides away. He looks far too big on a girl's bike, and it gives the illusion that he just floats away from me.

I get through the last hours of my shift by avoiding deliveries. I consider telling the callers to avoid Pepe's like the motherfucking plague, that they should get themselves to a doctor as soon as fuck possible, but instead tell the no-taste-buds fools on the other end that our ovens are down, sorry for the inconvenience.

Pepe comes out every now and then, asks about the calls. I tell him they're wrong numbers, and he heads back to his room. When one o'clock rolls around, I flip the closed sign, lock the front entrance, lock the back door behind me.

Packy's right on time, strolls into the parking lot with two duffle bags, one slung on his shoulder, the other in his hand.

I move toward the Fulton side of Pepe's parking lot and gesture Packy to follow. "Disguises?"

He nods, lines up on my right side, and swings the duffle off his shoulder and into my hand.

We start the walk up Fulton, head toward the spot. We aren't going to meet Fal and G, of course, but we need to beat them to the area, give me and Packy time to prep, watch Fal and G in action. Packy texts G about our delay, backs their ability to take the truck without us, that we'd meet up after they stashed the truck.

Packy slides his cell shut. "I tell you what, I can't wait to drive this thing."

"Hold up." I reach my hand out and press the back of it against his shoulder, stopping his walk, turning him toward me. "Your dad fired you last year, didn't he?" I can't believe this had slipped my mind. "Fucking hell, Packy, you hit, like, thirty parked cars over by Prog—"

"It was *six* cars. And it was the truck's fucking fault. You know that, told you before. Besides, *you* can't drive." He pushes through my hand and walks on. "I got this."

I look up at the stars, what few I can see, sigh, and follow.

C-F is in as bad a shape as the Yards. It's a nice mix of houses, stores, old-time businesses, but a bunch of the houses and mom-and-pop stores are burned out, a bunch vandalized, a bunch condemned, a bunch all three. A spray-painted smiley face with a cocked-to-one-side halo on one boarded-up door gives a kind of odd hint of hope, or at least attitude, that something might change for the better.

Passing St. Rocco's gets me thinking about my short baseball career. Initially, coaches saw the name Boland, remembered The Donor in his almost-Indian glory, excitedly signed me up. Didn't take but a few practices and games to see I sucked. The players' and coach's obvious disappointment made me skip the rest of the season. The Donor made me practice with him, told me no son of his would fail at baseball—his own failures lost on him—but I would not get better. It was like a string of his DNA, the baseball string, failed to pass to me, and no matter what effort or desire was put forth to add that string, it wouldn't take. I couldn't catch, I couldn't throw, I couldn't run, I couldn't hit (which made not being able to run not as big a deal). In short time, wasn't a tee-ball or little league or Metroparks team that wanted me. Only St. Rocco's would put me on their team, and that only after The Donor promised a donation. The coaching priest pulled me aside, told me he knew all about me, and that as long as I stayed for the season, he'd have a talk with The Donor about my early retirement. Only grandpa's declaration of his desire to be a grandma saved me from The Donor's full disappointment. But disappointing him was a fine path to walk.

Packy tugs my sleeve, pulls me out of my memories and through an empty lot. We head west toward 40th.

"I'm thinking, OK," Packy says, "so the, the truck's coming down this way." He points to the way we'd just come. "Fal's using your bike—"

"Sally's."

"Sally's bike. He's going to be in the street, down, girl in distress. G's waiting in the bushes." This time Packy points to a brick warehouse, thick bushes overgrown near the intersection. "And you and me are there." The large cemetery, opposite G's spot, runs the length of the street for blocks. "They do their thing. We there in a heartbeat if anything goes wrong, there for sure if everything goes right."

"Time?"

"It's one-thirty now, G said truck at two."

A six-foot stretch of chain link, crossbar free from posts, droops to a foot high, gives easy access to the cemetery. A huge tree stands guard over the dead, serves as our hiding place until the truck shows.

I fling my bag at the tree's base; Packy does the same. I unzip mine to see the disguise: a Lebron mask, and a Browns jersey, pants, and helmet. The jersey bears the name Sipe. A baseball glove's inside, too. "What the fuck, Packy?"

He pulls out an old Cleveland Barons hockey jersey, the name Stewart stitched on its back, an old Jason-style hockey mask, goalie pads. "My cousin's basement is full of this stuff. In this town? *Everyone* owns this crap. Thousands of suspects, bro."

Huh, yeah, not bad, I think. I slide the pants over my shorts, the jersey over my shirt. I swap my shoes for the cleats Packy'd included, makes me taller. "Christ, Packy, don't put those on." He stops lacing the hockey skate. "Right, right." He shakes his head, shoves it back in his bag.

I throw the glove at him. "No baseball."

He tosses it back. "Use it."

I hear a bicycle's bell ring, unable to tell its location. I push Packy, who'd just finished dressing, behind the tree.

Riding down the middle of Clark is a ski-masked Fal, Sally's purple bike an ant under an elephant. G's fifty feet behind, jogging to keep up; he wears a black hoodie and a ski mask that's folded up on his forehead. They are down by a self-storage building, a few hundred feet away, but I hear G say, "Stop ringing that fucking bell."

"C'mon, bres, who am I gonna wake? The dead?" His right arm gestures toward the graveyard and us, and the motion throws off his balance. He runs into the curb, yells.

G knocks the crotch-rubbing Fal off the bike and the two of them walk the rest of the way. I catch Packy's attention, tap my wrist. He flashes his fingers: one-five-zero. Ten minutes. G and Fal lean the bike against some bushes and pull out pieces of an old police barricade: two pieces of wood that serve as legs and a wooden crossbeam. They head toward 41st. Don't know how or where they got the barricade, or even when they stashed it. My guess: the Fulton station, or maybe LW; I'd heard the high schools needed more and more cops to control the students. Kids today.

Me and Packy watch them set up the barricade. It effectively blocks any traffic coming from the west, and with 40th a no-go for incoming traffic—it isn't a through street—it looks like G and Fal's plan isn't horrible. Who knew?

As they return to 40th, I hear G say something like he was sure we'd show, but Fal makes one of his air-escaping noises, a "fuck them," and retrieves the bike. G pulls a glowing something out of his pocket, checks it. Packy signs one-five-eight to me. G shoves his cell away and from his hoodie's pocket pulls a dark object: Fal's sap, I hope.

As I slide my Lebron mask over my face, line up the eyeholes, Packy slips his hockey mask on over a wool Browns cap. G is in the bushes—I barely see him—and Fal has the bike on its side in the middle of the street, the delivery rack propping the front a little higher, as if a kickstand had failed and caught hold at last. Fal puts a pink-ribboned blond wig over his ski-masked head. He grabs his chest like he's adjusting his make-believe tits, pats his hair, and lies next to the bike, back facing east, blond hair vibrant in the streetlights. Fal calls to G. "I hope you've a crane to lift me up, bres."

All four of us, we wait. And, this plan, I realize, it's nonsense. Too many things have to line up. I mean, how lucky are we that no other traffic's out and about?

Packy's fingers signal two-zero-two when I hear the truck's engine, see its headlights, see it pass Mazza's Bakery, watch it head right for Fal. Me and Packy press closer to the tree, tighter into darkness.

The speed limit's twenty-five, but this truck moves faster, as if its two-minute delay is a serious concern. I am uncertain the truck will see Fal, and if it does, I am uncertain it will see him in time. As it crosses 38th, the east edge of the cemetery, the truck shifts gears. There are only about two football fields left before it gets to Fal. I wonder if Fal, hearing what I hear, will get up and run, blond hair flowing behind him, or if he'll stick it out till the end, even if that end means getting run over. Fal isn't moving; he's in character. Or asleep. As much as he could frustrate the fuck out of me, I don't want to lose him, not yet, not like this. I push off from the tree, ready to leap the low fence and rescue him, but the truck's brakes whine and smoke billows from underneath the truck as it stops a few feet short of Fal.

I pull the helmet on over my Lebron face and grab the baseball glove. "Let's go."

The driver's door growls open and a man says, "What the hell is—" The slam of the door cuts off the rest.

The truck's trailer had stopped in line with our hiding spot. Me and Packy, the heroes and ghosts of Cleveland sports, step over the low fence and move to the back of the truck.

I don't see the whole thing, only imagine it: the driver bends over Girl Fal—"Girlie, you all right?"—the driver sees the ski-mask-covered face as G rushes out and whacks him in the back of the head with the sap. From the shadows behind the truck, I watch G and Fal carry the knocked-out driver to the cemetery fence and chuck him over. Sally's bike soon follows the driver and

I almost rush at Fal and G, ready to blow the whole plan. Packy grabs my arm. "Later," he says, "later."

It's our turn. Me and Packy'll thieve the thieves, go on to The Hoof. And we'll talk about this shit for weeks, laugh about it for years.

Packy takes G and I take Fal as each steps up into the truck's cab. At first I didn't think the mitt was a good idea, but it makes a great fake gun to poke into Fal's ass as he climbs.

I rough up my voice. "Where you think you're going?"

Fal stops his climb, a climb that has forced his breathing to become heavy, ragged. "Bres, bres, we's just *borrowing* it." He still wears his wig, and one hand grips the open door, the other a handle on the outside of the cab.

"Down." I step back so I won't be crushed. He stays where he is, either ignoring or thinking. I grab his waistband and pull. He falls to the street, catches sight of me. "No, Bron, bres, don't." His arms cover head, knees protect groin; he balls up like a potato bug.

"What are you doing?" Packy is beside me. "Let's go."

"Where's—?"

"Ran off," Packy says. He slaps Fal on the top of his head, grabs the wig after the last slap. "Off."

Fal rolls under the open door toward the front of the truck, struggles to find his feet. I tap Packy's shoulder, point to the huffing and on-his-hands-and-knees Fal, give him a do-something look—it's a look that can't fully be seen from under the mask, but Packy gets my meaning anyway. Packy kicks Fal in the ass. Fal yells, "No, bres, don't kill me!" But the kick works and he's on his feet and running. He bumps into the police barricade, knocks it over, side-staggers a moment, then straightens himself out.

"There he goes," I say, "a beeve dripping fat all the—"

"What the fuck's a beeve?"

"A cow. You never listen to Hook's stories?"

"Beeve," Packy says, trying out the word. He laughs. "I like it." He punches my shoulder.

I retrieve our bags and Sally's bike, and I check to make sure the driver's still out. While Packy sets himself up in the driver's seat, I grab the sap that G had dropped, slide the barricade to the side, then work bags and bike into the space behind the seats.

As the truck gets going, Packy says, "Oh, bro, how that beeve *howled.*"

The Donor's idea, if it wasn't for what happened to Sally, would've been funny.

With no one willing to fund him, help his big comeback, he tried to grow pot. Thought he could make serious money. At least that's what he'd heard Early Ed had done to expand his empire, and that guy was legend.

Most growers, they try to hide it. Grow it in a garage or use that netting. Not The Donor. He had heard the best way to hide something was to hide it in plain sight. Thought that was smart, intelligent, genius. So he grew his plants in our fucking yard. He tore out the bushes that ran around the entire house, widened the beds, and planted.

The Donor, not all dumb, thought he could disguise the plants. He plucked petals and leaves off of a bunch of plastic flowers, affixed them to the real leaves. Most people just shook their heads, called him a character, enjoyed his stupidity.

Until The Donor set fire to the flammable plastic camouflage. His whole field—and our house—went up.

Firemen came. Cops came. They initially laughed so hard when they heard what The Donor had done that the roofs of two more houses started smoking. Laughter stopped when a fireman came out with Sally. The Donor had thought no one was home, told the firemen and the cops nothing was worth saving. Never mind that he held his Indians memory shit in his arms. But Sally had come home early from school, sick.

He was sent to LorCI, been there ever since. And I hadn't visited him once.

Inside The Hoof, I smell death. Maybe a holdover from the slaughterhouse days, or maybe Captain Hook is finally nearing his end. Two semi-regulars, as skeletal as the owner, argue in the shadows of one corner of the bar about some chick named Ginger and the size of her tits.

Me and Packy sit at the end of the bar.

"I need to drink deep tonight, cap." I tap the bar with my fingers. He pours two beers. "You a fan?" He points at Packy with his hook hand. Packy still wears the Barons jersey.

"Damn, you idiot, take that—"

"Aight, aight." Packy removes the jersey, sits on it.

The captain puts two deteriorating cardboard coasters that read Cleveland Union Stockyards under our beers.

I feel high about our take, feel excited about Fal, his reactions, but sometimes The Hoof, Hook, piss me off. "How long you gonna hold on?" I finger-flick a stray bit of coaster off the bar. It sticks to the mirror for a beat then drops into the collection of dusty liquor bottles.

"That's me, son. My history. All of this." He gestures to the walls, the flags, the old pictures of the Yards, but I think he means everything outside—the old killing grounds across the street, the old packinghouses, the entire Yards.

"Really, this?" I gesture like him. "You want *this*?"

"It's all I know. Who I am. What more—?"

"There's other parts of Cleveland, parts ain't dying. Shit, other parts of the country, the world, better than this." I pick up the coaster; it nearly rips in half, drops on the floor.

"It's home, Hal. Takes courage to stay."

My family, my situation, Hook knows it all. I don't get why someone with options would stick. Me, always felt like I had no fucking options. Until tonight. But my high is wearing off. I force air through my lips, make a noise, Fal rubbing off on me. "Courage? Try being a scared-ass bitch, Hook. Run the fuck away." Packy nods, takes a drink. I'm not sure if he's agreeing with me or Hook.

"At one time, maybe." He rubs his nose with his hook. "But, no, this"—he taps the bar—"is home. Been here sixty years, not leaving her now."

"But—"

Packy's phone vibrates. "Fal's almost here."

Hook moves off to the tits. Their argument had led one to dump his beer on the other.

I laugh. "Bets?"

"Fifty."

"Fifty? Fuck, no way he'll say fifty."

"How many?"

"Twenty." I think for a second. "No, no, fifteen."

Packy leans off his stool, picks up the part of the coaster that'd dropped to the floor, replaces it on the bar. He takes another drink, wipes his mouth. "Why you do that?"

"Do what?"

"Bully the captain."

"Bul—? I don't bully him. I just—look at him." The captain moves one tit away from the other and mops the floor, his hook hand slipping up and down the handle with each pull and push. "All his work, back and forth. First he killed cows, now he herds sheep." I point at the tits, then softly tap Packy's chest. "Fuck, us included." My hands drum a nervous rhythm on the bar. "Look, maybe I'm not Icepick or, or, or Early Ed, guys who create opportunity—maybe I'm not even like Early's kid Harry—but, you know, I got a, a, a mind that goes beyond this, beyond The Donor. I got—"

Fal knocks through the door so hard it knocks over a coat rack. G follows and replaces the rack before the captain has a chance to react.

"Bitches!" Fal says. "Pussies! I hope every last one of them gets what's coming." He sees me, pulls a chair up to the bar and our stools, and sits level with my feet. "Every. Last. One." He slaps my shin to the beat of each word. His breath smells of alcohol. He claps his hands. "Give me a drink, Hooker!"

The captain rolls the mop bucket behind the bar, leans the handle against the register, and pours Fal a beer. He sets the beer in front of Fal who stares at it as if answers can be found inside.

"Pigeon-hearted, bres. No, not even my bres. Not even." He takes a gulp of his beer, spits the mouthful on the floor. "Hooker, shittiest fuckin' beer I've ever tasted." He slams the glass on the table behind him. "It's bad enough that there's nothing but, but, but—" He points at me and Packy. "Still, a futless gucker." He clears his throat. "A *gut*less *fuck*er, is worse, much worse, than a foul beer. A cowa—If courage and, and, stand-up men are not gone from this world, then I am a, a, a—" Fal repeatedly raises his arm straight over his head, lets it fall to his lap. "I am a dessi—, a decim—" He sighs, lets his arm fall one last time. "I am a dead dick."

Packy snorts, covers his mouth.

"Fal," I say, "what's up?"

"Bres, there are only three—" He holds up four fingers. "Three good men left in all of Cleveland and one of them is a fat fat man." He points at himself. "Beer, Hooker, I need another—a better—beer."

"Fuck, Fal, tell us."

"You, bres—" He points at me, then snaps his fingers at G who's leaning against the low gate that leads downstairs. "G, give me the sap." G shrugs his shoulders, shakes his head. Fal says, "It's lost. *Lost*, bres. If I had it I would beat the piss out of you." He thrusts his arms out to his sides, uselessly punches the air. "Chase you *out*."

I spin my stool, face the bar and the cloudy mirror behind, give my back to Fal.

"Tell me," Fal says. He stands between me and Packy, his face staring down at the bar. "Tell me, bres. Are you a pussy?" He jerks his thumb at Packy. "And this one?"

Packy chuckles. Fal turns my stool to face him.

"Nice to see your face, bres." He says it with disappointment, his anger and boldness drained for the moment. "I must admit, bres, I got used to your back tonight."

I put my hand on Fal's shoulder. "Fal, sit. Tell us."

Fal drinks half his beer, burps. "You—we—we'd be rich." The boldness returns, his voice louder. "A truckload of fags, ours, if we'd had more than—" He points to G. G hangs his head.

"Where is it, Fal? Where is—"

"Taken, bres. From *us*." He finishes his beer and sits. "Fifty. *Fifty* against me and G. At*tack*ed. Took took *took* the truck." With each "took" Fal beats the back of his right hand into the palm of his left, loud smacks that crack inside The Hoof. The tits watch it all, their argument second place.

"Fifty?" I say. Packy wins.

"I, we, G and me, bres, we held them off. They had *guns*. Shot at us." He makes his thumb and finger into a gun, fires. "I shot back. I, look at this." Fal shows us holes in his sweatshirt. "I was *shot*, bres, and then *beat*." He points to his head, but there are no injuries, no wounds. "But I fought. We, we, *we* fought!" He stands for emphasis. "But you pus—*cowards*." He looks at Packy. "Fuck 'em, *all* of 'em!" He sits. "Hooker, another."

"Easy, Fal," I say. "Your lips aren't even dry from the last one. And from the looks of it you've had more than enough." I look at G for confirmation and he pulls out an empty flask of whiskey.

"Fuck you, bres. Hooker!" A full beer appears on the table. "We had them, all of them, tied up. G was in the truck, ready to *roll*. Then six or seven men—athletes, I think, *huge*—show up, attack us." He empties his beer in one long swig. "First," Fal says, "they untied their friends. They all—*twenty* of them—attacked us."

"Twenty?" I say. "I thought it was fifty."

"It *was* fifty." Fal slams his hand on the table. "Aren't you listening? And I *got* some."

"You—?"

"Shot. Hit. I'm certain. I never miss, bres." Contrary to the gun he'd shown me earlier, he'd never shot a gun before. "Two dropped in the graveyard, dead as fuckin' Hooker over there. If I'm lying, Hal, if I'm lying, sic 'Pick back on me." Fal looks at G, looks at us. He gets down on all fours, unsuccessfully attempts to pry himself under a table. He gets halfway under, gives up. "I'm under that truck, we're under attack, four of them down—"

"Four? You just said two."

"Four, Hal. Pay the fuck attention, bres."

Packy says, "No, he said four, Hal."

"Four," I say, awed. "You're a bad mother—"

"These four, out. I shot and shot. Reloaded. Shot and shot. Bres, three more, down."

"Oh, it's seven now. You shot seven?"

"Quiet, Packy," I say, "we'll have more in a heartbeat."

"When I heard the sirens, I had to work quick, bres. Shot more, dropped more."

"How many?"

"Fo—eight. *Eight* more."

"Seven and eight. Fifteen. These men fuck like bunnies when they came at you?"

"Bres, we escaped. G, he—but you, the two of you, you limp-dicked weaklings. We could've taken fifty, all hundred of 'em."

"One hundred." I pat his shoulder, help him up off the floor. "Fal, you lying, back-breaking, greasy pile of flesh." I wipe my hand on his sweatshirt, gently push him into a chair.

"Don't start, you, you, you cow cock. I tell you, one hundred.

Look, bres, look, the *holes*." He holds his shirt out. The holes are there, all right, but they look more like moth damage.

Packy throws his Barons jersey in Fal's lap. "I—" Fal says. G loses his balance and falls over the gate he'd been leaning against. Fal's eyes go to G to me to Packy to the jersey. He touches the jersey lightly, then snatches it and holds it open in front of him. He flips the jersey back-front-back-front. His eyes meet mine. They look moist, shiny. He closes his eyes for a few seconds, seems to be trying to process the whole thing, and when he opens his eyes they look dry. "I—" Fal says again. I pull out Fal's wig, place it on his head. He tosses the jersey on the table, blows a piece of blond hair away from his face. He sniffs and smiles. "I knew it was you from the start, bres." He laughs, a loud boisterous one that fills the bar. "That mask, that helmet, the jersey?" He coughs. "Who else could it be?"

Fal shuffles toward the bathroom. He always seems heavy, but the weight, or the alcohol, appear to drag at him more than usual, pull him first one way then the other. He seems lost. When he returns he appears lighter somehow. "I am glad you have the truck, bres," he says. "Fucking thrilled."

Me and Packy slap Fal on the back and order a round, including two for the tits.

The single-room basement of The Hoof is dark, lit by a soft combination of a long lamp suspended over the pool table and lights that glow in varying states of operation inside the display cases on the cement-patched walls of red brick. Two glass-block windows look down on us; in the daylight, they reveal the Stockyards in distorted outlines.

The table's as old as Hook. When G breaks, a good cracking one, the fourteen balls scatter and slam into rotted rails, bounce in untrue directions. When the motion stops, when the balls should have come to a rest, they slowly slide to the right until most rest against one rail. Packy lines up his shot, a six-ball combo that will drop the twelve into a corner pocket if all goes well.

After celebrating upstairs for a bit, we came down here, played several games, really just knocking balls around, enjoying the night as it eased into morning, enjoying our success. G taps my foot with his warped cue, says he wishes we had told him our plan, that we'd nearly made him piss himself. But the more he drinks, the more he doesn't give a shit about us leaving him out. And once he joins in mocking Fal, all is good.

It is odd spending so much time in The Hoof. This had been The Donor's castle and he haunted every corner. I hate him, but for reasons I don't understand I shadow him, shadow his life, surround myself with him and his world. I think about it a lot, about why I hang here, about why I let him fill me so much when all I want to do is forget. The reasons always escape me.

The glass-encased Indians hats cover the walls and represent each year's team. Most are signed by one or more players. When Captain Hook opened this dump in the '60s, a friend of his worked at the stadium, gave him the hats, started something, a tradition. Now he has fifty-plus years of hats—from Tiant to Thornton, Perry to Alomar. And in the middle of one wall, below the glass-block windows, The Donor's hat, the only minor league one. I stare at it; my reflection stares back.

"Yo," G says. "You should tell him."

"Yes, bres. He needs to *know*, you know?"

"Why? I don't fucking care what he knows. The Donor's a—"

"What was the last time—"

"Years." On the bill of the hat I can read the overly large and faded signature of Henry Boland. "The trial." My stomach and chest tighten. I tap the cue tip against the case. My mind closes around Sally, around my hatred. The drink and the hatred make a bad combo, cloud my head, merge into rage. I flip the cue around in my hand, tighten my grip, and swing the weighty fat end at his case and the glass cracks and again and the glass shatters and I hear screaming and yelling and cursing and again and the frame cracks and again and the frame and the cue splinter. I turn to see who had screamed and yelled and cursed and realize it was me. I pant, wipe sweat or tears or both on my shoulders, try to catch my breath, pick bits of glass out of my hair.

G, Fal and Packy stand near the stairs, unsure if they should leave. They look everywhere but at me. Hook comes down the stairs, looks at the carnage, seems to understand—hell, he probably wonders why it had taken so long—and retreats. Fal takes a step toward me, seems to think better of it, then comes at me again. "Bres," he says, "easy?"

I toss the broken cue on the floor and grab The Donor's hat out of the case. I smack it against my leg, pieces of glass fall, bleed onto the floor. I wave the hat at Fal. "It's what I fucking have to deal with."

"Just a hat, bres."

"Fal?" I say.

"Look," Fal says. "Just a hat." He takes it from my hand, puts it on. It doesn't fit him, just sits on his head, his hair jutting out from underneath.

"You look ridiculous," I say.

"Like one of those, what do you call it, gnomes," Packy says. "With a bottle cap on his head."

"Bres, let me be him."

"Who?"

"Your fa—The Donor. Let me be him. You, you talk to him. I'll pretend."

"Stop being an ass." Glass and wood crunch under my feet.

"Hal. My *Hal*," Fal says. His voice attempts to mimic the gruff voice of The Donor, the odd way he overly emphasizes syllables or words.

"Fuck off, Fal," I say.

"You suck at baseball, so I have only your mom's word that you *are* my son." Fal rubs his beard, considers something. "Well, that and your *eyes*. You have my eyes." He points at Packy and G. "But you hang with *losers*. You *waste* your *time*. Here. At Pepe's. You steal from the *dead*. Don't look at me like that, Hal. I know. I *know*. You, you *stain* me, Hal, you dis*hon*or me, Hal, you disap—"

"Enough, Fal."

"Ahhhh, Fal." He smiles. "Fal. Now *there's* the bright man in your circle. Fal. He charms with his 'bres' this and 'bres' that and he is a *fat* one, but his weight speaks to his, to his thick *char*acter. *His* experience gives you di*rec*tion. His experience you should honor. You should keep him, this *Fal*, with you at all times. The rest," he says, pointing again to G and Packy, "*get rid* of the fuckers. They're no *good* to you."

I swipe the hat off Fal's head, push him back with the other two, and put it on. It fits but pushes my ears out. I lower my voice, roughen it. "I hear no*thing* but bad news, Hal." I point at Fal. "Even here, in prison, I hear you're *worth*less."

Fal claps his hands. "I'm you now, bres, I'm you." Fal's enjoying his dual-role performance. "Go. Go. *Action*, bres."

"You, Hal, are a worthless piece of shit. But there is one—a *knuckle*head, a *devil*—worse, way worse, than you. For fuck's sake, the man eats and, and, and—reach for his food? Lose a hand. Sleep if he's hungry? You won't wake *up*."

"That's true," says G. "This one time, I—"

"And his life, Hal, is a *waste*. Tell me, why does a forty-year-old *man* hang with *chil*dren?"

"Father," Fal says, "Fal's a good—"

"He has no worth, your Fal. He's an, an, an *abom*ination, Hal."

"But," Fal says, now mimicking my voice. "Yes he's older, yes he eats, yes he drinks, but he is *good*. If leading his young friends is a crime, then I—I mean, he—*he* should be in jail with *you*, you—"

"The pictures should have put him in *jail*. Hal, son, *you're* useless, but Fal, that one's more than useless." I take off the hat, hold it by it's bill. "Get *rid* of him."

"No," Fal says. "Get rid of G, of Packy. Get rid of Pepe. But *good* Fal? *Kind* Fal? *Faithful* Fal? Don't get rid of him, bres. He gives Hal—I mean *me*, he gives me—life. Get rid of *him*? You get rid of the *world*."

I throw the hat into the case's wreckage. "I will," I say, my voice my own, the playacting done. "I will."

Upstairs, one tit's passed out, head on the table, a thin layer of drool puddled around his head, and the other tit's writing on his friend's face with a permanent marker: "Ginger = C."

The guys had left after the drama, but Fal had lingered. He had swept up the glass, dumped the dustbin outside, trying to help, he said, and he kept talking to me. I didn't respond, he left. Whatever.

For the rest of the night—morning, really—I sit at the end of the bar, not even drinking, just sitting, Hook leaving me alone.

A mixed night. We'd taken down a truck loaded with profit, we'd had fun with Fal, we'd drank. But The Donor nags.

Hadn't seen him since the trial—I made it clear I wanted nothing to do with him—and he had never reached out. Until that postcard.

It's early light by the time I leave, sun barely hitting this side of the Yards. Morning traffic dodges the potholes on 65th.

I find myself at a strange spot. Behind me, The Hoof. To my left, my street, the tiny ironic baseball field behind my house shiny from the dew. To my right, the old Rollercade, an abandoned building; behind it, the truck we thieved sitting in the Ca$h for $crap yard. In front of me, although I can't see it, the south edge of the Yards and where Sally slept in her grave. Even in death she couldn't make it out.

A couple blocks out, Mrs. Brud heads away from me, a cup of coffee in each hand. I'd heard she visited her dead husband every morning. She'd been with the guy for fifty years, had coffee with him every morning. Some fucking habits, they die hard. I realize I hadn't visited Sally in a long time.

Gramps waits for me. She looks like she has some shit to tell me, but then her face changes, she hugs me, and tells me to come into the kitchen. I pull back, say I need sleep, but she grips me tighter and I find myself at the kitchen table, a cup of coffee in front of me. I keep turning my head toward the front, then back to gramps, toward the front, then back to gramps. I probably look like I'm jonesing bad, but I only wonder if—

"Where you been?" Gramps tucks the sides of her apron under her. She'd obviously been through an all-night painting session. They came in fits. She'd sometimes go months without painting, then, she said, a dream would pop or a vision would appear and she'd have to get it down. Most of her paintings were of these fucked up, non-sexed figures closed up in a box, a room, a cave, a stage; some featured male figures with their junk cut off, drifting away. Gramps'd seem surprised when I pointed out the possible symbolism of it all. I have no idea what she painted last night; blues, blacks, and yellows smear her apron. "Well?" she says.

"You know, around." I rub my face. "The Hoof."

"The captain shouldn't let—"

"Yeah, well. He does."

"Who were you with?"

"Usual."

She puffs her cheeks, looks out the window, blows the air out, brushes her hands on her apron. A corner of a paint tube or tip of a brush or something pokes out of the front pocket. "Here, Hal, let me show you something." She pulls me up by my elbow so quickly I've no chance to check my room. I've been in and out of here so many times over the weeks, all hours, exhausted, beat, I can't remember if that postcard still exists or not.

In the hallway upstairs, a finger to gramps's lips tells me mom's actually home but asleep.

Her makeup, fake eyelashes, a few scarves, and a couple wigs cover her dresser, and the art supplies dwarf the number of pill bottles on the nightstand. Plants and flowers in various stages of growth rest in plastic planters on the sill. Seeds and bits of black soil sprinkle the floor under the window. On a large canvas are two painted figures. One sits inside the other, a yellow-tinted figure living within the larger blue-black figure. The outer figure has a large dick. At first I think the smaller one's is missing, but a tiny flick of yellow paint rests in the corner. I don't know what to say, so I don't say anything.

"Slavic myth. Byelobog and Chernabog."

"Buy-la-what?"

"Deities. Gods. One good, benevolent, full of light; one evil, wicked, full of darkness. They created the world together, had a falling out, fought. Stories like this, two halves fighting, they've been around millennia. Myths travel. Gods travel. Continents. Time. Native Americans—Iroquois, I think—had similar. Sky-woman, Flint. The other one, Flint's brother, I can't remember." Gramps sits on the bed. "Remember Jacob?"

Gramps, when she was a kid, would go up the St. Lawrence River five, six times a year. Gramps's mom and her fourth or fifth or sixth husband always hired Jacob, this kid Indian guide. Gramps liked to boast that Jacob knew the best fishing holes, that they'd come back with chains so full they could feed the world. Jacob and gramps hung out a lot on those trips. I met Jacob once. His face, brown and weathered, creaked when he spoke. And I knew where gramps was heading when she held her arms up like sockless puppets.

"Not the two fuck dogs story."

Some kids, their grandparents would read and reread Dr. Seuss or *A Christmas Carol* or *Watership Down*, drink hot chocolate, eat cookies, all cozy and shit. Me and Sally? Maybe a Dixie cup of water and the same two dogs. Every fucking year. Two dogs inside of us fighting, one hope, one despair, one that wins is the one you feed the most. Bark fucking bark. Gramps would use her hands to illustrate the two dogs going at it, snapping, lunging, retreating. As kids, me and Sally loved it, ate it up, asked for more. I mean, I knew how the story worked for gramps: she'd said she'd had twin souls inside of her battling it out for too much of her life. But I didn't want to hear that dog story no matter how much it meant to her.

Gramps drops her arms, settles them into her lap, her apron.

I look out the window. The cranes hang their heads, a morning break keeping them motionless. Even giant machines are ashamed of me. "Gramps, I—"

Gramps runs her hands over the apron, straightening and flattening the folds, smoothing them all out. She clears her throat and reaches in her apron pocket. She holds up a short stack of postcards. "These have been coming for you." She pushes the stack into my hand. "For weeks. All there, Hal. Including the one you apparently threw at the wall."

My grip isn't firm and the postcards flicker to the floor. There are, like, fifteen of them. From: Lorain Correctional. To: Hal Boland.

"I have other stories you know." She grabs a packet of seeds, taps some into her hand. She looks up at me, tears in her eyes. "You want to hear the one about watering seeds?"

I want to backtrack, redo time, let her tell me the dogs story, take back what we'd done to Fal, unheist the truck, give everything back to Mrs. Brud, give everything back to all of them, de-deconstruct, put houses back together, just go back and back, pull The Donor out of jail, pull Sally out of the grave, put out the fire, put my family back together, just fucking restart.

I shake my head. Gramps and my mom? They deserve someone not me, someone not doing the shit I'd been doing. I knew the whys of my actions, somewhere, maybe, how all my shit connected. But I couldn't dig that deep. Fal made me go there once; I wouldn't go there again.

Gramps wants me to say something. Or to just fucking listen. Instead, I find myself downstairs on my couch, crumpling one postcard after another in my hand, thinking about feeding dogs and watering seeds, and never, not ever, seeing The Donor.

I have time to kill. Pepe'd cut my hours. G's uncle, who assured us we'd be rich, wanted to wait to sell the truckload, let any heat pass. So I'm at one end of the The Hoof's bar, a half-empty beer in front of me. Hook's at the other end, washing glasses. Molly, a waitress Hook had hired for reasons unknown, mops the floor. At a nearby table, Packy and Fal talk.

Watching Hook's like watching a magic show sometimes. His old hand and his taloned hook flow, fluid and confident, as they move a row of glasses one at a time from off the bar and into a soapy dishpan. A few submerged movements and the glasses reappear in a water-only dishpan. A few more submerged movements and the glasses reappear on a flaking drying pad. The final trick: he flips each glass into the air and catches it by spearing his towel-covered hook inside. After he towel-dries the outside of the glass, voilà, the glass shines as best it can and takes its place on the warped shelf behind the bar. All of this rapid sleight of hook yet barely a drop of water hits the floor.

The show over, I wrestle with The Donor, Sally, Mrs. Brud, my work, my life's track. I have my mom, I have gramps, I have my friends, my crew. I have plenty. But that seed shit. Back in the day, gramps read this underground magazine, *The Buddhist Third Class Junkmail Oracle*. She showed me some. Crazy poetry and art and shit that hit a range of topics and that led gramps to out-there spiritual Zen-type understanding, she said. The seed story, it came from there. Gramps had always told me to water the wholesome—she liked to say *salubrious*—seeds in my mind, my heart, my soul, to stop watering the bullshit thoughts, the dwelling, the hate, the anger, to stop what I'm doing before I end up like The Donor. I fear that, yeah. But I fear nothingness more. Doing nothing. Being nothing. A waste. I drank, I deconstructed, I stole, and I am sure—I am sure—I hurt people. But it's in those moments, only in those moments, that I feel anything. I don't have any other choice. Not really.

"Look, bres, look. At me." He holds his arms out at his sides. His sweatshirt hangs off of him. "I'm thinner, bres, I'm thinner. I'm wasting away. Since I fought those—"

Packy pushes him. "You weren't attacked, Fal. It was me. It was Hal."

Fal grunts and pulls at his patchy beard. "Nightmares, bres. And horrible friends." He picks something out of his beard and wipes it on his sweatshirt. "They're ruining me."

"You're going to waste away to nothing, Fal, you're not careful," I say.

"There it is, bres. Truth. Capital T, capital R, ooth." His hands pat his stomach. "You know, before you, I was a good person. Virtuous: *enough*. Cursed rarely, bres, never more than a few times: a fucking *sentence*. Got with a hooker once: a *month*. Paid off all my debts: *twice*." He sucks in some air, expands his cheeks, lets it all out. "I think."

"Fucked up long before me."

"He's right," Packy says.

Fal grabs Packy's face between his sausage-fingered hands. "You, my bres, here's the deal. You fix your mean mug and I'll fix my life." Packy was an ugly fucker. On his eighteenth we had to pay a stripper double to dance for him, triple to smile. Fal slaps Packy's cheek lightly. Packy shoves Fal. "You." Fal turns and grabs Molly's mop. "You, my dear? Have you found out who robbed me?"

"For fuck's sake," Packy says, "she wasn't even here."

The Hoof isn't the most frequented bar in Cleveland. It is unsigned, unadvertised, unwelcoming. And if you somehow stumble inside without an escort, without someone in Hook's circle vouching for you, Hook'd run your ass out. I guess Hook has his reasons for hiring Molly—maybe her Irish accent, maybe her Irish charm—but I sure as shit can't say for sure.

"I know her, bres." Fal dances with the mop, a gorilla wrestling a rope.

Molly cuts in, takes the mop, slaps Fal with the mop's wet end. Tendrils of damp slither across his ass. "Hook's told me about you, how much you owe. The drinks? That wreckage downstairs?"

Fal points at me. "He owes. Not me. He pays."

She looks at me. I shrug and drain the last of my beer. The warmth of it burns.

"He always talk about you like this?" she says.

"Always." Hook sticking up for me.

"I knew it, I knew it." Molly pokes the mop at Fal's feet. "And I know you, you and your slick mouth."

"I wish you did." Fal licks his lips. The effect is unpleasant.

Molly hits Fal again then walks behind the bar. Fal pursues. Hook steps in, steers Fal away with a fresh beer. Fal crashes into, and then drapes an arm around, Packy and sits, dragging Packy down with him. "Bres, you barely feel me, am I right? Wasting away, bres, I'm telling you."

I head back to the bar with my glass to get a refill, but something has me. One of Hook's talons has caught my belt. Hook tugs and ushers me to a small alcove. Pictures of the Yards, old and new, surround us. "Hal, you do owe. Not letting Fal hear this, Hal, but you do owe. Mess needs to be fixed."

I unhook his hand from my belt. "You know I'm good for it, captain." I tap his chest with my glass. "A few weeks. I'll pay for it and more." I take a few steps out of the alcove, toward Packy and Fal, but Hook heads me off.

Hook opens and closes his clawed hand—really, just spreads the two metal fingers apart, then back together. "I don't want dirty money, Hal."

"It's fine, captain. It's fine." I push past him to the bar and retake my stool. "Trust me."

"Trust him?" Fal says. "No one even fears him, bres. His father, now that was a man to fear. If I fear Hal, bres," he reaches under his gut, "may God snap my belt in two."

Molly, cleaning the beer taps, laughs.

"Fal," I say, a bit of warning in my voice. "Hook, a few weeks. Promise."

"Don't be him," Hook says.

Back in the old house, the summer before it burned, me and Sally played in the yard sun up to sun down. The Donor was busy fucking up a councilman comeback campaign. We didn't care. I was nine, Sally five. We just played our asses off.

On the tree lawn, a huge-as-fuck maple grew, popped the sidewalk into jagged and broken teeth. If me and Sally held hands, tried to wrap ourselves around it, we couldn't reach the other and complete the tree hug. We didn't have much of a yard and that year the grass was overrun by dandelions. Sally picked some, placed them at the base of the tree. When I asked what she was doing, she said she was making a fire, that I needed to help. I loved her weirdo imagination, so I picked dandelions, too, placed more on the roots, into the trunk, the dandelions licking up in thin flame-like strands—I could reach higher than Sally; she liked that the fire got so big, so quick.

And as we pretended to warm our hands on the fire, to cook marshmallows speared with sticks, she started screaming. "Too hot," she said. "Too hot." She yelled at me to put the fire out. I was confused, scared. Didn't know what she was on about, but I pulled a few dandelions out and Sally slapped me in the legs, said I'd burn myself, that we needed water, lots of water. Near the porch was a small kiddie pool—it barely fit her anymore—and I went up to it, splashed water toward the tree, and Sally came and, her tiny fingers gripping the lip of the pool, tried to tug and pull the pool down the short sloping front yard, but it wouldn't move. She kept screaming. I pushed while she pulled and we got the sloshing pool down the front yard, across the sidewalk, beside the maple. Both of us on one side, we picked up the edge of the pool and dumped the water onto the dandelion-inflamed tree trunk. The splashing water soaked us, flooded the dandelions away. Hundreds trickled along the curb and toward the sewer.

Sally stopped screaming and her breathing finally slowed. She sat in a puddle on the sidewalk, wiped her face with one hand. "What was that?" I had asked. "Just playing, goofy," she said. It didn't seem like playing; she seemed seriously deranged.

I'd remembered none of that until I saw Brud's granddaughter playing next to that pool. "Just playing, goofy." Life was simpler then, easier, when you hadn't yet seen that the adults you looked up to, that you thought knew shit, that you thought held some secret knowledge of the world, were just fucking frauds. But maybe the crazy lady with the tinfoil hat, maybe she knew stuff. Maybe crazy was the only way to get by.

I pushed my glass across the bar, pushed my stool back. "You know what I've been thinking about?" I say. "Teaching."

Fal laughs. Hook looks interested.

"Teaching, you know, kids." I don't know why this is coming out here, now. Maybe I need Hook to understand.

141

Fal's about to speak but Hook waves him quiet, waits for more. I offer nothing. The clock over the bar strikes twelve.

Fal says, "Hooker, how many times? We've heard that, that, that, that *ringing*." He claps his hands twelve times. "Every night, bres, like, like *clock*work. I mean, we know it's late, bres, we know we're fucking losers, but that clock, bres, that clock needs to come the fuck *down*." It isn't the first time Fal has gone off about that clock. It never bothered me.

Hook scars a thin line into the rail of the bar with his metal hand. "Fifty years ago I thought about working with kids, doing something different." He clears his throat, holds up his hook. "Then this." He taps the bar, metal on wood. "The chimes, Hal. When the chimes of midnight toll? It's too late."

"Fuck, bres," Fal says. "I'm tired." And he is out the door.

The rest of us follow. Outside, Fal heads north, is already fifty yards away, like he doesn't want anything to do with any of us anymore. I yell after him. He lets out a belch and holds out his arms. He does look thinner.

"What you doing tomorrow, Hal?" Packy says.

A full moon lights the skeletal brick buildings. Out of a broken third-floor window of The Hoof, a tree's thick branches, green leaves pushing into the sky, has busted out. I'd seen it before, never thought about how odd it was, like nature was attempting to take this all back for itself. I really do have nothing but time to kill.

The school sits across from one of the old packing buildings at the north edge of the killing fields of the old slaughterhouses.

As I walk past Ca$h for $crap, our truck still safely inside but not yet turning a profit, I almost turn back home. I feel stupid. Really fucking stupid. Like, who-the-fuck-am-I? stupid. Across the street, Molly leaves the Hoof, locks up behind her. Good for the captain, I think, good for the captain. I keep on.

I tell the lady at the main desk I am there to see Aisha Williams and then I wait on a low couch that fits a five-year-old. My knees bounce in front of me at eye level.

I'd come by weeks earlier, said that Mrs. Brud had sent me. Basic paperwork that time, only the LW diploma and Pepe's to put down. The background check they'd run concerned me a little, but I'd never been arrested, and I sure as shit wasn't giving them a 1099 rundown of my other income.

It's now the second week of school. Through the office window I watch groups of kids move—some rushing, some slow-walking—from one room to another. A few wave. I don't. And I don't see Brud's granddaughter. My knees pick up speed.

When the secretary says that Mrs. Williams would see me my knees stop and I stay rooted. "She'll—?" She eye-nudges to the open door to her left.

"Right, right." Instinct tells me to walk out the door, but instead I walk into the office.

Aisha Williams is a dark, thin-fingered black woman. Her long, braided hair rests on her desk as she leans over to scribble a few words on a folder. Also on her desk, besides her hair: a Rock and Roll Hall of Fame tin filled with pencils, pens, highlighters; my paperwork; a short stack of referral-looking forms that show some students haven't been behaving; my paperwork; a checkerboard of neon Post-it Notes peppered with swooped and swirled letters; my paperwork; one of those miniature Cleveland Indians hardhats you get when you order ice cream but it contains paperclips instead of ice cream; my paperwork; a cube holding pictures of smiling faces, some young, some teen, some old; my paperwork. I reach out and spin the cube. She says, without looking up, "That's my family." Then she gestures toward one of the two leather chairs in front of her desk. "Please, sit." She smiles. It's bright, warm. "Why are you here?"

I shrug. "Mrs. Brud." My knees bounce again. I look at the wall to my left, to my right. Pictures of groups of smiling kids in matching shirts stare back at me.

Williams follows my eyes. "Those are the last few years' classes. Good kids. Many told them they weren't."

I nod, eyes back on her, her smile.

She moves a Post-it Note from one side of the desk to the other, seems to reconsider, moves it back. "It takes special people to work with kids, Hal. They have to care, connect, respect, you know?"

I put my hands on my thighs and try to will my legs to stop.

"Mrs. Brud, she and her husband helped start this." The picture she holds up of Mr. and Mrs. Brud is nice. Brud isn't wearing her tinfoil hat. She looks dignified. "She tells me you're someone we need." She points a long finger to indicate the school, I guess. "That those kids need."

I think I've known, maybe once or twice in my life, happiness. I certainly know anger. I know sad. I know jealous. I know bored. I know hopeless. I know frustrated. I know scared. I know love. I know pain. I know loss. But nervous, goddamn, I've rarely felt it. Not when The Donor got convicted, not when gramps came out, not when we deconstructed, not when we robbed those houses, not when we took that truck. But here, now? I clear my throat. Shake my head. Then say, "She thinks I'm good. With kids." My knees start again. "My, uh, sister."

"I know." Her smile turns sympathetic. "About Sally."

That morning, I'd gotten up early, wondered if I'd be here now, in front of this lady, at this moment. I stood on the front porch; the penned-in ice cream trucks glowed in the early morning light. It had rained during the night and puddles spotted the short yard, the broken sidewalk, the potholed street. The wind pushed around a hairless Barbie head that floated and bobbed in a puddle.

Around the corner, Mrs. Brud headed home from her morning coffee with her dead husband. At first I made to follow Mrs. Brud, ask her more about this school, why the fuck she thought of me, but I soon found myself outside the sandstone pillars of West Park Cemetery.

It took a few minutes to find Sally's marker. A lot of trees, a lot of leaves, a lot of dead people made the whole place look the same. I remembered, though, it was close to some girl's memorial: Beverly Potts. She'd disappeared, never found, in the '50s. At Sally's funeral, gramps couldn't stop talking about her, maybe helped her avoid the reality of Sally, maybe gave a false hope that Sally was only missing.

Sally's marker was about a foot across, half a foot wide. It was flat in the ground, the years of her birth and death visible, "Sally Boland" and "Gone too soon" covered by grass and weeds. I kneeled and pulled weeds, ripped grass, made it look nice, crisped and cleaned the edges. It was the least I could do. And it wasn't enough.

Now, Aisha Williams explains how Mrs. Brud's word carries a lot of weight. If I am willing to hang around today, she wants to give me a try in a classroom. The first-grade teacher, a lady named Mrs. Hernandez, is on maternity leave and the teacher's aide, a young lady named Genevieve, needs help running lessons, keeping the kids on task. They'd been trying out replacements, hoping to find the right one.

I wipe my palms on my pants and nod dumbly.

She walks me to a classroom and on the way tells me about the school's history, which is short, and the school's plans, which are long.

I remind myself to watch my fucking mouth.

Inside the room, no kids. At breakfast, Williams explains, a lot of kids' families unable to afford food. The classroom is a world in miniature and I am its giant. About twenty tiny bolted-to-the-floor desks and their tiny chairs are arranged in a circle. On each desk are little tented cards with a name on one side, an animal on the other. The walls are decorated with motivational posters ("You're People Not Sheeple"; a bunch of goldfish swimming in one direction while one laughs and swims in the other, "There's Always One. Be the One"), several signs filled with rules ("Respect Each Other"; "We Are A Team"), and alphabet and number posters.

Williams walks me over to a regular-sized desk. "Here's where you'll be." On the front of the desk, another sign: "Gangs are not your friends." At LW, everyone in my crew, which I guess could be a gang, had been approached, threatened. Didn't expect an elementary school to have a gang problem.

I tap the sign, raise my eyebrows.

"You'd be surprised how young they start. We had one father initiating his ten-year-old just last year. We're in a fight here, in this city, in what many call Thieveland. Our kids, right out from under us, are being stolen."

I think of the funeral jobs, our heist. I think she has Thieveland all wrong, but I can see her point. Councilman Donor, having blown it with Joe Loose and Early Ed, tried the smaller gangs: South Siders, Broadway Boyz, Madhouse Chasers, The Houghers, The Two-One-Six. He first tried extortion then simply went after them, hindered their moneymaking operations. He made enemies and had to play sick more than once from city events because of hits put out on his life. His work, though, cut out a lot of gangs, left Early Ed and his son running most of the show. But new gangs always filled the vacuum.

"One reason we exist," Williams says, "is to get these kids through unaffiliated."

"Not easy."

"Not easy." She hands me a list with about twenty names on it. "Here are your kids. Knowing names helps." She heads toward the door. "Kids will be back shortly." I open my mouth to ask about Genevieve, but Williams says, "I'll check on you."

It makes no sense, being here. I tell myself I have better things to do, but I don't. I tell myself I'm making up to Mrs. Brud—robbing her, that locket with her and her husband's pictures inside—but that isn't true. Maybe. I scan the list of names. What am I going to do with these kids? Before I can figure an answer the door opens and kids, followed by a young lady I guess is Genevieve, stream in. The first kid flips the light switch—I didn't even realize the lights were off—the last kid closes the door. All twenty stand behind their desks and when Genevieve says sit the kids sit. She asks them to get out their workbooks and notebooks, approaches me, introduces herself. I'd been sitting in the chair and stand to shake her extended hand. My leg catches the corner of an open drawer, pain shoots through me, and I say, "Son of a bitch." Genevieve frowns, takes her hand back, says, "I'd heard good things."

"No, no." I rub my leg. It doesn't seem like any of the kids heard me, but one boy, head buried in his workbook, says, "Son of a bitch." The rest of the class giggles.

"Luis," Genevieve says. The class stops giggling, but I swear I hear Luis say the phrase that pays one more time.

"Look, won't happen again," I say. I stick my hand out.

"See that it doesn't." Her smile seems stale. Then she shakes my hand.

She brings me to the front of the room. "Class, we have a new member to our family. Mr. Boland will be helping us today and, we hope, for many days." The class cries out, "Hello, Mr. Boland" in more or less unison. Makes me feel big for a moment, like I fit the room. I give a two-fingered wave from my hip.

Genevieve tells me to walk around the room, look at what each kid's doing, help where I can, and get to know them.

I work around the circle a little at a time. I kneel beside them, get to their level. It has to be fucking intimidating to have a big person loom, figure being eye level might be a good thing. Less scary. I want to work toward the Luis kid quickly but don't want him to feel like he's in trouble.

I meet Aimee, who has beautiful handwriting; she'd written her name over and over, every letter a perfect imitation of the letters in the workbook. I meet Josh, who fills his paper with drawings of stick-figure people and dogs; a small figure has "me" and an arrow pointing at it. I meet Juliana and Jose and Miriam and Zachariah and Avery and Stacy and a girl named Shithead—it's apparently pronounced Shuh-*thayed*, Genevieve tells me later, but it was a fucking mean thing to do to a kid, I think.

At Luis's desk, I say, "What you doing?"

He hums. Maybe he thinks what he's doing is obvious. It is. He's copying words like dog, cat, son, ball.

"You know," I say. "Some words are good. Like those." I point at his work. "Others aren't." I wait to see if he gets it. "Words like I said before? Those aren't. You shouldn't say those, aight?"

"Why?"

"Because—." I don't really have a good answer other than that I don't want him to get into trouble because of me. These kids probably hear worse on an hourly basis at home, on the streets. "It, uh, shows you're uneducated. Always find better words. Show you're better." What the fuck am I talking about? He seems to buy it, though. At least he goes about copying the words king, yard, school, clock.

Genevieve tells the kids to put their books away, grab a carpet square, and gather around a stool near the front of the room. She tells me to pick a book from the shelf under the window.

I scan the spines. They're all the greats, shit I remember mom or gramps reading me, well, when gramps wasn't doing that two fuck dogs thing. I don't see the one I want, the one I hadn't thought about since Brud's granddaughter, the one Sally would ask me to read over and over again. I realize I'm glad it's not there. I also realize I'm taking too long. I check the kids. I'm losing them. One little fucker's apparently bitten a thumbnail off and pokes the kid next to him with the jagged shard. "Hey," I say. Two fingers at my eyes, two at him. The kid tosses the nail, pouts. The rest of the kids' eyes are on me, waiting.

I almost reach back for *Where the Wild Things Are* or *The Very Hungry Caterpillar*, use one as a crutch to just get through this moment, this now, to then push on with my life, but I remember a story The Donor used to tell, used to perform, about a king who, like, wants the secret to life or some fuck thing. I'm caught by a thought: The Donor's in me more than I want to believe, maybe. But it's a good story. Fuck it. Let's freestyle.

"There's a great and mighty king," I say. "Let's call him King James." The mention of LeBron hooks a few of them a bit. He may have taken his talents to South Beach, broke hearts in this city, but kids can have short memories. "King James feared failure, feared it like a city fears Godzilla." I let out a roar. The last few inattentive kids are with me now. I stalk around the circle, Godzilla-like, short-armed and stomping, their heads tracking me. I stand straight, raise my chin, attempt what I think is a king's, whatdoyoucallit, regal bearing.

"King James realizes that if he could know three things, three simple fu—" Genevieve, who had been working at her desk, head down until my roar grabbed her attention, glares at me. "If he could know three easy-as-your-ABCs things, he would never, ever fail."

I hold up one finger toward the group. "One," I say. "When is the right time to act?" I take a few steps, lunge toward a smiling girl, Miriam, I think. "Two." I hold two fingers a few inches from her eyes. She doesn't even flinch. "Who's the most important person in my life?" I hold three fingers high. "And three: What's the best, most right thing to do?"

In the story, the way The Donor told it—although Fal once told me The Donor'd stolen the story from some Russian, which, yeah, of course The Donor'd stolen it—the king fields answers from various people. He doesn't agree with any of them and he seeks out some wise hermit. While with the hermit, a man stumbles out of the forest, wounded, a gash across his stomach, and so the king helps him, saves him. When the king asks the hermit, again, for the answers to his questions, the hermit tells him he already has the answers.

But I couldn't have King James talking to random people and some whack-ass hermit, and I couldn't have some guy's guts spilling out on these kids. In a bit of storytelling inspiration, maybe the gramps in me this time, I instead populate the king's land with Cleveland mascots. I act out encounters with Chomps, with Moondog, with Sir C.C.; King James asks his questions, the dogs and the swashbuckler fucking clueless. The hermit becomes Brownie the Elf. Slider, starring as the injured, belly-waddles into the middle of the kids' carpet squares where he collapses, exhausted. King James heals Slider, and Brownie the Elf reveals the answers: When? Now. Most important person? Who you're with. Best, most right thing to do? Doing good for who you're with. Simple.

I expect applause. This was a Playhouse Square-worthy performance. The kids just stare at me; one kid checks his watch. What the fu—

"OK, kids," Genevieve says, "thank Mr. Boland and put up your squares nice and tidy." She gives me a silent clap, though, as the kids move about.

And the story hits me. Now: a truck full of money. Most important people: the crew, Fal, gramps, mom. Best, most right thing to do: helping me, helping them, doesn't matter how.

A kid's hugging my leg. I look down at her. She looks up at me. She rubs her nose and knocks her glasses crooked for a beat. "Thanks for saving Slider," she says.

The rest of the day's a mix of walking the room, chatting with a kid here and there—I even bust out gramps's two dogs story to one little shit who keeps acting up—being a warden during nap time, putting a Band-Aid on a kid's knee during recess. Williams checks on me once. "Don't look now," she says, "you're smiling."

More shit dreams. Nightmares. Always Sally. Always trapped.

I sit on the front porch, white plastic chair listing with the deep sag in the wood. Ice cream trucks pull into their fenced-in and razor-wired home. In a few hours we'll be meeting G's uncle, finding out how much the truckload will get us.

Fal strolls around the corner. Wood creaks under each step and when he sets foot on my level the porch sags deeper. Fal flicks his hand toward the house. "Your grandma home?" He's mesmerized by gramps's transformation. Enjoys it in an odd way. He'd once told me if something like a sixty- or seventy-year-old's sex can change, anything can.

"At a meeting."

"With others?"

"Yeah, others." The fact that gramps isn't the only trans in the neighborhood really fucks with him. "G ready for tonight?"

"Yeah, bres, yeah. Uncle tests the merch, negotiates, done deal."

"'*Tests* the merch'? They're fucking cigarettes."

A few hours later, me, Fal, Packy, G and G's Uncle are inside the Ca$h for $crap yard. Piles of crushed cars and cars to be crushed hide our truck, surround us, the moon giving it all an odd glow. G's uncle, who likes to be called the Scrap King but whose real name I learn tonight is Walt, wears a necklace dangling a large diamond-encrusted dollar sign. He waits for Packy to cut the trailer's lock.

"Boys, could be a big deal for you, for me," Walt says. He gestures to Packy, a ladies-first motion.

Packy's bolt cutters snap the lock. He flips the latch, pulls the doors wide. The truck is full—floor-to-ceiling, front-to-back—of master cases labeled "h-cigs."

"Open one up, let me see," Walt says.

I climb up, cut the shrink-wrap with a key, peel it away, grab a case, throw it to Fal. It hits him in the chest, bounces off, lands on the ground, one corner crumpling.

"Bres, I wasn't—try me again." He spits into his hands, rubs them together, and puts them up like a catcher behind home plate.

I jump down, right the box, and slice the packing tape. I pull a carton of cigarettes out, open it, and flip a pack to Walt. He unwraps the cellophane, smacks the pack against his left palm, and jerks the pack so a couple cigarettes pop out. He takes one, offers one to me. I don't smoke but think it'd be impolite if I decline, and take it, smell the tobacco, tuck it behind my right ear. Walt sticks the cigarette in his mouth, takes out a Zippo, flips it lit, holds the flame to the cigarette's tip. I know this bullshit is formality, the Scrap King putting on a show, acting big, but when the loose paper at the tip catches and smoke snakes into the air, I feel relieved.

And then it goes out.

Walt attempts to light it again; he sucks in, trying to get the tobacco going, but it's no good.

G says, "C'mon, yo, stop fucking around." He laughs, but it sounds forced. He kicks at a few rocks, a few flakes of metal, and they scratch and ping into the night.

Walt tries again. Nothing. He says, lips moving around the cigarette, "I'm not fucking around. Shit's not working."

How does a cigarette not work, for fuck's sake? I pull the cig from behind my ear, grab the lighter, try for myself. Same thing: paper lights, goes out, try again, can't inhale through the filter. It's like breathing through a plugged straw. I take the cigarette out of my mouth, look at it from end to end, notice a bit of shine coming from the burnt end, exposed when the papery tip had caught. I tug at it, and a sleeve of aluminum foil pulls free, clouding the air in front of me with a puff of brown.

Packy says, "What the hell is that?"

Walt does the same with his cig: pulls a piece of tinfoil loose that releases another cloud. He takes another cigarette out of the pack, carefully pulls the foil tip free, dumps a bit of the brown powder on his finger, tastes it. His eyes go wide. He tells us to crack open each carton and each pack in the case I'd opened, being careful not to dump any powder out. "Don't waste it," he says.

The case holds fifty cartons, ten packs per carton, twenty cigarettes per pack. Each cigarette we check is capped with a millimeter or so of tobacco, underneath the tobacco a small tin foil cylinder filled with about a gram of heroin.

"You know what a gram of brown streets for?" G says. "Eight or nine per."

"Eight or—" I say.

"Eighty or ninety dollars," he says. "More if it's pure."

The truck holds what looks like four pallets of sixty-four master cases each. I try to do some math. No matter how I figure it, we are fucking millionaires.

"Boys, you've done good." He looks at us as if we've just won the World Series or something. "Now, tell me again about this shipment?"

Walt had said, when all is said and done, he'd get us *each* a million for the H. Way the fuck more than the fifty g's the cigarettes would've brought.

Of course, it also explains why I'd not seen or heard of one cop from the Second asking questions about the missing truck. What the fuck would you say? "Uh, officer, can you help? Someone stole my truckload of heroin-smuggling fags."

But someone would be looking for it. G's uncle said he'd move it fast, but had to do it carefully; couldn't afford to alert the original owners by reaching out to just anyone, and sure as shit couldn't sell it inside Cleveland.

The door opens and mom comes in; haven't seen or talked to her in weeks, maybe longer. Only know a little of what's going on from gramps. I close my eyes, fake sleep, and hear her click past me into the kitchen. There are a few hushed whispers, glasses rattling, a few more whispers. She can only be talking to gramps, but I can't make out what they're talking about.

I open my eyes, strain a bit to listen. I instead focus on a thumbtacked print above where a TV used to be. Gramps had hung it recently, said the painting inspires her. It's called *Christine's Life* or *Christine's World*, like that. It's striking. That poor fucking girl, on the ground, looking, reaching: For her home? For someone to help? All I can picture when I look at it is Sally. Pick her up, calm her, get her to safety.

The heels of my hands press harder and harder into my eyes. From the kitchen, mom says, "Oh, stop, of *course* he'll like her. She's gorgeous. She's going places."

I don't like the sound of this. Back in high school mom had gotten the idea that I needed to date. She'd show at school, chat up girls outside and in the halls, and, as she'd said, try to pick me out a winner. Her seamed-stockinged legs, a walking two-legged Christmas Story lamp, ensured the MILF jokes never stopped.

"Ma, you're not fixing me up." I pull out a plastic chair—it matches the one on the porch—and sit. She looks beautiful, as always, but, as always, given her work, she's a bit overly done. Too-short plaid skirt, a blouse tied off showing her flat stomach, youthful skin, her face covered with too much makeup, her makeup kit apparently set on whore. Makeup can't fully hide the circles under her eyes, the result of lack of sleep, stressful and shitty hours, and whatever else is bothering her. Her hands, about the only feature that look old on her, cradle a cup of coffee close to her red lips. As she blows on the steaming coffee she eyes me over the cup's rim. Even in her forties, she still causes some serious fucking chaos in a roomful of guys.

"And where've you been?" she says. "Haven't seen you in weeks and weeks and weeks, it seems."

"We keep different hours, you know?" I pick up a loose packet of ketchup—we get ketchup, mustard, mayo from fast food joints, free shopping—and flip it through my fingers. "Ma, not going out with her. Don't care who it is."

"Told you." Gramps peels bits of paint off her fingers.

"She's gorgeous, Hal."

"Don't care."

"Smart. College."

"Don't care."

She puts down her coffee cup, walks behind me, her hands grip the back of my chair. She leans down, says in a sing-song voice, "She's going places, Hal."

"So am I."

She laughs. "Where, where are you going, Hal, huh?" She doesn't sound angry, but I'm not sure.

"Where'd you meet her?" I ask.

"Work."

"Aw, ma, she's a *stripper?*"

"A dancer. She's saving money for school, going to be a therapist, going to get out, Hal. You play your cards right, take you with her."

"I'm not dating a stripper, ma." I stop fingering the ketchup packet. "No offense. I mean, seriously, it'd be like I was dating my mom."

Gramps watches the cranes lurch to life over the Yards. She's keeping out of this one.

"Your friends would call you their hero, you dated a stripper. Fal? Wouldn't know what to do with himself."

I snort, know exactly what he'd do.

"That mean you'll do it?"

Look, I want to say, don't need your help or some stripper's help to get out of here. Plus, I find myself thinking about that Genevieve teacher a lot. She was … something. A possibility, maybe. We'd had some nice moments that day, I think. Maybe. "Thanks, ma, but—"

She pushes off my chair, knocks me forward an inch, and paces back to the window, biting a fingernail. "Delivering pizzas, Hal, that the plan? Or is it the shit you do you think I don't know about? The shit I ignore?"

The noise of the cranes' first mouthfuls of metal drowns out my response. She raises an eyebrow, waits for me to repeat it.

Gramps holds my arm, takes my hand. When I look at her all I can see is a plea. My knees bounce, stop, bounce, stop. I shout over the outside noise. "How would I even pick her up? Sally's bike?"

Mom's face softens. "She's got a car, too. I'm telling you, Hal, this girl? Go with her."

Mom figured I'd give in. She'd already set the date with Monica for seven.

Me, mom, gramps, we sit on my couch-bed together and wait. I am nervous again, a new habit I'm not fond of. Mom senses it, I think. She taps my thigh, smiles some kind of knowing smile. That smile, it tenses me up, doesn't calm me for shit.

I hear a car approach. I turn my head, nudge the curtain a little, take a look. She owns a car, all right, a piece-of-shit Olds Cutlass, rusted holes eating doors and fenders, the back bumper a bolted-on two-by-four. But what was I complaining about? I have a bike, the buses, the Rapid.

She parks in the street—like many of Cleveland's old houses built before cars were a thing, our house doesn't have a driveway or a garage. She steps on the sagging porch, and knocks.

Mom is right: she's gorgeous. Her large, long-lashed blue eyes cut through me, and her classy, form-fitting clothes both hide and high-light her tight and attractive body. A tattoo peeks out from under her short-sleeved shirt. What I could see suggests horse hooves.

She hugs mom, shakes hands with gramps—Monica seems unsurprised and indifferent to the lipstick and high heels, which I appreciate—and off we go.

The front bench seat of the Cutlass has several tears in the vinyl that have been closed with thick baseball glove-like stitches. It makes me think of an old Frankenstein movie Sally liked. Next to Monica, on the seat between us, sits her purse, a small hand-held thing covered with My Little Pony stickers and patches.

When she turns north on 65th, her tattoo, an exact duplicate of one of the Pony stickers, gallops out.

"Where we heading?" I ask. Don't care what mom says, I have a hard time getting that a girl with a cartoon character purse and a cartoon character tattoo is going anywhere. But I know I'm not really one to judge. My tattoo, on my shoulder blade, is a misspelling of Sally's name.

"My aunt owns a little place off Detroit. Italian. Great food."

Her aunt greets her with a hug and a two-cheeked kiss. She looks me up and down. I stick out my hand, she ignores it. What gives? I have on my nice clothes: black denim jeans, black T-shirt, black sneakers. It's my job interview outfit. Cartoon characters and a rude fuck aunt. Great date.

She seats us by a window, but out of sight of other customers. If she hadn't already been so rude, I'd think she was giving her niece and her date some privacy. But she's hiding us, embarrassed of me, embarrassed for Monica. Nerves aren't the issue anymore. Anger's riding in on a colorful pony.

The place is nice, though. Tables and chairs all match, white tablecloths, carpeting unstained. Complete opposite of all things Pepe's.

Outside, telephone poles are striped red, white, green. Little two-foot banners stick out of the poles: "Johnny Kilbane—Celebrating 100 Years." The Donor used to talk about that guy, some even compared the two. But that little Irish motherfucker boxed his way to a ten-year run as featherweight champ. The Donor? He fucked his way to ten to twenty.

Me and Monica stare around each other. Food comes—good shit—and we eat. I say, "This is good." She says, "You should try this." And we seem to repeat these types of sentences for a while, no real communication.

I feel like I'm already checked out. I think of gramps, her silent plea, and after a while decide to try. "So," I say, "you're a stripper, yeah?" Fuck, I am an idiot.

Her blue eyes stare at me, I think measuring if there's something more to my question, but for the first time I also pick up on an "I know this girl" feeling. Her expression stays flat. "For now. Saving for school."

"Yeah?"

"Yeah." She pops a piece of garlic bread into her mouth. "CSU in a year, physical therapy."

"Why?" After my first stupid-as-fuck question and now my weird feelings that I know her, one-word comments seem in order.

"Why am I a stripper or why physical therapy?"

"Yeah." I glance outside. Damn, who is she? "Both." Two words; big man.

"Means to an end. I don't like guys grabbing me. But money's good. If it wasn't for that casino downtown I'd be making more. Now, instead of the sure thing of a naked lady, they blow money on the long shot." Monica says, "But I make three hundred a day, most days, fifteen hundred a week. Have the first year saved up." My eyes must have jumped. "A lot of money, right? But my dad, after his accident? This therapist helped him walk again. I can't imagine bringing that to someone, you know?"

"That's," I say, "great." I mean it.

"What about you? You going to work at that pizza place your whole life?"

"No." Our heroin truck's my ticket now. "No," I say again.

"Good," she says. "You seem better than that, everything your mother tells me."

"I feel like I know you." I've given up trying to figure it out. "I mean, you seem to know me."

"Hal." She laughs. "We went to school together. I was three years ahead."

Monica … Monica … "Monica? Fa*brizio*?" I look at her, take her body and face in again more carefully. "You did *not* look like *this*," I say.

She chuckles, a beautiful throaty thing. "People change."

"Jesus."

Things seem to click. We talk about school, old teachers, including Fal, graduation, life since. She tells me how she first met my mom the year she'd prowled the halls looking for dates. They became friends, kept in touch. Later, when her father got in that accident, her family needed money, she was desperate. Mom reluctantly suggested The Velvet Lion. Monica took a job at the front, quickly became a dancer, money too good to leave.

I relax. I tell her about Pepe's, delivering pizzas on the bike, Mrs. Brud, the guys, The Hoof. Don't know why, I even tell her about our funeral jobs. She tries not to show anything, I think, but she fails. "What?" I say.

"Nothing."

"Your face changed."

She winds a straw wrapper around her fingers, wrapping and unwrapping it until it breaks. "It's just—" she says. "Hal, that's horrible."

"Yeah, well, what'd you say? Means to an end."

"No, it's not. I—"

"Take your clothes off for money. High standards."

She bites her lip. I look outside. The Kilbane posters flutter in a light breeze.

"Hal—"

"No, Monica. Who the fuck are you to judge me? You got your plan, your way out. I do what I do because—you know why I'm here?" My voice is rising. I'm losing it.

"Because your mom thought we'd—"

"Because my mom thought you could help me get out of the fucking slaughterhouse." I point out the window at one of the posters. "And let me tell you, the only way out is to fight. Legal, illegal, don't fucking matter."

Her aunt appears, cliché checked apron and all, hand on my shoulder, trying to calm me, quiet me.

Monica dabs a napkin at the corners of her mouth. Purple lipstick mixes with red sauce on the whiteness. "What would Sally think?" She stares right through me.

I flip her aunt's hand off my shoulder, reach into my pocket, pull out some money, dump it on the table. "I'll walk."

I get turned around coming out of the restaurant, the food or the mention of Sally or the fight making me unbalanced, and I head north a few blocks—the wrong direction. Fuck it, keep going. I half expect and half hope Monica will come after me, and I prepare some words: How dare you ask about Sally? How do you judge me and what I do? Me? *Me?* You're a, a, a goddamn nightmare bitch. Like that. But none seems right, that last bit too harsh even for her. No Monica anyway. Lucky her. Unlucky me.

Light still hangs on, late summer making the days long. My

walk takes me toward the lake, through some old neighborhoods. Peeling paint, sagging porches, chipped and broken steps, the screen doors torn and hanging by hinges' single nails. Couple of guys work on ladders and paint the second floor of one house. Drop cloths drip off bushes that are likely thankful for not having to look at the neighborhood anymore. Idiots didn't even scrape the old paint, just slap on the new. Shit will peel right quick, winter hits.

Last house on the block, before cutting under the Shoreway, two old-as-dirt guys, mangy cats in their laps, sit on filthy plastic chairs, red and green and white faintly striping the legs, and talk about better times. Given their age, those times are probably one hundred fucking years ago.

On the paved walk that leads to the lake, I think maybe Monica has followed, decided to apologize. It'll be good. I've cooled off, the earlier words gone. But it's just some guy in black sweats out for a run.

Walking into Edgewater Park gets me thinking about when me and The Donor used to go fishing off the pier, which gets me thinking about Jacob, which leads to gramps's story and that question. The shit dog, gramps, and the shit seeds: those are the ones I'm feeding and watering. It's what I'm good at, yeah?

At the end of the pier, I sit on an old bench, watch three old guys work their rods and reels. Each wears faded and ripped jeans, hoodies, no shirts. The one standing at the railing wears a sweat-stained Indians hat that has long ago lost its color. Chief Wahoo, that smiling fuck-awful caricature, looks sad. Gray Hoodie digs through a tackle box at his feet. I get the sense I'm looking at everything they own, that they fish not for fun but for survival.

I close my eyes, feel the breeze, smell the mix of somewhat-fresh water and foul fish, hear the water slap against the piles and the concrete slabs that make up this end of the shore. "Any bites?" I say.

When I open my eyes, Wahoo speaks. "Nibbles, man. But they fight." He works his rod up and over his right shoulder. "Like this one."

"Pffft." Gray Hoodie flings his rod out toward downtown and the haze that clings to the tall buildings. "White bass, they don't do that, fight."

"You prolly got a snake." Black Sweats has walked up the

ramp at the base of the pier, hands shoved in his pockets. For someone who's been jogging, his breathing's slow, steady, not winded at all. No sweat covers Black Sweats.

"Snake my ass." Wahoo pulls a fish up over the railing, puts it on the concrete pier, pulls the hook, and puts the fish in a blue plastic drug store bag. He ties the handles to the railing, but the wind kicks up and the fish flops out, smacks the pier, hops twice, and drops twenty feet back into the lake. "Fuck a duck," Wahoo says. Gray Hoodie bends over laughing.

Watching these three, I can see me, Fal, Packy sixty years from now, nothing changed. Part of that vision feels good, part of it feels like the saddest fucking thing in the world.

"You fish?" Black Sweats sits beside me. He looks in his forties, smells like a can of Axe. "I fish," he says. He pulls a deck of cards out of his pocket, shuffles the cards, cuts it with one hand. He flips over the top card, ace of spades. He pretends to deal himself a hand. Every three cards or so he flips the top card, always the ace of spades. Cool trick. He has 216 tattooed on the inside of his lower lip.

"Good for you." I stand, head back down the pier.

Behind me I hear, "You know what I like for bait?"

"Don't care," I shout over my shoulder.

"Your grandpa does." I stop. "Or is it your grandma? Hard to tell, that one."

I turn and rush him, cock my right fist. He holds up his arms when I swing and the cards—hearts, diamonds, clubs, spades— burst free and scatter across the pier and blow into the lake. As Black Sweats grabs my arms—his grip is tight—I hear Wahoo say, "Fuck a duck." Black Sweats pushes me down, my head clanks a railing. I am dazed.

"Do you know who I am?" Behind him, Wahoo, his pole bouncing on his shoulder, and Gray Hoodie, his tackle box dropping hooks and sinkers behind him, hustle past and off the pier, nothing biting for them anymore. "Your father does." From his left pocket he pulls out the ace of spades—I swear I saw that card float off the edge of the pier—and from his right pocket he pulls out a crumpled ball. "Whenever he hears my name I'm sure he wishes me to hell."

"Who—"

"Shhhh." He holds the ace to his lips. "Did you know when I was born the river burned? All for me. For Owen."

"Where's gramps?"

"He's safe."

"What do you—"

"You should've seen him when he asked. Maybe could've prevented this." He hands me the crumple. It's one of the LorCI postcards gramps had given me. On one side's a picture of the Terminal Tower. On the back, in The Donor's all-caps block handwriting: "We need to talk. Before you do something stupid." I look a question at Owen. He gives me the ace of spades. On the card's face, where seconds ago I know, or think I know, there hadn't been any writing: "Too late. Tomorrow. Airport. Noon."

"You will return what's ours," Owen says.

I shove the cards into my pocket. This Owen has to be lying. I mean, gramps has to be home. She has to be. Behind me, as I flee the pier: "Next time you rob a truck, Hal, leave that bed-breaking mountain of a man behind."

Houses blur past as I rush down 65th. But one detail sticks: someone has painted on the four front steps of one house, one word per step, Honesty, Unselfishness, Love, Hope. The words were meant to inspire. They make me afraid.

I run through the house, yell for gramps. Her room's trashed, her paintings scattered, torn, the wood floor spotted red. I hold my finger out to touch the blood, connect with gramps somehow. Paint. Red fucking paint. Not blood. I wipe a streak across my jeans, breathe some relief.

Her nightstand's turned over. Her makeup litters the floor. And her pill bottles are gone. Gotta love her: kidnapped, she somehow convinces them to take her pills.

Mom's working. Go and tell her? Not tell her? Fuck. She'll kill me. Tell me I'm no better than The Donor. Bullshit, right? Goddamn right I'm better. Right?

Tomorrow: I have another job at the school. Mrs. Brud told me I'd done so good they'd asked for me again. Those kids, man. After that first day, I had figured I'd never go back, but something pulled. Now: I'll skip school, no chance to tell Brud or Williams, and I'll cancel my shift at Pepe's. Comes down to it, if I can get gramps, still score the H's sale, who the fuck *needs* Pepe? Or those kids?

I head out, grab Sally's bike, unsure where to go. The Hoof only a few blocks over. The Velvet Lion a few miles down. A drink sounds good. Telling mom doesn't. The Hoof it is.

I stay up too late, drink too much, sleep too little. The hour I do get is drunk unconsciousness.

Up before mom, I ignore her note with the question about gramps, head to the 65th–Lorain Rapid station, a twenty-minute walk.

The noise of the street jars my head, churns my stomach. Behind a sign pitching the Cleveland Food Bank ("Struggling to Pay for Food?") I kneel down and throw up. A few assholes driving by honk their horns, yell. I wipe my mouth with my fingers, wipe my fingers on my jeans, stand on shaky legs, and move on. Today it'll be a forty-minute walk.

Past the old killing grounds, stores, both open and abandoned, and houses, both lived in and condemned, dot the landscape. Signs in store windows pump the holy trinity: WIC Accepted, Cigarettes on Sale, and OH! Lottery. Survival, death, and bullshit hope all in one. Outside of one abandoned storefront, three kids sit. One shirtless, one in diapers, one eating fingers of dirt. The shirtless kid picks up an empty Doritos bag, tears it open and licks its insides. Staring at the kids nearly gets me run over by an overweight lady in a wheelchair. I dodge her as she tamps out a cig, slips what's left back into a crumpled pack. And there you go: the signs, those kids, that lady, me, this neighborhood in a fucking nutshell.

At the station, I wait outside and ask people coming out if they're done with their pass. The ninth person gifts me his card, I swipe it, go down to the platform. A mix of urine, coffee, mold, and plastic. Garbled music plays overhead while two tattooed guys talk about trains in other countries. "Check it, dude, check it. Watching this video on YouTube? These Pakistanis just climbing on roofs of trains." The one with the giant eight-ball inked on the back of his hand says, "Naw, naw. Get the fuck out." The other smacks Eight-ball's shoulder: "For real. Crazy, *crazy* shit.

Think we—? Fuck, man, watch that fucking video. Blow your mind." His hands go to either side of his head and his fingers widen as his hands pull away. His mind, blown. Fucking idiots, all of us.

Inside the train, most people press to the sides, leave the aisle seats open, antisocial. The ride's mostly uneventful. Stops, entrances, exits. Repeat. Eight-ball and his friend stay on longer than I like. I'm lucky enough to hear Eight-ball: "I do *not* think of you when I masturbate, dude." And a Transit Survey Team member's unlucky enough to ask me about my RTA experience: "Fuck off."

The train pulls into the airport an hour before pickup.

I haven't seen The Donor in seven years. I missed school a lot then; the funeral and the trial and the trauma ate up all our time. Mom thought we should stand by him, show our support. At first that made sense. But I think I was in shock, too. Sally was gone. She wasn't coming back.

The days after the fire, we moved in with gramps, the same house we live in now. The house was filled with sadness, anger, fights—my father saying it was an accident or blaming Early Ed, my mom's hands pressed tightly against her ears while she screamed at him to shut up. Gramps's house truly belonged there, near the old slaughterhouses, where shit went to die. But then a detective came with a warrant, took dad to city. There was talk that dad would be charged with aggravated murder, that he set the fire intentionally to kill Sally, as if he was throwing gas around the steps, the porch, the inside of the house like some fucking maniac, and the murder coupled with the arson charge would get him the death penalty. Prosecutors ultimately figured the grand jury wouldn't buy it and, besides, my dad, former councilman, had a few friends left, and they true-billed a package of involuntary manslaughter.

The truth, though, the part of the trial that killed my father for good, was when it came out that shortly after the fire started, the flames climbing the porch and the right side where Sally's room was, the pot-filled smoke blanketing the house giving him and the neighborhood a crazy high, he went up to get his old Indians shit, passed by Sally's room, saw her through the smoke, but couldn't get through the flames.

"But you got your Indians hat?"

"Yeah."

"You got your jersey."

"Yeah."

"Your signed bat?"

"Yeah."

"But not your daughter."

"My, uh, my *arms*, they were *full*, yeah?"

"Excuse me?"

He had seemed to reconsider. "I couldn't get to her. I didn't even know—" He cried.

At trial's end, when the time came for his defense to ask for a Rule 29—I was told the defense always asked for this, for the judge to dismiss—the judge snorted. And later when he was sentenced to LorCI for ten to twenty, I smiled for the first time in two months. If it wasn't for Fal, my teacher, who got me through a lot of the school setbacks, helped my grades even when I didn't do a bit of work, I wouldn't have moved on, would have felt stuck in that time and that school I shared with Sally for another year.

The only time I saw The Donor, talked to him—well, he talked *at* me—was after he was first arrested, sitting in city. Mom talked through the slitted partition, telling him about Sally's funeral arrangements. He ignored her, looked me up and down. "Why you *dress* him like that?" I had on torn jeans, a Cavs tee, an Indians hat with the bill slanted over my ear. "I got a repu*ta*tion. *He* reflects on *me*." Mom had pulled me up and out we went.

Watching the luggage wind its way around the carousels, I think about going shopping. It's been years since I've done it, but it's so easy—grab a suitcase right before it tracks into the back again, cross your fingers you get lucky with clothes that fit. Did my Christmas shopping like that once, me and Packy making off with some nice clothes for the family. Got mom a nice skirt, gramps a great blouse, me a pair of shorts.

A folded and unclaimed garment bag slides toward the end. I grab it, go into a bathroom. The shirt's a little tight and the suit's a little big, but they fit well enough; I have to cuff the pants. The shoes seem made for a ten-year-old. I tie the tie—gramps may be more woman than man but she taught me, teaches me, things—slip back on my high tops, shove my jeans and tee into the garment bag. I check myself in the mirror. I look good. *Sharp.* Eat it, Donor. I chuck the bag back on the track and wait outside.

I don't wait long. A black SUV approaches, salt stains still brushed up the sides from a winter that had ended six months ago. The window rolls down. A large black guy in a tight black T-shirt, sunglasses lowered on his nose, says, "Hal?" His eyes track me as I get in, stops at the shoes. "You weren't what I was expecting."

I expect the inside of an SUV being driven by one of The Donor's men to be a mess. I expect cigarettes in the ashtray, garbage in the seats and on the floor, used condoms, crack pipes, empty beer cans. His is clean. "You neither," I say.

He tells me his name's Blount. "Half hour, traffic holds," he says.

"Whatever," I say.

Traffic doesn't hold. I-480's a mix of stop-and-go cars and trucks, on-their-break construction workers, and a thousand orange barrels. Blount raises his hands then lets them fall on the steering wheel. That's the max of his road rage. They are big fuck hands, though. Hands that can crush, I'm sure. I cross my legs, right ankle on my left knee, foot-tap the dash. "You mind?" Blount says.

I uncross my legs, exhale loudly. "Look," I say, "here's what I don't get. Why now? After all these years?" Blount stares straight ahead, as if he can will traffic to move, to part, to make way. "Hah?"

"You should see him. More often."

"That's what you got? 'You should see him more often'?" The SUV jumps forward. We break free of the jam. "Useless," I say.

Once off 480, the empty stretch of single-lane flat rural roads moves us quickly through green farmland. My eyes track the double yellow lines and the thin strip of blacktop that stretches endlessly down the road's center. LorCI nears and the SUV bounces over railroad tracks. I laugh.

Blount says, "What?"

"That's it, right?" I point at the low run of buildings off in the distance. "Donor fucking hates trains. The sound. Everything. Always has."

"Siderodromophobia," Blount says.

"What?"

"Fear of trains. It's called siderodromophobia. Everybody's got something."

I attempt to repeat the word, own it, fail. "You're full of surprises."

On LorCI's grounds, Blount parks and points to a low wood-paneled trailer that looks like one of the portables at Sally's old school. A short snaky line, four women, several kids, and an old man, dangle out of the propped-open door. "Get processed first." I step out of the car, wait for Blount. He just points again.

One teenager, my age maybe, he slips a small plastic baggie into his crotch. Jesus, he does that here, now? Stupid fucker. A few of the kids are quiet, emotionless; others are wild and require mothers to sharply tug arms and ears, keep them in line.

A hundred yards away, the jail's fencing and discolored brick seem to push toward me, and when the clouds cover the sun the shadows worsen the feeling.

Inside the trailer, two COs sit behind a short desk: Paperwork CO moves papers around, Keyboard CO taps at an old computer. A metal detector and another CO holding a wand stand near a set of double doors in the back. Once checked in and scanned, any bags searched, visitors sit on a church-like bench on the other side of the metal detector.

Keyboard CO asks without looking up, "For?"

"Henry Boland," I say. I tug at my tie. I'm suddenly hot.

"Name?"

"Henry Boland," I repeat.

"No, son, *your* name." He eyes me over his glasses, seeing me for the first time. I regret the suit.

"Hal," I say. "Hal Boland."

"Relation."

I pull at the collar, give my Adam's apple a break. "Son."

"Purpose?"

I lean forward, prop my hands on the table. I can see on his screen a list of names: my mother's name, gramps's, Early Ed's (a surprise), and a few names I don't know. To see a prisoner, you have to submit paperwork to the sheriff's first, get checked out ahead of time. I'd never done it, but somebody has because there I am on the approved list. Keyboard CO looks at me again, waits patiently. "To catch up." I show my high school photo ID. No driver's license is one reason I deliver pizzas on a bike.

Paperwork CO asks me to sign my name, write down the "time in," and says, "Wait there." He points to the short line behind the metal detector.

When I go through, the alarm pings. "Anything in your pockets?" the CO asks and holds out a plastic dish. I pat my pockets, drop some coins in the dish. I hope the suit doesn't have something that'll get me on the wrong side of the inside. I step back through the detector, hold my breath. The CO pats me down, tells me to collect my things, radioes The Donor's name to someone, and tells me to sit and wait.

I want to greyhound the fuck out but figure Blount, for all his quiet, would force me back. But that Owen fuck. And gramps. I don't want to do any of this. But I dealt myself this hand, I made these bets.

After about eight of us are cleared, another CO comes through the double doors and ushers us single file down some stairs at the back of the trailer, across a parking lot toward the front entry building. There is nothing: long flat runs of grass and dirt and farm, that's it. Nowhere to run. I imagine what this looks like in the winter. Blinding white snow, untouched, anything but pure. Inside, an old lady stands at a kiosk, talks to a CO about getting funds deposited into an inmate's account; her son, I guess.

One of the kids stares at me and scratches his arm nervously. I realize, after a few seconds, that I'm scratching my own arm, thumbnail scraping shoulder to elbow just as the kid had done. Catching each other in the act we stop at the same time. I raise my thumb to my arm, the kid does the same. I scratch, the kid does the same. I touch my finger to my nose, the kid does the same. I put my finger up my nose and stick out my tongue, the kid does the same, giggles. His mom looks at him, then at me, yanks his arm and tells him to stop fooling around. A few of the other kids know what they're doing, been through this before, and dart into a book-filled room where an inmate reads a picture book to a small group of kids. A tag on his prison-issue states: "Inmate Narrator."

Soon the rest of us stand outside a large room populated with a series of bolted-to-the-floor powder blue hard plastic chairs. The chairs face each other in groups of two, a three-foot gap between them. The room's lit in that eye-fucking fluorescent, a few bulbs

still twitching. At each end of the room stand two COs oversee-
ing the meets. The inmates are already seated, waiting.

At the doorway a CO asks each visitor's name, announces it
to the CO on the other side, and then escorts the visitor to the
corresponding set of chairs. Crotch-bag goes ahead of me, is led
to a stringy longhaired guy whose eyes zip back and forth so fast
I think they'll jackhammer out of his head. The CO returns and
stares.

"For Henry Boland."

"*Bo*land? Call me 'Stockyard King' or nothing." His voice
echoes and bounces around me; I can't see him.

The CO's voice echoes, too: "Shut it, Boland." At the same
time another voice rebounds: "Fuck your royal highness." I can't
tell if that's the other CO or another prisoner. I feel disoriented.

The CO takes me to a chair across from a man who's older,
grayer, and more wrinkled than I expect. The orange jumpsuit
makes his skin waxy. Circles under his eyes make him look tired
and sad; it all, almost, makes fake his confident declaration of
Stockyard King. Glasses stick out of a breast pocket; he'd never
needed glasses before. His legs, straight out in front of him, are
crossed at the ankles and his right foot Morse-codes his left. His
eyes dart and look everywhere but at me. He smells like cigarette
smoke, but a small nicotine patch clings to his upper arm, just
below the orange sleeve.

Part of me wonders if I should have come to see him sooner,
before shit went down. But not for the regular reasons people
might think. I don't want to cry or hug or get all sad and shit, I
don't want to tell him how much I miss him, how much I wish
he wasn't a fucking idiot, how I hope his life in prison isn't full
of beatings and rapes—hey, I saw *Shawshank*, I know what goes
on. I don't want to hear him tell me how he knows he fucked up,
how if he could do it all over again he wouldn't, you know. How
he's sorry, although he's never, as far as I know, ever said that. And
I certainly don't want him to tell me that I look good or that he's
proud of me or that he loves me. No, none of that shit.

But here, with him in front of me, not even making eye contact, not even acknowledging me, I want to punch his fucking
face, kick his motherfucking balls. I figure the CO won't let me
do that. Maybe if I palm him twenty?

The Donor finally scans me. "*Who* the *fuck* are you, eh?" He turns toward the CO. "Fuck is *this* guy?"

My hands shake. I press them against my thighs, try to calm them. I had run through a lot of scenarios, thought of all the things I'd say, do, not say, not do. But this? I'm drowning. The CO doesn't return my look. Crotch-bag adjusts his low-hanging jeans, moves his junk. A lady hoists a gurgling baby up to her own imprisoned donor. Did he really just—? I mean: The fuck am I? The *fuck* am *I*?

"*Dick*head, I am *right* the fuck in front of—. *Je*sus, Mary, Joseph. *Sit*, Hal. Hal, sit." The Donor smacks his lips. He points at my stolen clothes. "*Fuuuuck* me, *al*most didn't *rec*ognize you." His lips purse as if he makes to whistle. No sound.

I have visions of strangling that smirk off his face, life in prison not a bad tradeoff. I stay standing, ready to motion the CO that I am done, but he is preoccupied: he holds crotch-bag by the elbows and pushes his screaming ass out the door as he struggles to free himself. I sit.

"Cleveland Zoo, son, can't compare to LorCI." He looks at his fingernails then back at me, waits for the noise to die. "I don't *get* it. Why you throw these shitty fucking knuckleballs at me, Hal. Swear to *God*, you're here to *pun*ish." He sighs. "All your actions make me think you *birthed* to disap*point* me."

"The fuck you say? Repeat: Who's a disap—"

"—*point*ment? Son of mine, you do unworthy, foolish deeds. Be*neath* you. Hal, my fucking blood, you've bound yourself with dolts, buf*foons*. Unless you were in*ten*tionally hurting me. And your po*ten*tial. Hopes, Hal, *hopes*. I *ruled* that neighborhood. I'd hoped you'd come into your *own*, you know? Supposed to do me *proud*, Hal."

"Go fuck yourself and fuck your pride."

"*You're* the one in trouble. Who's—"

"Know nothing, absolutely zip, about my life and—"

"*Friends*, Hal. Checking. What you're *doing*, who you're *with*, and how you're badly fucking up, boy." He uncrosses his legs, leans toward me. "Heard about that truck you jacked. Be*fore* you took it down, son. Kiting you with all those *post*cards? Had to see you, set you *straight*."

"But—"

"Taking that much H? Could not be*lieve* your balls had

dropped, Hal. Honest. Fucking *proud*est ... That was *my* boy, *my* son. Should have *seen* me." He taps my knee, holds his head high, looks down his nose. "Cock of the motherfucking *walk*. But *now*, Hal? *Ev*eryrone knows. Early Ed knows. His son, Harry?" The Donor gives me a look I've known for much of my life, the look I've seen hundreds or thousands of times, the look that said he wished I was someone else. "*He*—"

"The situation," I say, "it is handled. I—"

"'*Hand*led'? Shit, Hal, outside's simple, easy." The Donor looks around the room, leans back, recrosses his legs. "No idea you could fuck up simple."

I think about strangling him again, this time picturing my tie around his throat, his eyes popping.

"Do you even *know* what it's like *in*side? LorCI's mostly Level 3. Shit's tame compared to other joints." He holds his arms out at his side as if he's embracing the entire prison. "But let me tell you: *con*stant racket, paranoids by the *hun*dreds." He sucks in his breath, a wet slippage of air. "How you *walk* can be a challenge. How you *talk* can be a challenge. Fucker *props* you, son? Get beat or turn the fucking tables." The Donor claps his hands together and the crack quiets the room for a heartbeat.

I shrug. Strangling him seems unimportant all of a sudden.

"Fuck, Hal. *One* guy? Let me tell you, he will pass your cell, say, all sweet-like, 'Through the bars, give me your cock.' And if you *don't*? He throw a cup of *piss* at you. And that's the *same* damn fucker who'll be *jerk*ing it in the *mid*dle of the *yard*, in front of God and everyone, before, *may*be, a CO tackles the fuck out of him. My life, Hal. I'm surviving it. *In*side. In this motherfucking place. And you out there in the simple-as-fuck real world tell me you can handle it? You can *han*dle it? My *ass*, Hal. You," he looks at the ceiling, "you're an embarrassment."

I stand, ready to claw or punch or kick or stomp or run. I see his mouth moving but I am not hearing it. My ears ring. I rant. "You asked, you fucking *asked*, for me. To what? Do what? For this? You bring me here. To fucking disre—"

"—spect, Hal." The Donor stands, faces me. I feel some of the air come out of the room, as if all eyes are on me, him. I expect a pair of big hands to grab my elbows, escort me out the way of crotch-bag. "Said you got to show re*spect* in here, boy.

Got to *calm* yourself, eh? Otherwise?" He nods at a CO who has taken a special interest in our discussion. He taps the chair leg with his plain white tennis-shoed foot. "There you *go*, Hal. Easing it down."

We sit. Being desperate makes me do surprising things sometimes.

"Twenty-*two*. Did you know that? When I left baseball. Twenty-fucking-two." He wipes his face from brow to chin and the sigh that escapes blows through his fingers and hits me in the face. "Pulled myself together any way I could, Hal. Even worked for Early Ed, Joe Loose. Fucking hated them, the fucks. But I was making my way, making my *name*. When I got voted in as *council*man? I ended up running that shit from Rabbit Run, up through the Yards, up to the *lake* and Whiskey fucking *I*sland. *You*, son?" He waves a hand at me.

I've clocked his use of "son" since I got here. My jaw clenches a little tighter with each one. I hear my teeth.

"Smarten *up*. So many others doing *more* than you, son, doing *bet*ter than you. Fucking *think*, Hal."

I look at my feet. I look at my hands. I find a loose piece of skin on my palm, pick at it. "I, uh—they've taken gramps."

"What do you mean, 'They've taken gramps'?"

"Said his name was Owen. Do you know him?" The Donor nods. "Crazy fucker took her. I think."

The Donor stares off into space. For once, it seems, he doesn't know everything. Feels good to have one on him even if at gramps's expense.

He's gone for a bit, lost. He used to do that when we were kids; weirded me out then, makes me uncomfortable now. "Normally," The Donor finally says, "I'd say to talk your way out. Made a living doing just that: *talk*ing. Making people *lis*ten. *You're* a talker. Talked those morons into following you." He slides to the edge of his seat; our knees touch and he leans in close. His glasses drop out of his breast pocket, land in his lap. He doesn't notice, his gaze locked in on me. "This is *dif*ferent, son. Owen? Works for Ed, for Harry. These guys, they aren't Packy or Fal. Talk won't cut it. *Fuck* talk. Need to hit hard. I mean, swing the fuck a*way*, batter." He slaps my cheek lightly, three quick taps. "The Yards are *ours*, Hal. Take what's mine, what's *yours*."

We stare at each other while one by one the prisoners are escorted out. The Donor stands to leave. "Take every fucking bit."

Inside the SUV, Blount says, "How'd it go?" I tap the dashboard, point for us to leave. Blount nods, turns the engine over.

I don't give a shit about The Donor's past or his kingdom. Don't give a shit about Ed or Harry. Don't give a shit about being a good son, at least not to him. I've carved out my own world, did what I did, do what I do, out of necessity. I need to help mom. I need to help gramps. I need to help myself. I need to feel something. I fucking need. And I'd thought—goddamn it to fucking hell—I thought I had hit it. Solved it all. That dumb-as-fuck-luck heroin was the answer to a question I'd carried since Sally. I was somebody. I wasn't that waste-of-a-man's loser son and I wasn't that dead sister's poor brother. I was going to be the guy who had made it out. Who had escaped. Who had rescued the only family left that mattered to him. The dead I'd carried inside? Fucking exorcised. But none of it matters now. I am who I am and that's that. I put someone I love at risk. I *need*, all right, but right now, all I *want*? Gramps.

"Swing the fuck away," I say.

"I could help, you asked," Blount says as we pull away.

The ride back from LorCI is uneventful. I ask Blount to come by the Hoof later. No clue if he'll show or not; doesn't much matter. We are going to bring it to Ed to Harry to Owen, get gramps. After that?

I have to tell mom. As much as I don't want to, I know that.

I hop the bus, the 81, down Storer to Fulton. The outside of The Velvet Lion is all purple and pink lights. A driving bass pours through the propped-open and heavily tinted glass door. A few guys in front of me wait to get in, tall crew-cutted douche-bag meatheads. I'm glad mom doesn't dance anymore but unhappy she has guys like this, any guys, really, eye-banging her. The guys in front of me pay their cover, go through the next set of doors, past Andrews the Giant, the fatherly, muscle-bound Hispanic bouncer all the girls love. I think about catching his eye, point out the meatheads, target them for a beating, maybe, or at least some harassment—I feel like seeing someone get hurt—but mom, dressed in a see-through negligee over a sports bra and Spanx, grabs my arm, smiles.

"What a surprise," she says-yells over the bass as the inner doors finish closing behind the meatheads. "Andrews, look. Hal."

Andrews nods hello, I nod back. Such a big fucker, Andrews. Forget the meatheads, I think about talking to him on the side, seeing if he'd be down for helping, decide I need to keep this close to me.

"What's wrong, Hal?"

She can always read me. Might be why I avoid her so much. "Nothing."

"Look, Hal, if it's about Monica, she told me all about it." I really hope Monica hadn't told mom all about it. "She's really sorry, said she wants to see you again."

"Naw, that's not it. Besides, she didn't do anything wrong. It's on me." I look outside, not really looking at anything.

"What?"

"Nothing, I said."

The door opens, an older guy in a suit, tie pulled loose, pushes by me, pays mom, goes inside. Prince's "Sexy MF" blares through the open door, fades as it closes.

"Look, Hal. She's here. Monica's here. She's on now, but I can get her. You can talk to her."

I finger-tap the counter mom sits behind. Try to figure out what to tell her. How to tell her.

"I'll make it right, Mom."

"Oh, Hal, I know you will. She's a sweet girl. I'm telling you." Prince is winding down. She reaches to pull open the door. "Let me get her." Andrews steps aside.

"No, not that." I take her hand, hold it.

"What are you—?"

"Gramps, mom. It's gramps."

"Do you know if she had a meeting last night? It's not like her to not come home. I mean, there was that one time she made friends with Esther and lost track of time, she said. I think they traded makeup secrets because, I swear, after that? Her makeup looked a million times—and did you see her room, Hal?

I can only make out part of this—her volume changes and shifts with the loud music coming through the wall and door—

but by the end her face changes, her smile's gone. "What did you do?"

"I'll fix it," I say. "Mom, I'll—"

"Tell me."

Andrews now hovers directly behind mom and his muscles seem to double.

I tell her everything. About the heist, about the H in the cigarettes, about that Owen guy and what he said about gramps, about meeting with The Donor. I'm not expecting to tell her all of it, and with each detail, as her eyes close and her head shakes and her mouth tightens, I think about leaving the next thing out, protecting her, but everything keeps right on coming. It feels good for Andrews to hear it all, too. Even though he looks like he wants to crush me, I know he'll keep mom safe. All of these thoughts are out of my head when mom backhands me across the face. "You're no better." I taste blood, feel my cut lip. She's never hit me before. When she winds up to hit me again, Andrews grabs her arm. "Monica's too good for you," she says.

I want to tell her I have a plan, that gramps will be safe. I feel lost, more uncertain than ever. I can only say, "I know."

At the Hoof, I wait in the basement. The Donor's hat sits on the pool table, its case unrepaired. As old as the building is, as much death as it's seen, part of me wants it all to collapse, take me, take Hook, take the tits, swallow us all, just get it fucking over with.

I hear the main door open upstairs, a slurred "bres!" followed by the cracking of the wood stairs straining under Fal's weight. He loses his balance and slips down the last two, lands in a few stray pieces of glass that give his palms tiny cuts. "Fuck, bres."

This, this is my team, my crew.

I help Fal up. "Where's Packy? G?"

"What I came to tell you, bres, what I came to tell you." Fal wipes his hand on his face, droplets of blood hang in his beard. "G's shot."

I imagine G squaring off against Harry, the two drawing guns. Or maybe G was jumped, shot in the back as he tried to run.

"Cops, bres." Fal cocks his finger and thumb into a gun.

Fal tells me how Packy and G had decided to test the market,

173

nicked some of the heroin from the truck, took to the streets. Jesus Fucking Christ, I think. A zone car saw them, pulled up. Packy and G took off, ran into some shithole apartment building. Cop followed. G threw rocks and bricks. Cop opened fire. Packy got away, found Fal, told him what happened. He waited for us at the scrapyard.

"And G?"

"Think he's at Metro."

I pull Fal toward the steps and we make the short walk over to the truck and Packy. I want to slap the shit out of him, but it won't do any good; he's a nervous mess.

I tell them we need to get rid of the truck, that it's caused problem after problem, nightmare after nightmare. At first Fal protests—"Bres, our money"—but when he hears about gramps, he's in.

We leave Packy to get himself together. Hook knows where Ed and Harry headquarter; I hope we'll find gramps there. Tonight, I'm putting everything right.

It wasn't long after Licavoli's big fuck-up in killing Danny Greene that Ed was able to bust through. This was before the Joe Loose days. Ed sat back, watched the two factions fuck each other in the ass, bomb the shit out of Cleveland, waited. Greene, dead. Nardi, dead. Licavoli, arrested. Big Ange, arrested. Ed was early to the table, feasted on the opportunity, took a small chunk of the mob's drug business. The mob, temporarily weakened, just let the chunk go.

That was in the '80s, when The Donor was dicking around in Class A, when he wasn't even thinking about councilman or dealing or any of that shit. Other than boosting a few cars in high school, The Donor had lived a clean life. (The judge, whose son was also on the high school team, gave The Donor ten hours of community service teaching kids to play baseball.)

While The Donor struggled, Early Ed thrived. Carved out a nice niche, he and his son. In Clark-Fulton, Ed and his son had founded The Shrewsbury Club, an underground gambling house that, before the Horseshoe opened, cleared a million a year. Add in his drug sales, Ed was one of the main players on The North Coast.

And I'd managed to thieve one of his trucks, get gramps taken, prove The Donor right.

Back at The Hoof, Blount waits. Over the years, The Donor'd sent fuck-up after fuck-up to help mom and me, and every one of them had been cockless wonders. Maybe Blount'll be the same, but here he is and he looks ready.

I'd thought of a number of ways to go: negotiate, attack, run, cops. The Donor had said to fuck talk, to just hit hard. What the fuck does he know? In my mind, talking was a can't-hurt-could-help sort of thing. I say, "Head over to The Shrewsbury Club. I need a peaceful way out." Blount nods. I kind of like his big-and-silent routine. Better than Fal's never-shut-up routine. "I'll wait here." Another nod and he's gone.

Hook pours me a beer. I chug half of it, exhale deeply. My shoulders loosen and I realize I must have been pinching them to my ears for days. I roll my head around, loosen my neck, rub it with one hand while my other grips the beer. I conjure images of gramps safely at home, painting, just doing her thing. I picture letting her tell me all about dogs and seeds and whatever else she wants to tell me. Bring it all on, gramps. Mom takes us both in, smiles at us. The imagined scene scores me some calm. Yeah, this shit can work itself out, I think. It just, man, it all—

Fal bursts through the door, announces, "Bres, bres, an army." Behind him, a sorry looking group. They look like they're still in school, homeless, or both.

My shoulders pinch again. "Fal, who the fuck are—"

"I recruited, bres." He orders two beers, one for himself and one to be shared by his army of three. "I trust every one of them, bres. They'll do everything we need." Hook looks at me, I wave my hand, he starts pouring.

I sigh but my shoulders stay up. I chug the balance of my beer. My stomach hurts.

Fal walks in front of one of his recruits. He says, "This, bres, this is Bottles." Bottles wears jeans that are missing one leg so the white of the pocket pokes out; the intact leg is covered in dirt and oil. "He recycles. A lot." Fal walks behind a boy whose face looks babyish and whose glasses seem to cover half his face; he pats the boy on the shoulders. "This here is Specs. Bres, he can spot pepper in fly shit. Or is it fly shit in pepper." He flutters his

175

hand away; it doesn't matter. I am unconvinced Specs could find his cock if it was in his hand. The next boy props his feet on one of the tables, rocks his chair back on two legs. Fal pushes his feet off the table, and the chair, with boy, fall. I think Fal says something about respect, but it's lost in the crash. The boy straightens his chair, settles back in, and Fal's about to introduce him when I call Fal over.

"Aren't they great, bres?" His breath reeks.

"Fal, you've got to be kidding. How old are they? What could they possibly—"

"I know people, Hal. These boys," he points, takes them all in with the gesture, "are perfect, bres." The one who fell picks his nose, wipes it on the edge of the beer glass, marks this single beer as his territory.

"For what?"

"You want to go into Shrewsbury first? I don't, bres, I don't. They, they will. Fodder, Hal, fodder."

"Fal, I'm not sending kids in to be—"

"Rethink it, bres. I taught some of these kids. We'd be doing them, us, Cleveland a favor."

"Cut 'em loose."

"But—"

I push Fal toward Bottles. "This is our deal, Fal. It's not, you know, honorable to get others into our mess."

"Honorable, bres?" Fal says. "There's no honor in getting ourselves killed, either. You know how many honorable men are buried in Cleveland? None." Fal rubs his stomach. "Honor sure as hell isn't what's been making me thinner. Doesn't make them smarter." He indicates his army. "What the fuck good does honor do when you're dead? It's an empty fucking word, bres. We need them."

"Now."

Fal goes up to each one, whispers something, and as a group they leave. Specs, his sharp eyes leading the way, nearly knocks into Blount as he comes through the door.

Fal eyes Molly as she sweeps under some tables. "Bres, I bet she's like the highway. Lots of wide open spaces." He burps. "With a lot of potholes, if you know what I mean."

Blount looks at me. "Ignore him," I say.

"Nice place, Shrewsbury." Blount's voice is so low and deep it feels like the room shakes. "My great-grandfather worked at the old Harvard Club, told me stories. Seems just as nice."

"What'd Ed say?"

"Wasn't Ed. Harry."

"Whatever." I feel a stab in my stomach. "What did *Harry* say?"

"I offered the truck. Harry laughed. I offered the truck and money. Harry said you were too kind. I think he was being sarcastic, Hal." He orders a beer, Hook pours, and Blount waits to take a sip before talking again. "He asked for you, Hal, asked that in addition to the truck, the money, you leave the Yards, give up everything."

Fal's eyes leave the sweeping Molly, flick on my face.

Blount says, "Let me get this right. He said, 'Not that we fear him, no, just that Hal, intentionally or otherwise, fucks our lives up.' Said it's best if you're gone."

"Anything else?" I say.

Blount looks away.

"Blount ..."

"Called your mom a whore, your dad a fuck, and your grandpa a freak. Threatened to cut off his cock and balls if you don't comply."

I wonder if gramps would be thrilled by that threat. "Did you see her?"

"Upstairs. The old prostitute rooms." Blount cracks his knuckles, each pop a gunshot. "She looks OK. Told me to do whatever you said. Harry wants a fight, Hal, to settle everything from your father's past to your future."

I'd only truly been in three fights. One was because a student had bullied Sally. One was because Packy had made it with a girl I was interested in. And one was because of gramps. Her first time going outside as herself, gramps had picked me up from school wearing a lacy flower-patterned dress, a bright gold lamé purse, heels. Her cheeks were pink with blush, her lips glittered with lipstick. Gramps had greeted me with a hug. Some fuckhead parent had called gramps a hideous girl, angrily said she should stop being a deviant. The kid he was with? Followed his parent's lead. I threw my backpack at the parent and tackled the boy. It took gramps and a teacher to pull me off. I was suspended the rest of the day. I remember gramps told me I was not to fight, not for

177

her, not for anyone. She told me she'd stop dressing up. I told her she had to be whatever she wanted to be. She ended up staying indoors for years. I hoped she wouldn't mind one more fight.

"What you're feeling?" Blount says. "It's atychiphobia."

I'd almost forgot about his weird-as-shit knowledge base. I raise my hands, impatient.

"Fear of failure, Hal."

The instructions I give Blount and Fal are simple, and I tell them to give Packy the location, tell them what to do with the truck. They can have the truck. Leaving the Yards? It's what I've always wanted. But not when I'm ordered.

I peddle by Pepe's on the way to Shrewsbury. I call Pepe from out back, tell him I quit. No more deliveries. He takes it better than I think, even gives me a slice on my way out the door. I almost take a bite, think better of it, and throw it in the dirt. I swear I see a roach turn its nose up at it, too.

I'd never been to Shrewsbury. Not like I had money to gamble. And drinks? No need, not with The Hoof. I straddle the bike seat—the ride over did me good, gave me time to think—take in the building. Old brick, new mortar, the place takes up about three lots at the dead part of a dead-end street. According to Blount, the short steps to the porch lead into a homey-as-fuck fake living room complete with a nylon-legged lamp in the window. In the back, an entrance to the upper bar and a stairway down to the gambling area: blackjack, poker, craps, roulette. Back in the day, the upstairs was a brothel. Now the rooms go to out-of-town high rollers. Or to hold my transgender gramps prisoner.

I lean my bike against the right corner of the house, climb the steps. Fal and the others will be here soon.

The door opens as I approach. Two large men in suits greet me.

"I'm here to see Ed or Harry," I say. "I'm Hal." I smooth my hair, slick a bit of sweat from my forehead through it. "They have my fucking grandma?" I add.

"The old lady?" Suit One says with genuine pleasure. He goes inside while Suit Two pats me down. Chest, arms, up one leg, down the other, cups my larger-than-normal junk. When he comes up empty, he looks disappointed.

178

Downstairs, gamblers sit at various gaming tables. Stacks of chips decrease as I watch. One roulette table drops a 22 and the loser, near tears, looks like one of the Browns. Man, if I could have a tenth of what these fuckers are losing, throwing away?

Inside his office, Harry looks good. His bright red hair pops in wavy strands from under his hat and his Hollywood face pisses me off. I hate and admire this guy. Good looks, a father who isn't a child-murdering dumbass, moneymaking businesses, talent. The Donor loved to compare the two of us, me and Harry. Told me, more than once, he wished him and Ed could swap sons. I want to pull Harry into my fist but I keep my cool; he has a gun fake-hidden under a tented *Plain Dealer*.

"Where's your father?" I sit in a chair across from him.

"Sick." He adjusts the *PD* with his right hand.

I plow into it. "We have your truck. You have my grandma. Even trade."

Air puffs his cheeks and Harry removes his hat, scratches a spot of matted curls. "No time to be wickey-wickey, Hal. You don't do what you did without paying for it. You pay. Or your grandpa does."

"She had nothing to do with any of this."

"It was either him or your mom. Owen heard you were closest to him, him we took."

"I need to see her. Before we agree to anything."

Harry nods to one of the guards. He goes out, returns a minute later. No gramps. I say, "Where—?" at the same moment he flicks his right arm, a pitcher delivering a baseball to first, an easy underhand toss guaranteeing an out and no mistakes. A bloody glob slaps the desk, spatters.

"Your grandpa's down one testicle, Hal."

When I try to stand the guard presses me back into the chair. "You fucking—" A large sweaty hand slaps me and holds my mouth shut.

Harry comes around the desk, sits on the edge and faces me. "When I was sixteen my dad brought me a whore. Some father's get their son a car." He shrugs his shoulders and rolls his eyes. "I didn't pay her. When she argued about it I hit her. Quite a few times. My father took it as a personal insult, a mark against his good name. He took it out on me. He always took it out on me."

179

He cups his crotch. "You can live without one, Hal. If treated fast enough. Before you bleed out."

I mumble through the hand.

"What's that, Hal?"

"All of it," I say, the hand removed. "Truck. Heroin. Whatever money we have."

"And you?"

I hesitate. Harry slaps his desk, the testicle jumps. "Gone," I say.

Here's what I picture: Packy driving the truck; Fal and Blount seat-belted in across the bench seat; the back open and trailing cases of heroin-tipped cigarettes behind it; the truck barreling through intersection after intersection; Fal sighting Sally's bike that marked where to strike; the truck heading straight for that corner, straight into Shrewsbury Club's living room. The three of them would pile out, get gramps to the hospital (although that wasn't part of the original plan), and I'd get lost in the confusion.

The house shakes but not nearly as much as I expect. Harry flattens his palms on the desk, gets his balance. "What the fuck was that?" He straightens his cap and moves around me. "Go, go." He opens the door, pushes the guards ahead of him. Gamblers scramble to the exits.

I think about grabbing the gun, shooting Harry in the back. Instead I pull Fal's sap out of my crotch, stand and spin and swing as hard as I can. Harry drops to his knees, holds his hand to the side of his head, and I keep swinging. I work out a lot of anger on Harry. Feels good. Blood spots the door, the desk, my clothes. I kick Harry in his one-nutted crotch and run through the casino. A car's front end has blown through the ceiling, one tire on the living room's level, the other tire hanging into the now empty casino. Inside, Fal's recruits—Specs, Bottles, Booger—look dazed through the cracked windshield.

I scramble up the stairs, hope the others have found gramps.

On the main level, Shrewsbury Club's a mess. In the front room, where I had expected to see the truck, is the rest of the car. The rear of it points out the broken main window, points toward the truck, on its side in the yard, and toward a trail of cases and cartons of cigarettes that litter the street. Beside the truck, on his back, is Fal. Sirens ring in the distance. I jump on the car, slide through the window using the car's trunk, and rush to Fal.

His eyes snap shut before I reach him and his chest and whiskers move with each exhale. The fuck. "I'll miss you, Fal. Heavily fucking miss you."

Fal sits up, sticks one stubby finger in his ear and wiggles it. "No need to miss me, bres. When they ran out I thought it best to, uh, rest, bres, rest. I was resting."

I push him back down. "When gramps is—"

"Bres, you misjudge me. That Blount fellow has your grandma, dress and all, carried her out of the house. Packy yelled that he'd be at Metro, don't ask me why. I waited. For you."

I tell Fal why as I help him up and survey the house's damage. It's a mess, just not as big of a mess as I'd hoped. Plan was for the truck to hit the house—Fal had obviously missed the mark. "You guys can't aim?"

"Bres, my recruits, they were brilliant. Until they cut in front of us."

Fal heads indoors. Specs, Bottles, and Booger trickle outdoors. "Where you going?"

Fal says, "Money, bres," while the boys each point in a different direction.

I chase after Fal. He moves fast when free food or abandoned money's involved. I catch him halfway down the stairs. "Fal, you hear that?"

"My ears are ringing, bres. I barely hear you."

As he walks by each table, Fal stuffs chips in his pockets. Don't know what good they'd do seeing as he'd have to come back here to cash them.

"Fal, let's go," I say.

"Whoa, bres, what have we here?" He's in the office, has discovered Harry. "Is he dead?"

I shrug. I didn't know.

A gun fires. I jump back, hide behind a fallen chair. "Fuck, Fal," I yell. "What are you doing?"

"Making sure, bres." He fires again.

"Stop it stop it stop it." A fog of blue-and-green-tinted smoke hangs over Fal and the doorway to Harry's office.

"Dead, bres. No doubt. Your father, you think he'll reward me?"

"Sure, whatever." I pull Fal through the door, don't look at the body. "I'll tell him whatever you want."

"That's my Hal."

We pop through the back porch's cellar doors as sirens stop and tires squeal and we head toward the hospital.

The *Plain Dealer* initially made little of what went down that night: it was a truck accident that plowed a carful of reckless teens into a nice old house in Clark-Fulton. The teens suffered minor injuries. No mention of any deaths.

As police reports came out and reporters dug deep, Early Ed and the heroin jumped to the front page. At home, at The Hoof, at Metro, the only places I go, I hang nervous, wait for shit to reach me.

Gramps is fine. She's understandably upset at first, a bit traumatized, but one nurse has a friend at the Cleveland Clinic, tells her that his friend has done numerous reassignments, that he'll set something up with her; the nurses and doctors even take up a collection. Gramps can charm anyone, given the chance, and being in the hospital for four days gives her plenty of chances. Her story? She tells them she'd become so lost as a man, so desperately wanted to be a woman, that enough was enough, took a knife, passed out after the second cut. Metro'd seen plenty of crazy shit and her story's both crazy and sad. They even let her paint during her stay. She shows me watercolor images of ladies wading in lakes and of women holding umbrellas. I am happy for her.

Mom alternately hits and hugs me for days. Andrews comes by for support. One look pins me to the kitchen chair and I wait for one of his muscled hammers to drop. But he just holds mom as she tells story after story about gramps. Says it's time to start calling her grandma.

While at Metro I hear that G had only been clipped in the shoulder, that he was suing the police. I haven't seen Fal or Packy, not sure I want to. I still can't believe Fal had shot Harry.

Weeks later, the noise of the scrapyards pushing through the walls and rattling plates and cups, I go out back to the miniature baseball field that wasn't really our property but might as well have been. I'd avoided it in the past and on this day I feel like an explorer, the first to set foot on a new untouched piece of land. It had rained the night before, the sky's Cleveland gray, and the weed- and grass-overgrown infield is muddy and puddles run down the third base path. A plastic Wiffle ball bobs in one of them. I pick it up, toss it into the air with a spin to flick the water off of it, and go to the pitcher's dirt pile. I fire a whistling pitch, grossly high and outside, that slaps the rusty green chain-link backstop. This was the only fucking field, the only kingdom that ever mattered to The Donor. And that's sad. When he couldn't have this? He fought for any power that would make him a star in the Yards, a star in Cleveland. He was a joke, a murderer. Yet, aren't I both those things now, too?

Mom yells from inside that someone's at the door. On the porch stands an odd pair: Blount in a black suit and Mrs. Brud in her tinfoil hat.

The three of us just stare at each other. I look at Blount, Blount corner-eyes Brud, Brud looks at me then looks up as if she's received a transmission. Her chin droops to her chest.

I hold up two fingers and tick-tock them Blount to Brud, Blount to Brud. "You two, you know each other?" I say.

Blount shakes his head. Mrs. Brud nods.

Mom pushes by me, takes Mrs. Brud's hand, and invites her in to have tea with her and grandma. I step on the porch with Blount.

"You need to see him again," Blount says. Inside his SUV, through a tinted window, I see Fal's oversized head.

"I got nothing to say to him."

"Not him," Blount says. "Your father. He's got words for you. And him."

"Now?"

"Now."

I go into the kitchen. Mrs. Brud's foil hat is on the table. Mom and grandma and Brud talk so low and the noise from the scrapyards is so loud I can't hear them. An envelope sits on the table in front of mom. She looks up, sees me. She's, I don't know, beaming, she looks so happy. "You, Hal? A teacher?"

"Ma, it was one day. Like, two, three weeks ago. No big deal."

Grandma, also smiling, says, "He says it's no big deal."

"Look at this." Mom holds the envelope out to me. Inside is a check for one hundred dollars. It's slightly more than I'd get from a night at Pepe's, not even close to what we could've gotten from that truck, heroin or no.

"I got to go," I say.

"Work?"

She doesn't know I'd quit Pepe's. I keep a fake schedule by going to The Hoof. "Yeah," I say, "work."

Mrs. Brud puts on her hat, deflecting my lies, maybe. Mom's eyes narrow. "I'd rather you didn't, Hal."

"What?"

"Whatever it is you're—"

I hold up my hand. "Mom, it's nothing, OK?" I give the check back to her and give mom and grandma each quick from-behind-the-chair hugs. "I'll be back."

On the porch, I walk past Blount and down the broken steps. Inside, Fal says, "Bres, it's—" and I tell him to shut up.

At LorCI, processing goes different. No one else is here. No visitors, I mean. Fal asks the female CO out on a date while her male partner pats him down. She doesn't even grin, not even a little. Fal grabs his crotch. "You don't know what you're missing." That nearly gets Fal escorted out, but Fal retreats and we sit on the benches and wait.

"Don't know why he wants you," I say.

"Bres, who doesn't?" He rubs his beard as if he seriously thinks on it.

Inside the front entry building, I half expect, don't know why, to find The Donor sitting in the children's reading room, his glasses propped on his nose, entertaining a roomful of inmate kids. The room, of course, is empty. A uniformed deliveryman dollies a stack of boxes labeled "Union Supply Direct: Inmate Packages" toward a CO with a clipboard. I wonder if mom had ever sent anything to The Donor, food or music or clothes. I have only myself to offer. And maybe Fal.

The Donor sits in the middle of the visiting room in the same chair as my last visit. But it is quiet as St. fucking Rocco's. Only one CO, no other prisoners, no other visitors. The Donor has apparently arranged a special audience. The fluorescents are over-powered by a few slashes of sunlight that cut across the room, that cut across The Donor. For a moment, he looks holy. Then he rubs a palm up and down his bare arm and tiny flakes of dead skin spin off into the light, flicker, and disappear. The chairs are spaced too far apart for all of us to sit. I take the chair, Fal takes the floor.

"My, oh, my, son. Son son son son son *son*," he says.

Fal smiles, I stay rigid. Don't call me son, you fuck. But before I've the chance to say anything, The Donor says, "You, Hal. Almost. *Al*most fucking did it."

"Bres," Fal says, "we did do it. You're right, you're right." I press a hand against Fal's shoulder, urge him to shut it. He brushes my hand away. "Hal tells me, bres, I get a reward?"

The Donor's smile evaporates. His color, it seems to me, is off, his cheeks an ashy shade of yellow. "What the fuck for, dickhead? Leading my son far away from—*lis*tening to *me?*—away from his, his *des*tiny? I get it, yeah? I get it. You took down Ed, Harry—"

"Killed him, bres." Fal looks up at us, a man-child seeking approval. He scrapes at a patch of beard. "I think."

The Donor stops. The look on his face, I imagine, is the one I had when I'd wished I'd a few bucks to get the CO to look the other way while I strangled him. "Yeah? Then who the fuck's the guy I saw on the news last night, Fal, sitting—just like I'm in front of you right now—in a motherfucking *wheel*chair?" He eyes Fal who looks like he's been given an advanced calculus question. "That's right. Give a *good* and *long* think."

I'd stopped reading the paper. We don't own a TV. Hoof doesn't have a TV. LorCI has a TV, apparently.

I think Fal, his eyes widening, has an answer. But: "Who, bres?"

"Harry." The Donor shoves Fal who roly-polys into me and rebounds off my leg and back into The Donor. "Fucking Harry, *bres*. You gonna do it, do it *right*, am I right? No, not with *you* involved." He points at Fal and then at me. "You finally get your chance, Hal. What you do? You bust him up and shoot his *knees?*"

"I thought you killed him." Fal turns away from me, looks at the wall. "*Fal*." That wall keeps his interest. "You shot him, I mean, I didn't *want* you to shoot him, but, I, I, I fucking heard. I *heard* it. You—" I am relieved, actually.

Fal snorts. "Hal, I ..."

The Donor looks at us, takes us both in.

Fal says, "I, you know, thought you'd killed him already, bres. Me, I couldn't—" He turns to The Donor. "I still get a reward?"

The Donor folds his hands in his lap, tries to stay calm. "You're *kill*ing me, Hal. I'm in *here* and this is who you choose to run with? Know what that *does* to me? I mean, this is your *time*, you know? Some of what you did was—god*damn*, I'd kill to see Ed's face, Hal. *You*, my son, did that to *him*, without a thing he can do about it. But." He holds up one finger, lowers it toward Fal. "He's got to go, Hal."

"Bres?"

I feel like my nerves are jagged edges warring inside of me. "Fal's always been there when I've needed him, no matter how much he fucks up. I owe him. Owe him more than you."

"Owe him shit," The Donor says. He claps his hands together then gives himself a hug, each hand holding the opposite shoulder. It's as if he's trying to squeeze himself into something. Or squeeze something into himself. He releases, shakes his arms out. He removes the glasses from his shirt pocket, plays with the sidepieces, tosses them to the floor. "I'm a walking fucking cli*ché,* Hal. You know that?" He chuckles. "I might be dying, they tell me. Gotten some treatments. So far it's, yeah, no good." He puts his hands out in a what-do-they-know kind of gesture. "Listen to me: I need to know that my world is mine. Out *there*. Be*fore* I'm gone. In *here*."

Knowing The Donor might be dying does nothing for me. Fuck, he could be lying for all I know. But those jagged edges of my nerves, or whatever they are, feel like they break, shatter, reassemble, and break and shatter again. Fal must've felt it. I barely register the squeaking of his sneakers on the tile as he scoots away from me, from us. "That's what you care about? For real? The shit we just went through. That *gramps* just went through. That you put us through. Our lives, dad, our motherfucking lives." Waves upon waves of anger flush my cheeks, pit my chest, clench my fists, tighten my groin. I stand and bend over The Donor, my face a few inches from his, and spit. The CO has a quick hold of me. I jerk my shoulder away and spit again.

I'm dragged out, Fal trailing behind. I never even hear if The Donor says another word.

I stare through the SUV's window at the prison, wonder

how different, how truly different, everything can be. Fal says, "Bres—"

"Fal." The window holds my face's reflection over the prison. As we pull away, the sunlight shifts and I disappear.

In the back seat I hear Fal say, softly, "I'm sorry, bres."

Blount drops us at The Hoof and takes off. Hook slides drinks in front of me and Fal. On the ride back from LorCI, Fal kept trying to talk; when I didn't respond, he'd leaned from the backseat into the front seat and kept fucking with the radio. I felt jammed up. This was my life. And that fucking sucked.

Packy sits alone on the couch. He holds The Donor's hat, spins it around one finger.

From my spot at the bar, I say, "Packy, what the fuck?" I haven't seen him in weeks and here he is pissing me off.

Packy stops his hand and the hat hits the floor. That hat, that hat was the beginning of the end. It gave The Donor everything, it took from The Donor everything. I want to burn it.

Fal goes over and picks it up, flicks dirt off it with one hand. "Bres, with him dying, with Harry out, we can run it all." Fal puffs up. "We, we can be great."

Packy says, "No one's greater than you, Fal." He blows out his stomach, slaps it. "It'd take a piano box to bury you."

Fal lets out a short, sharp, scraping breath. My interpretation: "Packy, blow me." Fal taps me with the baseball cap, its brim ticks my shoulder. "Listen, bres," Fal says, "think what we can do."

I think about it. Try to run this sorry-ass crew the way I'd been doing, small-time heists for short-term cash. Or something bigger. The Donor was right about one thing: Early Ed's shit was crippled. So, apparently, was Harry. Owen had disappeared. We could take over in our way, money never a problem. Sure, sure, one of them could come after me, but despite everything that'd happened I didn't think that a real thing. Besides, Ed and Harry, they were prison-bound. Fal's been with me for years, helped me through some heavy shit, but—

"Fal," I say, "why are you here?"

Fal holds up the beer, finishes it. His answer, I guess.

The mirror behind the bar clearly shows Fal, but large spots of dirt and wear hide me from myself. I think of Mrs. Brud, what we did to her, to the others. Think of that classroom, those kids, that tiny-as-fuck paycheck. Think of Sally, always Sally. Me sitting there, these thoughts looping, when the creepiest of images bangs into my head: just above Sally's grave, just above her headstone, floats a baby, a months-old Sally. She hovers, living, crying, giggling. Right there: birth. Just there, right below her: death. That space between? That split-second time it takes her to fall? Her life. Gravity pulls hard, fast. A blink, maybe. Baby Sally falls and pops into her grave. Life's over. And I imagine baby versions of all those dead and gone, all floating above that whole West Park Cemetery, spread out, some high, some low, all falling—pop!pop!pop!pop!pop!—right into their graves. Wasn't a fuck of a lot of time.

Fal's beard's whiter than I remember. The years with him, without Sally, feel faded.

I push my untouched beer away from me. "I'm done."

"Done, bres?" He taps the bar, asks Hook for another beer. I shake my head at Hook. Fal grabs my beer, drinks a third of it. "Beer, bres." He wipes his mouth and pushes the glass toward me. "It makes fools smart, makes the mind creative, makes the weak brave. It gives *heart*, bres."

"With you, with Packy. All of it."

"Bres?" He smiles, but it's unsteady, that smile.

"No, Fal. Just no. I'm not who I was. Anymore. That fuck who was just, I don't know, *lost*? He needs to go. And that means I'm done with all of it, with you."

Fal roars a laugh that turns into an angry demand to Hook for more beer. Hook crosses his arms, his hook hand visible under his armpit.

I push Fal. "Go," I say. "Don't, don't come near me, OK?"

"Bres, you're just—"

"Go!" I say. I push him with my feet, knock him off the stool. He lands hard on his back and he gasps for air. "And take him with you." Packy's been silent through it all, but his expression indicates he understands.

It takes Fal a few seconds to catch his breath, to stand. He tugs at his beard nervously, looks around The Hoof.

Hook busies himself, refuses to even look at Fal, but says, "Fal, he deserves better."

"And I need a better Hal, bres. I just—and I've *tried*—I just can't get rid of him."

I keep my focus on a spot on the bar in front of me, but I see Fal hang his head out of the corner of my eye, hear him sigh. I look up and watch him slowly exit.

I sit alone. Options swirl in my head. Tomorrow I'll see if Mrs. Brud will take me down to the school, help me apologize. I'll give her locket back to her. Maybe. Maybe.

I stare at the mirror, at the spot where Fal had been. Panic sets in. "Waitaminute," I say to myself. I look at the door Fal had left through. "Wait, goddammit." I try to move—at least I think I try—try to get off the stool.

I stay still.

AFTERWORD AND ACKNOWLEDGEMENTS

While these stories are steeped in Cleveland's rich history, and while I've attempted to depict time and place with fidelity, I confess there may be some inaccuracies. These either are due to my own failings or are intentionally committed to suit the needs of a particular character, scene, or story.

Perhaps only five percent of my research found its way into these pages, but every resource helped shape the work, helped me dive into the city and, I hope, helped the reader dive into it, too. Resources that were most useful: the Cleveland Public Library (which provided access to old copies of the *Press* and *Plain Dealer* and which opened up its photograph collection to me); The Cleveland Memory Project (courtesy of the Michael Schwartz Library, Cleveland State University); Cleveland Historical (courtesy of Center for Public History + Digital Humanities, Cleveland State University); Teaching Cleveland Digital; the Western Reserve Historical Society; *The Buddhist Third Class Junkmail Oracle: The Art and Poetry of d.a. Levy* (Levy and Golden); *Cleveland and Its Streetcars* (Toman); *Cleveland: Prodigy of the Western Reserve* (Condon); *Cleveland: Then and Now* (DeMarco); *The Encyclopedia of Cleveland History* (Van Tassel and Grabowski); *Hidden History of Cleveland* (Busta-Peck); *History Detectives* (PBS, Episode 10, 2006); *Seth Pease's Journals to and from New Connecticut, 1796-1798* (Western Reserve Historical Society); *Stories of Ohio* (Howells); *Trolley Trails through Greater Cleveland and Northern Ohio: From the Beginning Until 1910* (Christiansen); *West of the Cuyahoga* (Condon); and *The Western Reserve* (Hatcher).

Thanks to Jeff Parker and John Dufresne, writers and teachers whose generous encouragement and guidance cannot be appreciated enough. Thanks to Erica Dawson for being Erica Dawson, which in itself says everything. Thanks to Glenn Kumhera, Shane Hinton, and R. Dean Johnson for showing the way. Thanks to Dana Greene, my sis, and to Tony Macklin, my guide, for sharing the passion. Thanks to those who read drafts early and whose feedback helped shape my writing: Maile Chapman, Tibor Fischer, Stefan Kiesbye, Cooper Levey-Baker, Annie Liontas, Jason Ockert, Padgett Powell, and the St. Pete Writers Group. Thanks to University of Tampa, especially Don Morrill and Lynne Bartis.

Thanks to Ann Sindelar at Western Reserve Historical Society for taking the time and granting permission. Thanks to the Cuyahoga County Department of Public Works for unlocking the gates to the lower deck of the Detroit-Superior Bridge and letting me run wild. Thanks to Dan Hudak of River Cruiser Kayaking for the up-close tour of the Cuyahoga River.

Thanks to my former students—too numerous to name but you know who you are—who urged me on. (And to you writers, creators, and dreamers: if I can do it …)

Thanks to Bob LaRosa, Ross Madak, and Pamela Madak for giving me a place to stay and/or providing transportation while I set off on my day-long walkabouts around Cleveland and its environs.

Thanks to Celeste McKeever for the love and for supporting this thing that ofttimes chews up mornings, nights, and weekends.

Thanks to my parents, John and Celene, the best research assistants and first, second, and, in many cases, tenth readers a writer could ever ask for.

Thanks to the Madville crew, Kim and Jacqui, for believing in this book and giving it a good and proper home.

About the Author

Brian Petkash was born and raised in Cleveland, Ohio. He holds an MFA in Creative Writing from University of Tampa and his stories have appeared in *Midwestern Gothic* and *Southword*, among other publications. He currently lives in Tampa, Florida, where he remains an avid fan of Cleveland sports.

. . . continued from page ii.

"The Cleveland depicted here is at once mythic and pedestrian. There's the familiar stuff—the stockyards, the Cuyahoga, Lebron—but there's also a werewolf (of sorts), a skywoman, and a remarkable Shakespearean duo known as Hal and Fal. Call it historical fiction if you must, but Petkash forges from the fire of a burning river a new view on the American city everyone loves to hate and hate on. *Mistakes by the Lake* is a fictional *tour de force.*"

—Jeff Parker, author of *Ovenman*

"Put simply, Brian Petkash is this era's Sherwood Anderson. The ten stories that comprise *Mistakes by the Lake* do for Cleveland what *Winesburg, Ohio* did for Anderson's fictional town. They present a cast of characters across historical time—characters beset by change, marital and familial difficulties, shattered dreams and loss. Often dark, the stories still manage one important infusion of light: a kind of momentary stay against despair. These stories mark Petkash as a necessary writer for this moment in our national life. Move over, Mr. Anderson."

—George Drew, author of *Drumming Armageddon*

"In this remarkable debut, Brian Petkash immerses his reader with textured prose that is as beautifully nuanced as it is brutally honest. The settings of these stories are authentically Cleveland, but the terrain is the full range of human emotion. From a trolley driver searching the tracks for purpose to a war veteran wounded by the loss of his wife, Petkash binds together a disparate cast of characters with threads of hope and humanity. *Mistakes by the Lake* is a collection that resonates long after the read, and Petkash is an author to be watched."

—R. Dean Johnson, author of *Californium*

"These are stories like I haven't read before, of mostly busted people in tough spots who usually come to weird, bad ends, threaded through a couple of centuries. They're dark, because that's what is within the Midwest if you look at it closely enough, and they're impressively researched and lived in. 'We honor others in strange ways and for strange reasons,' Petkash writes. 'And sometimes we don't honor them at all.' I for one will remember these souls and this Cleveland for a long, long time."

—Ander Monson, author of *The Gnome Stories*

CPSIA information can be obtained
at www.ICGtesting.com
Printed in the USA
FSHW010624280520
70364FS

9 781948 692328